No Tears For the Lost

Adrian Magson

CREME DE LA CRIME

Magson

First published in 2007
by Crème de la Crime
P O Box 523, Chesterfield, S40 9AT

Typesetting by Yvette Warren
Cover design by Yvette Warren
Front cover image by Peter Roman

Printed and bound in Great Britain by
Cox & Wyman Ltd, Reading, Berkshire

ISBN 978-0-9551589-7-1

A CIP catalogue reference for this book is available from
the British Library

www.cremedelacrime.com

About the author:
   Adrian Magson is a novelist and freelance writer, and lives with his wife Ann in Oxfordshire.

www.adrianmagson.com

My grateful thanks to Christie 'Eagle-eye' Hickman, my editor, for making sense of my words. Any remaining bloops are mine.

Thanks as always to Lynne, Jeff, Yvette and everyone at Crème for putting the book out there.

Thanks also to the members of Almondbury Library Reading Group, who created the character of Jacob 'Tristram' Worth, toilet attendant, who plays a key part: Elaine Harrison, Marion Holmes, Jean Jones, Hazel Hirst, Elaine Ashton, Dot Goodall, Vivien Bebb.

This one is for you…

They'd sent him a severed finger.

It lay on a bed of cotton wool like a grisly jewel, dark in colour and slightly curled, the nail torn and rimmed with dirt. The amputation had been made just forward of the main knuckle. The separation was ragged and crude, with a dried flap of skin left hanging on one side.

"Who delivered this?" The man couldn't take his eyes off it, his voice barely above a whisper. A faint smell of chemicals drifted up from the box, overlaid with something not altogether pleasant. The unstamped brown envelope which had contained the box lay discarded, the front bearing three simple words in bold print: **Sir Kenneth Myburghe**.

"I don't know, Sir Kenneth." The man in the smart grey suit spoke respectfully, his voice a deep rumble. He stood in the doorway, huge shoulders filling the frame, the fabric of his jacket and shirt strained by the bulk of muscle beneath. "I heard a noise and found it on the doorstep." His face, all angles and crags, stayed carefully blank. "There was nobody about."

"Go check again." Myburghe brushed at a stray lock of distinguished grey hair above one ear. A faint sheen of perspiration had appeared on the mottled skin above his cheekbones, adding to the already unhealthy appearance of a gaunt face.

The butler departed, silently in spite of his size, leaving Myburghe staring at the object on his desk. It took a moment for him to realise that the finger was a small one – a pinkie – and that in studying the cut, he'd been ignoring something else lying in the box. When he realised what it was, it was like taking a punch to the chest.

It was a gold signet ring.

He took a tissue from a drawer, wet it and dabbed at the ring. There was no mistaking the dull colour showing through the film of dirt – he tried not to think about what this really might be – or the gradual appearance of a crest worn down by time and use. When the full design became visible, he felt sickened and collapsed into a nearby chair.

The ring had been commissioned and manufactured over a hundred years ago, barely twenty miles from where he was now sitting. Originating with his great-grandfather, it had been passed down the line of what had once been a noble and honourable family.

But all that, he reflected with overridding feelings of despair and guilt, had been a long time ago. And the last person seen wearing this ring was barely nineteen years old.

His son, Christian.

1

"Die, you time-wasting bitch!" Riley Gavin stabbed the keyboard to eliminate another batch of spam email. The focus of her attention today was someone calling herself Morwena, no doubt a pseudonym for a pimply youth in a sweatshop computer room somewhere in deepest Michigan. Thirty-three junk mails, most of them cheap offers of Viagra for those suffering from something called an 'unflatering erectoin'. "And," she added, "try learning to spell."

As she sat back and sipped her coffee, which had gone cold, the incoming email tone announced another arrival. The name of the sender this time was Tristram. Untypically, the message box was empty, but the subject line contained a single line of type.

SIR KENNETH MYBURGHE HAS GOT A NASTY SECRET...

Lucky old Sir Kenneth, thought Riley. Whoever he is. She stabbed delete and sent Tristram's missive winging off to join Morwena's. At least this last one was a little subtler in his sales pitch. So subtle, in fact, there was no pitch at all. Maybe he was having an off day.

She glanced at the on-screen clock. It was almost ten and so far the morning had produced little in the way of interesting new work other than a vague rumour of an alleged call-girl racket operating out of a government building in Croydon. The girls were being run, her contact had insisted in her email, by a manager in the Immigration section, and featured teenagers from Nigeria, Uganda and Romania, all being supplied with papers and accommodation in return for 'favours'.

It didn't need much imagination to guess what those favours might be.

She wondered if the story had legs, or whether it had already been picked up by other hacks and was now doing the rounds in search of a home. She'd stumbled over two others like it within the past month, and each time they had led nowhere. But it had taken time and money to reach that conclusion. If she didn't come up with something soon, she was going to have to fall on the tender mercies of Donald Brask, her sometime agent, who played the airwaves with Svengali-like expertise to seek out stories and places to sell them.

Not that she begrudged going through Donald for work. With his uncanny nose for business, he knew more people in the media, government and police than anyone she'd ever met. But her innate independence meant she preferred to find her own assignments whenever possible, and set the terms accordingly. It made the work all the more satisfying, somehow.

Coffee, she thought. I need another belt of coffee, only stronger. It wouldn't magic up another assignment, but it might sharpen the thought processes and help get things moving with a bit more determination.

As she stood up, the computer beeped again.

It was Tristram. Again?

SIR KENNETH MYBURGHE ISN'T WHAT HE SEEMS...

Riley frowned at the screen. Was she supposed to be impressed? If the mystery sender was hoping to draw in a gullible user, why not include a hyperlink to click on? And who the hell was Sir Kenneth Myburghe, anyway? If there was one thing she hated, it was anonymous informants who dribbled information as if they were passing out gold dust. She hit the delete button with a hiss of irritation and shut down the machine.

It was the signal for the cat to appear. She hadn't seen it since yesterday, when it had gone walkabout as usual. It had evidently decided that it was Riley's day to play maidservant.

"Good timing, pal," she congratulated him. Walking obediently into the kitchen and taking a tin of meat from the fridge, she spooned some into a dish. He responded with a chainsaw-loud buzz and dropped his face into the food with the grace of a born binge-eater.

The cat, a solid and confident tabby with a broad head and the shoulders of a bruiser, had arrived courtesy of a former neighbour, adopting Riley by default and nominating her as a provider of food, comfort and convenience. It responded to her largesse with an occasional battered ear for her vocalised thoughts when it felt like it, and a strictly rationed show of affection.

When it wasn't using her first floor flat to crash in, located in a quiet house off west London's Holland Park Avenue, it toyed with the affections of Mr Grobowski, Riley's Polish neighbour on the ground floor. Unlike Riley, who hadn't felt able to saddle the animal with a name, Mr Grobowski called it Lipinski, in honour of a Polish musician, and fed it vast helpings of his native food, which he cooked for a nearby community centre.

Half an hour later, showered and changed from her house sweats to comfortable jeans and a jacket, and having run a quick brush through her collar-length blonde hair, she was immersed in the morning newspapers and an industrial-strength latte at her local Caffé Nero.

Then someone dropped heavily into the seat next to her. She caught a strong smell of mints and aftershave, rising over the warm aroma of roasted coffee beans.

"Why, if it isn't Riley Gavin, journo extraordinaire," said a dry male voice. "Just the person I was looking for."

The newcomer was tall and broad-shouldered, with brush-cut greying hair and high cheekbones. He wore a well-cut pinstripe suit and a crisp, white shirt and dark tie.

Matthew Weller was something high up in the Metropolitan Police. Riley wasn't sure of his current rank, and was surprised to see him. Senior officers from the Met didn't normally cruise the coffee bars of London in search of journalists, not when a beckoning finger would get most hacks running to them in the hopes of a story and glory. She wondered what he wanted.

"Morning," she said cautiously.

She'd first met Weller at a press briefing after a street crime initiative had gone sour a few months ago. The Met had been forced on to the defensive when the Home Office had left them high and dry, with months of hard work ruined by a sudden budget crisis. Weller had been wheeled out as one of the big guns to do some reassuring interviews. Rumour had it that he was now with the National Crime Squad.

"Am I under arrest?" she asked mildly. "Can I finish my coffee or should I duck under a blanket and let you drag me screaming to the nearest nick so I can sell my life story and claim police harrassment?"

"No, yes and no," he replied. "Anyway, the cells are at capacity again, so we're not nicking anyone at the moment." He showed her a line of uneven teeth and chomped down on a mint like a terrier chewing a rat. In the relative quiet of the coffee shop, the crunching was loud and intrusive. Weller stared bullishly at the few heads turning his way, then offered Riley a crumpled bag.

She declined. After researching a piece about how many millions of germs were transmitted through bowls of hospitality sweets, she reckoned the number could be multiplied several times over with Weller. Not that he was necessarily a health hazard, but in the course of his work, he shook hands with some very unsavoury people.

"How's your friend, Palmer?" he queried. He flicked a piece of lint from the knee of his pinstripe and crossed his legs, giving Riley a brief glimpse of fine burgundy wool above gleaming shoes. Weller's teeth may have been uneven, but there was nothing wrong with his dress sense.

"Palmer's fine," she told him, "as far as I know. I didn't know you were acquainted."

"We're not. But word gets around. You and he seem to be a team." He looked about him. "He's not here, is he? I wouldn't want to steal his chair."

"He's not. What can I do for you – Chief Superintendent, is it? Or have you moved up the greasy pole a bit further?"

Weller shrugged easily. "It'll do. You can call me Weller, if you like. Most people do." He sounded vague, even bored, but she wasn't fooled by the easy approach. Weller was after something.

"OK. Out with it. Has the Home Office dumped you since that last fiasco or have they just slashed your budget by a few million?"

"Nothing so simple," he murmured, popping another mint into his mouth. "I have rivers of information flowing across my desk every day. Most of it is crap – the need to know because it's there kind of stuff. But every now and then I spot an item which interests me." He crunched the mint and looked at her. "Like yesterday."

Riley sipped her coffee and waited to see if he'd tell her what it was. She felt certain she hadn't done anything recently that would have hit the official information channels. But when he didn't say anything, she nudged him by asking, "Are you saying my name cropped up?"

"Not yours – your mate, Palmer's." His eyes were blank, but it was clear he was waiting for the penny to drop. When she didn't respond, he said, "We know what Palmer does to earn a buck. And we know you two sometimes work together." He inclined his head to one side. "Ergo, it begs the question: what's he up to at the moment?"

"Why don't you ask him yourself? I'm sure you can get one of your boys to find his office. It's out in Uxbridge. That's a suburb to the west of London – just before you start seeing countryside stuff like trees and grass."

"I would ask him, but he doesn't appear to be around. Any ideas?"

Riley shook her head. Frank Palmer was a former Royal Military Police investigator, now private detective. He was also her occasional colleague on some of the trickier assignments she took on, where someone with a background in investigative work and a willingness not to be frightened off was a definite asset. Not that Riley shied away from the occasional spot of trouble, but she wasn't afraid to acknowledge that Palmer, a lean, tough forty-something, could handle certain things better than she could.

When he wasn't working with Riley, Palmer spent his life on surveillance or making security assessments for private or corporate clients. He was often incommunicado for days at a time, either playing with his computer or in a car somewhere, watching someone. His absence now was therefore hardly a cause for concern. On the other hand, she didn't see why she should help the forces of law and order dip their collective noses into his business.

"Is this official government interest, or do you have some common criminal reason for asking?"

Weller grinned and nodded. "Good question, Riley. Clever. If I say it's official government business, you'll get an attack of the goosebumps. Only you know it won't go anywhere because we'll sit on it. That'll get you more interested. If I say it's a criminal matter, you'll get the same goosebumps and as much interest, only with what you fondly hope is more chance of a story."

"Cynic."

"True." He pondered the question for a moment, turning to eye an unshaven youth with spiked hair, sitting against the rear wall. The youth wasn't drinking coffee, but appeared to be taking a close interest in a handbag lying on a chair at the next table.

Weller cleared his throat noisily until the youth dragged his eyes away from the bag. When he saw Weller, he shot up from his chair and walked out without looking back.

"These places are a playground for maggots like him," Weller said sourly. "What was I saying? Oh, yes. Palmer and you. Well, Palmer, anyway." He peered into his sweet bag again as if it might contain the secrets of the universe, although she knew he was merely giving her a chance to speak. He'd also avoided answering her question.

"I have no idea where he is," she answered truthfully. "Contrary to your information, we don't spend much time together, except when we're working – which isn't as often as you might imagine."

"But you would tell me if you knew. Wouldn't you?" His eyes had suddenly gone as flat as his voice, and Riley felt a chill descending. Weller wasn't joking.

2

"What happens if I tell you to get lost instead?" she asked evenly. "Do you stalk me until I break down in tears and confess all?"

He smiled blankly. "You got it."

Riley shrugged. "I'm a journalist, not a mother hen. I don't keep twenty-four hour watch on my friends."

"Fair enough." Weller shifted in his chair and yawned. "Just thought I'd ask. How about you – what are you working on at the moment? Anything juicy?"

"Sorry. No comment."

He sniffed. "Mmm… bad as that, is it? Never mind. Something will turn up."

Riley felt her ears prickle. Was there more to that comment than one might think or had Weller been reading Dickens? Somehow, she couldn't see him being a Micawber enthusiast.

"Do you have something in mind?"

Weller considered her reply, then stood up and stuffed the bag of mints into his pocket. Now he was standing, he looked out of place, as if he'd been beamed down from his eyrie off Victoria Street and wasn't sure where to go next. It reminded Riley that policemen like him were rarely in the habit of passing the time of day. It wasn't part of their social armoury.

"Right. I'll be off, then." He leaned over the table and tapped the surface with a strong finger. "Good luck with your work. But a word of advice: keep it to low-level crims or blushing brides and the colours of their corsages, will you? I'd hate you to trip over anyone's feet in search of a story that wasn't there. Know what I mean?"

Riley resisted the temptation to tell him to go sit on his thumb. He was pretending to be friendly, but she wasn't fooled: he'd come out to drop a warning in her ear. Now all she had to do was figure out why he'd bothered and what it meant.

"Anything you say, officer," she intoned meekly, and made a note to watch her step. But she couldn't resist prodding him one last time. "Tell me, Weller, what exactly do you do in life, when you're not pursuing innocent journalists?"

"Me?" He looked surprised, as if he'd never been asked before. "I suppose I'm what they call a floating voter. I can be whatever you want me to be, as the tart said to the padre." He grinned. "Take it easy."

Riley watched him disappear along the pavement, then took out her phone and dialled Palmer's office, where he mostly hung out when he wasn't working. No reply. She tried his mobile. He picked up after three rings.

"Frank Palmer. Bodyguard to the stars."

"Have you been a naughty boy?" she asked him.

"Dunno. I haven't looked recently. Why?"

"There's a big noise from the Met been asking questions about you. His name's Weller."

"Gosh, how cool," he murmured. "Do tell."

"He didn't say why, only that he thought we were joined at the hip and that I'd know where you were and what you were doing."

"And you said…?"

"I said nothing." Palmer didn't respond. "So what are you doing?" From the flat quality of his voice and a rushing noise in the background, which could have been wind in the trees, he was out in the open somewhere.

A dry laugh echoed down the line. "Jesus, you're so transparent. So's Weller. I'm on a job, as a matter of fact. Can't say what or where, of course, or I'd have to kill you. But I can confirm that it's a beautiful sunny day and I'm thinking of treating myself to an ice cream."

"Great. Can you tell me what country you're in?"

"Not even. If Weller comes round again, tell him to mind his own." He cut the connection, leaving Riley with the suspicion that she had just done the one thing Weller may have been hoping she'd do. Palmer, ever wary and quicker off the mark, had got there first and ended the call in case anyone was listening in.

Frank Palmer stuffed his mobile back into his pocket and wondered why one of Scotland Yard's finest should be taking an interest in his activities.

He wasn't unduly bothered by the news, as he hadn't broken any laws recently. But even the most innocent of citizens could be excused a small frisson of apprehension at finding themselves under the suspicious gaze of the authorities. And with all the extra legislation surrounding every aspect of life and the law, from the Data Protection Act to the current frenzied deluge of anti-terror laws, stubbing a toe on one of the new rules was an increasing danger for those in the private security industry.

He debated lighting a cigarette, but went for the healthy option and tore off a thick grass stem instead. He chewed on it, angling his tall frame round to study an expanse of neatly tended grass, flower borders and, beyond them, a thick belt of trees which formed the backdrop of his current assignment, near Tetbury in Gloucestershire.

Palmer didn't like open spaces. Especially like this, dotted with clumps of greenery large enough to hide a small field gun and backed by enough lush trees for an entire regiment to sit and have a brew-up without being spotted until it was too late.

He turned to study the large, impressive manor house in the centre of the grounds, one end of which was covered with scaffolding rearing against the sky like a giant Meccano set. That, too, was a problem, but of a different kind. He'd deal with it later.

For now, he was more interested in keeping the list of problem points around this place to a manageable length. If he itemised every area where security was a living nightmare, he'd run out of paper – and most likely a client in the process. Some people just couldn't stand bad news.

Risk assessments were a regular part of Palmer's routine. As a former RMP, he had a close working knowledge of security procedures and planning, as well as general investigative work. Advising nervous clients on aspects of daily risk-avoidance was something he did on a regular basis. Some were simple, such as advising on the fitting of lights or alarms, or buying a large, voracious dog; others were more complex, usually because the client had a chequered history or a background which meant their particular risk levels were outside the norm.

This current client, he had a feeling, fell into the second category, although he wasn't sure why. Maybe it had something to do with the fact that he had been contacted by phone with a follow-up email and a couriered cheque as an advance against his initial advice. No face-to-face meeting, no background briefing on the client, no contract specifying his operational parameters. Just get on with it and report back, the clipped voice on the phone had instructed him, preferably without asking questions. The man had sounded faintly hostile and had given his name as

Keagan. And if he wasn't a serving or former army officer, Palmer thought, he was ready to eat his hat.

All he did know was that a wedding was scheduled to take place here in a few days time, and his task was to identify any chinks in the armour around this building, and to list them with any recommendations. End of job.

In the brief time available to him, he had taken steps to find out the identity of the owner. When he'd seen the name, he'd realised he didn't need to do any more digging. He knew the family – one of them better than the others – from a previous assignment, and that Sir Kenneth Myburghe was a diplomat. That fact might raise the security stakes a little higher, but as long as he wasn't also a mass murderer or manufacturing chemical weapons in a shed at the back, Palmer didn't much care what he did.

His mobile rang, tinny and feeble in the open air. It was probably Riley with more bad news. Maybe she'd discovered the United Nations was bugging his office.

The name Keagan flashed up on the small screen.

"You done yet?" The man's tone was sharp and unfriendly and Palmer decided something must be biting him. Either that or he'd just lost a winning lottery ticket.

"Just about. I'll send in my report."

"No time for that. Come to the house. You can do it in person."

"Does that mean –?"

"There's been a change of plan. You're hired. You'd better be ready to start straight away." The connection was cut, and Palmer reflected that, all things considered, there were probably more formal ways of being offered a job.

Riley returned to her flat in a thoughtful mood, wondering if something was going on in the capital that she hadn't heard about. Senior coppers trudging around on their own feet and mixing with the public was a rare occurrence. Usually they had an army of junior faces to do that for them, rank being given to those capable of determining strategy, not asking basic questions.

As she pondered the intricacies of police thinking, she automatically checked her email.

There were two new messages: one from an on-line purveyor of steroids, the other from the mysterious Tristram. She deleted the first and was about to add the second, when she read the text on the subject line.

It was chillingly direct.

DID YOU KNOW SIR KENNETH MYBURGHE IS DIRTY?

J

3

Riley stared at the screen with an increasing feeling of unease. Her instincts told her this wasn't an idle spammer with time on his hands or some brain-dead computer nerd looking for laughs at someone else's expense. And the smiley face in the message box somehow made it all the more sinister.

She checked 'Properties', but it was just a Hotmail address. 'Tristram' would probably prove untraceable; it was simple enough to use an internet café and create a blind email address to send out messages to whomever you wished. She scrolled down the window to see if any other recipients were included. If there were, it meant Tristram was most probably a nuisance, spreading rumour like buckshot to see who got drawn in.

But her name was the only one.

She called up Google and fed in *SIR KENNETH MYBURGHE*. Microseconds later, she had a list of hits running off the page. At least the man existed, which was oddly comforting.

She scrolled down the page, occasionally checking the links. But whoever Myburghe was, he seemed to prefer staying out of the cyberspace limelight. Direct information about him was curiously sparse, and no more than she might have picked up from newspaper reports. There were mentions of his name, but nothing accompanied by anything more than events he had visited, and then only as part of a list of delegates or invitees. She soon tired of this and clicked on Images. These showed a tall, elegant, man with thinning grey hair and the magnolia skin of an ageing academic. In most of them he was sharing floor space with other figures in penguin suits at a range of charity or government functions. Some showed him with a thin, smiling woman. They were dressed for partying, in elegant clothes and jewellery and mostly holding glasses and smiling into the camera. But the accompanying information revealed strangely little in the way of background detail. And none mentioned what he did for a living or when the photos had been taken.

Curiouser and curiouser, she thought. It takes real work in the digital age to stay so low on the radar. It wasn't until she scrolled down the page and came across a Spanish-language site that the picture became slightly clearer. The site yielded clippings from a newspaper in Bogotá, Colombia, listing a clutch of British and American embassy staff and personnel. From Riley's limited fund of Spanish, it had been lifted from an invitations list for a Colombian Government seminar on the environment and local development issues held three years ago. There was no photo of Myburghe this time, but that might have been for security reasons.

At least she now knew what he did for a living: he was a diplomat. Or had been. While interesting, it didn't necessarily mean much, other than that someone called Tristram didn't like him. Maybe, she reflected, Tristram was an ex-Foreign Office employee with an axe to grind.

A site on another page led to a society column clip, announcing the forthcoming marriage of former British Ambassador to Colombia, Sir Kenneth Myburghe's twenty-six-year-old daughter Victoria, to Simon Biel, a banker. A photo showed a tall, pretty young blonde on the arm of a lofty individual with an impressive stomach and no discernible chin.

The wedding, Riley noted with interest, was in a few days time.

She chewed over what she had so far, which was that someone didn't like a shy diplomat whose daughter was about to get married. It was pathetically little, and most days she would have binned the idea and got on with something else. She sat back and ruminated. Was it a story worth pursuing – and if so, what propelled it to that level? Jilted putative son-in-law, perhaps? If so, why not take it out on the daughter instead?

The fact that the maligned Sir Ken was a former ambassador elevated him some way beyond Mr Average on the news front. By the nature of his job, it meant the source reason for any enmity might lie overseas. But apart from that, the only reason he seemed to be currently in the news was because of his daughter's wedding. It was hardly reason enough for somebody to take what appeared to be a more than passing and personal interest in him.

So why the unmistakable rancour?

She wondered what the mysterious Tristram was doing right now. Probably grinning smugly over his own cleverness and sending the same message to another sucker to see how many responses he could notch up.

Eventually, powered by a growing sense of curiosity, she hit REPLY and typed:

TELL ME MORE. WHO ARE YOU?

Three minutes passed before the machine beeped.

A FRIEND. J

The smiley symbol again. Two simple keystrokes, but enough to give Riley a renewed sense of concern. She paused, her fingers above the keyboard, questioning what she might be getting herself into. Simpler beginnings than this had turned into unpleasant situations in the past. But it was too late now; the connection had been made and Tristram, whoever he was, now knew she was hooked.

She typed back: SO TELL ME YOUR REAL NAME. She didn't for a moment believe it was really Tristram, but it was worth a try.

The screen remained blank. She gave it a minute and tried again.

ARE YOU WASTING MY TIME?

Still no answer. She sighed and switched off the laptop. If Tristram were serious, he would get back to her. If not, he'd get bored and try somebody else.

She checked the time and decided to call on Donald Brask. If he had any crumbs of work on offer, facing him down might get her a headstart on his other journo clients. Besides, she could do with some fresh air and the gladiatorial buzz that driving in London inevitably gave her.

She grabbed her car keys, told the cat to behave – it was pointless, but a habit she found hard to break – and headed for the door.

Donald Brask lived and worked alone in a large Victorian house in Finchley. Both home and office, it was his sanctuary from the world outside, preferring, he claimed, the company of his machines and their flashing lights, cursors and ring tones to people and places.

Over the years Riley had known him, Donald had built up an impressive array of computer power and electronic archives. Armed with this and his little book of contacts in commercial, showbusiness and governmental circles, he claimed to have a finger on the pulse of whatever scandal or intrigue might be in need of uncovering. With an address book of newspaper and magazine editors around the world, he was able to play the market like a virtuoso, seeking out the best offers and contracts for his clients.

"Sir Kenneth Myburghe," she asked him, when he opened

his front door. "Should I know anything about him?"

"Pahum?" Donald scowled blearily at her and closed the door quickly as she stepped past him. Unlike his customary attire of mismatched slacks and shirts, he was dressed in a garish dressing gown that made him look like an eastern potentate in a bad school play. He was also nursing a thermometer between pursed lips and looking distinctly peaky.

"What's up?" she asked, suddenly concerned. It was barely noon, and although Donald could be a bit of a drama queen, being too ill to get dressed was not something she had witnessed before. Illness meant time and time was money, and in Brask's book the two didn't quite gel.

"I've got a sore throat," he squeaked, whipping out the thermometer and frowning at the results. He held out the instrument for her to check. "See?" he cried dramatically, his ample belly quivering. "One hundred and six! I'm ill!"

"Donald, if it was that high, your head would be steaming," she told him bluntly. She felt his forehead. He was a little hot, but nothing out of the ordinary. Not that she knew what might be ordinary for Donald Brask. "Take some paracetamol, drink lots of tea and watch some day-time televison. We common folk do it all the time – it's called throwing a sickie."

She walked through to his kitchen, fitted with every device known to culinary man, and switched on the kettle. She might as well do it for him, or he'd be useless.

"Did you say Sir Kenneth Myburghe?" he echoed, trailing along behind her, bad throat and thermometer momentarily dismissed. When any kind of 'name' was involved, his nose, permanently set on 'Seek', was more sensitive than a truffle-hound on heat.

"Yes. I think he's something in the diplomatic corps, but I can't find out much more at the moment."

"I wouldn't bother, dear. He's one of Her Majesty's faceless men in far-flung places. Flour graders, most of them." Donald sounded faintly uninterested, and stared at the floor while calling up details from his prodigious memory. "Let me see… middle-ranking diplomat, sixties or thereabouts? Couple of kids. No, three. He has a country pile in Gloucestershire somewhere, near the Royal Triangle. His wife lives in London. Something about an amicable split, as I recall. He's been around a long time but I don't recall anything newsworthy about him."

Riley was surprised Donald knew even that much about the man. "How do you know all that?"

Donald waved a vague hand. "Lord knows. Some things come in and stick, others don't. It was a while back – probably in connection with a diplomatic fundraising event, I expect. Why the interest?"

Riley told him about the anonymous emails from Tristram. "It could be someone with a warped sense of humour or a personal grudge," she admitted. "But why would they bother – and why come to me?"

"Who knows, sweet pea?" Donald murmured sombrely, suppressing a cough. He watched as she poured water over tea bags and stirred them. "There are some odd people out there, as you know. And you're not exactly unknown. That Observer piece you did on procurement fraud last month got you a lot of notice. Who better to call, when you want to dish the dirt on a VIP, than a star reporter? Better than Hello magazine, although not as well paid, sadly."

"Is Myburghe still a VIP? I got the impression he was a former ambassador."

"Quite possibly. But a career in the diplomatic corps doesn't automatically end with retirement. Some embassy suits go on to even greater heights." He smiled wolfishly.

"Or depths."

"In that case, I wonder what he's been up to?"

"Are you sure you want to dip your little piglets into such muddy waters?" Donald stared at the thermometer one last time before dropping it into a nearby drawer. His voice was already sounding a lot better, as if the lightweight bout of verbal sparring had given him the energy he needed.

"What do you mean?"

"Diplomats, sweetie. It's a little too close to Her Majesty's embassies, isn't it? With all the terrorist activity at the moment, they've got them wrapped up like little cocoons and surrounded by armed heavies, in case Al-Quaeda come calling. I'm not sure it's healthy at the moment, taking too much of interest in somebody like Myburghe. You could find your pretty face appearing on a security department computer somewhere." He chuckled and touched her cheek. "Definitely not good for the complexion."

Riley stared at him. This didn't sound like Donald. He usually had the gung-ho attitude of a pit-bull, VIPs and terrorists or not. True, he wasn't above suggesting she get some backup if danger threatened, which was where Frank Palmer had first come in. But nothing about what she'd seen so far suggested it was a possibility.

Was it her imagination, or was he trying to put her off this job?

"If this Tristram has got something on Myburghe, we should find out, VIP or not."

"Maybe." Donald sipped his tea and grimaced as it went down. "But there are other avenues worth pursuing. I have a couple of hot tips you could follow up for me – one involving a rather libidinous pop star who's made a lot of fuss recently about how clean-living she is." He chuckled nastily, in spite of his throat. "Now there's a young lady who will go down in flames if she has to – and enjoy it." He sniggered at his crude double entendre, then doubled over in a coughing fit, his face turning purple.

Riley slapped him across the shoulders and waited while he regained his composure. "Thanks, Donald. But pop stars come and go, most of them briefly. I'll give this Myburghe a look first, just in case." She took a final swallow of tea and said casually, "I don't suppose you know what Palmer's working on at the moment, do you?" She knew he handled some of Palmer's assignments, although it would probably take wild horses and a weighted hosepipe to get him to give any details.

Brask wiped his lips on a silk handkerchief and created a drama out of a simple shrug, before subsiding into another coughing fit. She couldn't tell if it was genuine or whether he was simply trying to avoid answering her question. Never mind. She'd get to the bottom of it sooner or later.

"I'll take that as a 'don't know', then," she said coolly. A cold shoulder and a little gentle bullying sometimes went a long way with Donald. "Please yourself." She poured the rest of her tea down the sink and headed for the door. He was a lovely man and always full of concern for her, but she never forgot that he was first and foremost a businessman and therefore always on the lookout for number one. He'd soon come round.

"Dear heart," he began, his voice plaintive. "I really think –"

Riley patted his cheek and slipped past him into the hall-way before he could suggest any other stories she should follow up. She wasn't sure why, but instinct told her that, even if on the basis of dubious messages from a mystery source, the Myburghe thing was worth a look.

"Stand by, Donald," she told him. "If my instincts are right, we're up and running."

4

Back home, she switched on the laptop and waited for her emails to download. There was a message from Tristram, sent ten minutes ago.

WHAT DOES IT TAKE FOR A DIPLOMAT TO BE DROPPED FROM THE DIPLOMATIC LIST?

Riley typed back: IS THIS A 'KNOCK-KNOCK' JOKE?

The screen remained blank for a full two minutes before the reply came.

ANSWER THE QUESTION.

OK, Tristram, she thought. So you don't have a sense of humour. No need to get ratty.

She typed: I DON'T KNOW. WHAT DOES IT TAKE…?

The reply was instantaneous.

ASK SIR KENNETH MYBURGHE. HE KNOWS FIRST-HAND.

She sat back and read the message three times. Whatever the words said, there was clearly a hidden subtext. Unfortunately, so far only Tristram knew what it was. She decided to cut to the chase and hit the keyboard.

WHY DON'T WE TALK ABOUT THIS?

WE ARE.

I MEAN FACE TO FACE.

There was no reply, and by the length of the pause, it was clear Tristram either wasn't sure or didn't want to reveal himself. But that could be for any number of reasons; personal, professional or moral.

Even criminal.

Riley sat and wallowed in indecision. She wasn't going to get anywhere with a story based solely on unsubstantiated and anonymous hints about another man's honesty. Yet there was something very barbed about these messages. They hinted at something far more than a simple desire to gossip, or a haphazard smear campaign by a malicious spammer.

And the accused was hardly a nobody.

Maybe, she reasoned, it was the way the messages were coming to her in this spooky, veiled manner, feeding on to her screen like notes being slipped under the door. Nothing, after all, was calculated to spike any reporter's interest more than a drip-feed of innuendo, especially when the choice of other stories to work on was less than exciting. Or was she merely responding to a touch of vanity, her ego fanned into action by the thought that this Tristram, whoever he was, had selected her as his contact?

Her phone rang. It was Donald Brask, still sounding full of cold. "Sweetie, I've got you an appointment," he croaked mournfully, "at Colebrooke House. It's this afternoon, so you'll have to get your skates on."

Riley's head was still full of Tristram and his emails. "Where and what is Colebrooke House?" she asked, wondering if it was the latest glitzy pad for a headline-seeking pop princess, and whether Donald was intent on pointing her down the track of celebrity journalism.

"It's in the Cotswolds, off the M4," he replied. "Home to Sir Kenneth Myburghe." He sounded pleased with himself. "He's agreed to an interview about his daughter's wedding."

"Donald, you're a star! How did you manage that?"

Notwithstanding his stuffed-up nose and sore throat, Donald still managed to preen. "Influence, sweetie, influence. The only condition is, you stick to the wedding and nothing else."

"Word of honour, Donald – and thank you! I'll be in touch."

She rang off just as the intercom buzzed three times in quick succession. Moments later, she heard the creak of the stairs. She went to the door and opened it just as John Mitcheson raised his hand to knock. He was holding the downstairs door key.

"Hi, babe," he said, and leaned through the doorway for a kiss.

"Hi, yourself," she replied, responding in kind. She felt a strap curled over his shoulder, and followed it round until she encountered the bulk of a leather overnight bag. She pulled away reluctantly and with a mild feeling of disappointment. "You're off on a job?"

"Yeah. Not long, though. A day, maybe two at most, out of town." He followed her into the flat, dumping his bag on the floor. "If I can, I'll drop by."

She smiled and stood close to him. "We're like ships that pass, you and I."

"Better than not, though, eh?"

"I'll say." She leaned back and looked at him, pleased to have someone else to think about for a few minutes. Especially this someone.

John Mitcheson was in his mid-thirties, tall and tanned, with smooth, dark hair and an easy smile. A former army officer, he now specialised in security work, sharing some of the same working pastures as Frank Palmer. The difference was, Riley suspected Mitcheson ventured closer to the line than Palmer when it came to the risks involved and the sort of assignments he undertook.

A couple of years younger than Palmer, his military experience had been cut short after becoming unwittingly embroiled in arms smuggling by soldiers under his command in Bosnia. Although he hadn't been part of the ring, he had made the mistake of speaking up on the men's behalf, while most other officers would have kept their distance.

Riley had first met him in Spain, while she was on the trail of a re-emerging London gang trying to promote itself back to the premier league through the traffic in drugs and illegal immigrants. Mitcheson had been working with the gang, but had changed sides in time to prevent himself meeting the same fate as some of its members – ironically, some of them the same men who had caused his earlier downfall in Bosnia. He and Riley had subsequently enjoyed an exciting, if sometimes remote relationship, as Mitcheson had, for a while, been persona non grata in the UK.

"What's cooking?" He eyed the laptop as he sat down on the sofa.

"Something or nothing," she replied vaguely. "Rumours about a diplomat… might be pie in the sky. Donald's not enthused because of the security thing surrounding them at the moment. I had to twist his arm."

Mitcheson knew how stubborn Riley could be when following a good story. "Is it anybody I know?"

Riley shuffled up next to him and spun the laptop round so he could see the last message from Tristram.

"Myburghe?" He frowned. "Sounds familiar - I'm not sure why. What's he supposed to have done?"

"I don't know yet. This Tristram is either a spotty kid having fun winding me up, or he knows something and wants to spin out the story for as long as he can. It could be a complete waste of time. I won't know until I start digging."

Mitcheson slung an arm across her shoulders. "Go with your instincts, like you always do. But watch your back. Donald's right about the diplomatic scene – it's touchy territory. Get too close and they might burn you."

They kissed for a while, taking what advantage they could from snatched time together. It was a situation they had become accustomed to, and even Mitcheson's continued presence in London had not led them to share space together on a more permanent basis. He had a small flat in Islington, and they met when they could, touching base by phone when they could not. It wasn't perfect, but for now it was all they could manage, neither of them seeming keen to push for more. In the quiet moments when she was alone, Riley sometimes asked herself why, without coming to a firm conclusion.

Mitcheson eventually broke away and stood up. "Sorry – got to go. Will you be OK?"

"Of course. Aren't I always?" She followed him to the door and watched him sling the bag over his shoulder. She experienced a small stab of something akin to loneliness each time he left, and wondered if he felt the same. For some reason, it was something she had never been able to ask him.

"The Myburghe thing," he asked. "Is Frank in on it, too?"

Mitcheson got on well with Palmer, and understood the relationship Riley had with the ex-Redcap. If he'd ever harboured any feelings of jealousy about how close they were, he had long ago come to terms with them.

"No. He's off somewhere, doing his own thing." She smiled and leaned in for a parting kiss, aware of the subtext in his question. "Don't worry. If I need to, I'll scream for help."

"Liar," he said mildly, knowing she wouldn't. One thing he'd learned about Riley was that she was far too tough and independent to play the weak female. But he also knew she would calculate the risks involved very carefully before wading in without a thought – at least, most of the time. It was an aspect of her character that had been a definite attraction ever since he'd met her. "Take care."

When he'd gone, Riley returned to her laptop and stared at the screen. She was hoping for an answer from Tristram, giving her something more to work on, a hint, maybe, of what was driving him. But the Inbox remained resolutely blank. In the end, she switched the machine to Standby and stood up. Enough of this; it was time to do something constructive. She had just enough time for a quick spot of paper research before heading westwards along the M4.

She set off for the library, where the reference section offered a variety of valuable information unmatched by Google. The quiet, academic atmosphere always seemed to inspire her thought processes far more than researching on-line at home, and she still enjoyed the feel and texture of printed paper over the soul-less click of plastic keys. If she picked up anything useful, it might help her stray off the subject of the wedding and touch on other things.

'Tristram' stared at the screen of his computer, his forehead creased with indecision.

He hadn't been prepared for this development. Sending emails to the journalist, Gavin, had been easy; he'd picked the name off the page of a newspaper and trusted to luck. It was supposed to get things moving. It was part of the plan. But the idea of meeting face to face was something else entirely. He wasn't good at face to face. He hadn't been for a long time.

He looked up at a security monitor on the wall and saw two figures appear on the screen. One of the faces was familiar, the body language well known to him. Tristram momentarily forgot all about his computer and whether he should or could meet the journalist beyond the anonymous confines of his screen. He hurried out of the small room, banging the door back against the wall as he went, the sound echoing off the tiled walls like gunfire.

5

Colebrooke House was Queen Anne in design, according to the details Riley had uncovered in her research earlier in the day. Built around 1700 by the local landowner of the time, it was square and redbrick with large, high windows and clusters of tall chimneys, and she was sure she'd seen something like it in a bus tour of Hollywood a few years ago. That one had been a good two hundred and thirty years younger than Colebrooke House, courtesy of a major MGM star with more cash than dash, but the design was the same.

Unlike Hollywood, where houses vied for space close to droves of other celebrities, this place was located a respectable distance from its nearest neighbours, a clutch of impressive but obviously lesser, stone-built mansions with far fewer trees to shield them from prying eyes.

It had been a two-hour drive from London, made longer by heavy traffic and slow going once she was off the M4, but still a pleasant change from snarled city traffic. Riley had enjoyed the scenery along the way, persuading herself that taking a trip out on what appeared to be the flimsiest of evidence was worth the punt. If it came to nothing, all she had wasted was some petrol and a few hours of her time. But at least Donald would have some background information to tout to his editor friends.

She turned in through an impressive set of wrought-iron gates and crunched along a looping strip of gravel drive bordered by heavily-laden horse chestnut trees. There were no signs of the army of staff it must take to keep the place in order, but she did catch a glimpse of one old man with a rake. He was either being suitably deferential at her passing or merely scratching his head, but she waved anyway, and smiled.

The drive snaked between two slabs of pasture and into a thick belt of mature trees. The grass borders were uniformly short with precision-cut edges. If it was all the work of the lone raker, he evidently toiled a lot harder when nobody was looking. Every now and then, through gaps in the trees, she caught a flash of rolling countryside, like pastoral snapshots of the world beyond.

To the rear of the house, glimpsed as the drive curved level with the side of the main building, stood more gardens, with an array of terraces and colourful flower-beds, while lawned areas dotted with shrubs and trees swept down a gentle slope to a thick belt of woodland running into the distance. She drove on and passed to the left of a large, stone fountain with a cherub spouting water in the centre, and another hundred yards took her between lush explosions of laurel, until the drive opened out to a fan-shaped area of gravel in front of the house. In the middle of this stood another fountain dominated by a stone goblet centrepiece bubbling with water. She pulled up to one side of the parking area and climbed out.

Dismissing the front entrance as a door would have undervalued its purpose in life; it was tall, wide, glossy and black, and mounted with enough brassware to sink a tugboat. Come the revolution, thought Riley, if a modern peasant army rolled up here to address the natural order of things, they'd take one look at this solid, gleaming barrier and go home for tea and a re-think.

As if the grounds and house weren't indication enough of Myburghe's financial standing, parked a few yards away was a Jaguar in British racing green and a dark BMW

7-series, both polished to a ferocious gleam. Even the tyres had been buffed to their original black, as if the scene had been set for a coffee-table magazine photo-shoot.

On one end of the house an intricate cluster of scaffolding clambered up the stonework like steel ivy, the poles rigged with ladders and planks behind a partial covering of see-through plastic sheeting. Judging from the workmen and the high-pitched whine of power tools sending a fine cloud of dust swirling into the atmosphere, some major renovations were in progress.

Riley counted seven bodies in all. Evidently being an ex-diplomat wasn't hurting Sir Kenneth's wallet in any way. She couldn't see any activity related to a wedding party, but presumed that was all going on at the rear of the house.

She walked up the front steps and located a discreet bellpush. The sound reverberated inside, bringing the approach of heavy footsteps.

The door was opened by a huge man with impressively broad shoulders and a craggy face like a lump of granite. He looked down at Riley and waited for her to speak. He may have been wearing a sober grey suit and shoes with a shine he could have shaved in, but his manner was clearly that of a butler. If so, Riley thought, he was one of a kind.

"My name's Riley Gavin," she said, passing him her card. "I have an appointment with Sir Kenneth."

"He's not available at the moment. May I ask what it's about?" The man's voice carried traces of a northern accent. He appeared to be in his fifties, but the years sat easily on him.

"I've come to do a piece about his daughter's wedding," she explained. "My agent made the appointment earlier."

To her surprise, the butler gave a sly smile. "Do me a favour, love," he grated. "You'll have to do better than that."

Without another word, he closed the door with a firm thud.

She stared at her reflection in the shiny paintwork. What the hell was that about? She leaned on the bell again, but there was no answer. She raised her hand, this time to pound on the wood, then thought better of it. OK, so they'd had a change of heart about an interview. Now why was that? Still, there were more ways than one of picking up on gossip; given the right approach, the folks in the village might have something useful to say.

She walked back to the car, certain that she was being observed from one of the many windows, probably by the gentleman's gentleman having a quiet chuckle at her expense. She ignored it and drove back down the drive, trying to work out her next avenue of approach. There was always the staff, of course, although she doubted they would talk. Alternatively, she could tap whatever contacts she could find in London to see if there were any whispers about Sir Kenneth circulating the corridors of Whitehall and St James's, where these things had currency.

As she rounded the final bend in the drive, she found the gateway blocked by a car parked sideways across the opening. A tall, dark figure was silhouetted against the lighter sky, leaning casually against the bonnet. She swore and jammed her foot on the brake, and felt the tyres losing their grip on the loose gravel as the car began to slide. She corrected it in time and jabbed the brake again, bringing the vehicle to a stop against a grass verge as the engine cut out.

When she looked up, the figure had stepped away from the car and was walking purposefully towards her, head down. It was a man and he was holding a heavy stick.

Riley felt the choke of fear grip her throat. She still

couldn't make out his features. She checked her rear-view mirror. The drive behind her was empty, but there was too little room to turn round – and the man was only a few feet away. She ducked her head and scrabbled in the glove compartment, fingers brushing over paper, the car's information folder and some batteries, before she found a small can of de-icer. It wasn't Mace but would be painful enough to the eyes to give her a fraction of time to do something – as long as he got close enough for it to be effective.

Then he was alongside and tapping at the window. All Riley could see was a tall frame and a strong hand clasping a heavy stick, like a club. With a sick feeling, she realised she might as well face him down rather than wreck her car trying to get by. She pressed the button to lower the glass a fraction, waiting with her thumb on the button of the spray can as the man bent and peered through the gap.

"Bit heavy on the brakes, there, weren't you, missus?" he commented, and smiled genially.

"Palmer!" Riley felt a wave of relief wash over her, fighting to compete with the surge of puzzlement at seeing a familiar, grinning face in the middle of nowhere. Before she could say anything, he gestured at the car, a muddy Saab 95, blocking the gate.

"Follow me and I'll treat you to a cream tea."

"I don't want a cream –" Riley started to protest. But he was already walking away, tossing the stick casually into the bushes.

6

Palmer led her on a fast drive to an inn a couple of miles away and pulled into the car park. He climbed out of his car and disappeared ahead of her through the front entrance. By the time she joined him in the dark-timbered lounge, he was flicking through a local magazine, long legs stuck out before him in careless disarray as if he'd been there all day.

"What the hell is going on, Palmer?" Riley nearly exploded as she slumped into a well-worn club chair across from him. "And what are you doing here? You scared the crap out of me back there!"

A young woman's head poked out from behind the reception office doorway, then ducked back again when she saw no blood was being shed.

Riley's initial relief at seeing Frank Palmer at the entrance to Colebrooke House had now given way to a deep suspicion that Donald Brask had once again donned his Mother Hen cap and asked Palmer to keep an eye on her. He'd done it before and it would never have surprised her that an unaccustomed dose of flu in Donald had awoken some temporarily dormant feelings of concern for her wellbeing. Especially if he felt that going after Myburghe was fraught with danger.

"Going on?" Palmer dropped the magazine and flicked back the twin halves of a carefully rumpled sports jacket. The rest of his clothes were his usual blend-in, comfort uniform of slacks, soft shoes and dark cotton shirt, but no tie. Palmer only did ties under sufferance, although Riley knew he sometimes carried one with an alternative outfit

36

in the back of his car for making quick changes when on surveillance work. "Suppose you tell me. You're the one who was planning on assaulting me with a can of – what was it, hair spray? Tea's coming, by the way. I asked for extra jam and cream." He gave her an innocent look and a raised eyebrow, a signal she recognised as showing he was prepared to out-wait her for an answer.

"It was de-icer, actually," she retorted. "And how was I supposed to know it was you standing there waving a big stick?"

She had first been introduced to Frank Palmer at Donald Brask's insistence when embarking on a dangerous assignment a couple of years before. Faced with the lethal attentions of a criminal gang whose members had shown few reservations about killing people who got in their way, she had reluctantly enlisted his help. Her initial impression had been of a laid-back man with low energy levels and a marked reluctance to get involved unless absolutely necessary. Subsequent events had forced her to revise those first impressions, as he had proven himself capable of ruthless efficiency, and in the time they had been acquainted, they had come to know and trust each other. They had built an easy, if sometimes prickly rapport, more akin to long-term partners than occasional colleagues, although their relationship had never shown signs of developing into anything stronger.

"Why are you following me –" She paused as a waitress appeared with a tray of cups, saucers and the makings of a cream tea, depositing them carefully in the middle of the coffee table and departing quickly with a shy smile. "Why are you following me around?" she hissed at him, but found the lure of scones and jam, not to mention cream, reminding her that she hadn't eaten in hours. She reached for a scone

37

and a knife.

"Why the hell should I be following you?" he retorted indignantly. "I've got better things to do with my time."

"Yeah, right. So you being here is just a huge coincidence?"

"Well, I don't know about you, but I'm on a job. Tea, dear?" He reached for the pot and waited for her to nod assent. "And before you start again," he continued, "I hate to sound one-uppish, but I was actually at Colebrooke House first." He pushed a cup towards her. "Which means, technically, you were following me. Were you?"

"Mmm?" While she finished a mouthful of scone, jam and cream, Riley debated whether she should believe him. He actually sounded sincere, although she'd known Palmer lie convincingly enough when the occasion demanded. Maybe he was just playing dumb and knew what she was doing here all along.

"I said, were you following me?"

"I was actually on a story," she said forcefully, but her indignation was beginning to evaporate. "Remember? It's what I do."

"I can see that." He leaned round the table and stared pointedly at her legs with an appreciative grin. "New line of attack, is it?"

Riley felt herself redden and pulled in her feet. She rarely wore a skirt and high heels, preferring instead the comfort of slacks or jeans and a jacket. For this job, however, she figured it had been worth the effort to look a little more formal. "Very funny."

"So, what's the story?"

"Sorry?"

"The lead you're following."

"Why should I tell you?"

"Because if you don't you'll develop nosebleeds and have

sleepless nights. Come on, you know you'll tell me in the end, anyway."

She gritted her teeth. Had Palmer been another journo, there was no way she'd have considered it. Needs must, however, although she wasn't about to spill everything, just in case Tristram was perpetrating a huge hoax. "It's no big deal," she said finally, and settled on the only plausible reason for her being there. "It's about Sir Kenneth Myburghe."

He rolled his eyes with a pained air. "Christ on a motorbike, I'd figured out that much already. What about him?"

"His daughter's getting married. I thought I'd do a background piece."

Palmer lifted an eyebrow. "You. Covering a wedding." His tone was as flat as his gaze, laden with disbelief.

In spite of her toying with the truth, Riley's hackles rose in response. "What's that supposed to mean? I have to pay the rent, too, you know."

"Of course. I'm sorry – that was rude and insensitive of me."

"Palmer, don't patronise me. Donald called you, didn't he? He's suffering from a dose of flu and it's making him get all motherly in his old age. He changed his mind." Then she saw the ghost of confusion drift across his face and realised that Palmer hadn't a clue what she was talking about. She swore silently. "Dammit – what were you doing there?"

Palmer helped himself to a scone and took his time spooning on a thick helping of cream and jam. Typical, thought Riley savagely, reaching for her tea. Cream first – he has to be different.

"I've been hired to do a study of security around Colebrooke House," he said, with what she thought was a slight air of pomposity. Or maybe it was the mouthful of scone and cream that was making speech difficult. "It's an exercise called risk-assessment."

"Against what?"

Palmer swallowed and showed his teeth. "People like you, mainly."

"Really? Why should–?" Then it hit her. "It was you! You blocked my interview, didn't you?"

Palmer studied her for a moment, his eyes impossible to read. There was humour in there, and friendliness. But there was also caution born of long experience, even when dealing with friends. He said, "You shouldn't take it personally. In the run-up to the wedding. I decided to bar any press interviews."

"Why?" Riley was puzzled. With Sir Kenneth Myburghe high on the diplomatic totem pole, he would surely have a single man or a team of close protection officers around him. Yet from what Palmer had said, that wasn't the case. She wondered why. "And who are you taking over security from?"

Palmer sighed, aware that Riley would continue to gnaw away at this until she got the answers she was looking for. "Do you know anything about him?" he asked. "His working background, for example?"

"I know he's been in Colombia."

He nodded. "He spent years at the embassy in Bogotá. They've got some dangerous people over there, including the drug cartels, FARC or any number of other groups with a grievance to air."

"FARC?"

"Fuerzas Armadas Revolucionarios de Colombia." He supplied the translation easily. "They're conducting a war against the government and use drugs to fund it. There's always a risk of them taking action against a representative of the British or US governments, just to regain face among the locals."

"You seem to know a lot about them."

"Well, you know me – I read all the right books." He reached out a fingertip to scoop up a blob of cream and ate it with relish. "Next question?"

"Question?"

"Of course. I know you've got one – you always do."

"OK. Why would these groups have a grievance against Myburghe now he's retired? He can't do anything to them, can he?"

"Search me. He represents – or used to, anyway – British attempts to wipe out the drugs trade. And according to my brief, that's reason enough for me to check out everyone who comes near him."

"But I'm not a FARC person – and we're a long way from Bogotá."

Palmer shrugged. "If anyone wants to settle some old scores, he and his family are soft targets." He gave her another infuriating smile. "In any case, your trip down here has got nothing to do with the wedding, has it? You don't do that sort of fluff stuff."

Palmer knew her better than anyone else, but Riley had learned to read him fairly well, too. And right now she sensed there was something he wasn't telling her.

Then something else occurred to her. Weller.

"That's why Weller was asking questions about you!" she said, barely able to hide her excitement. "Your name popped up alongside a senior diplomat, and they want to know why." She frowned, trying to figure out what it meant. "Is that normal?"

Palmer gave one of his infuriating shrugs. "No idea, guv.

Maybe this Weller's put all his paper clips in a chain for the week and doesn't know what to do next."

"Aren't you bothered?"

"Why should I be? I've done nothing illegal. They're probably just dotting the tees and making sure I haven't got a bazooka in my back pocket and a grudge against people who insist on paying me to work for them. It's typical security department paranoia."

Palmer and his laid-back attitude made it all sound so reasonable and straightforward. A former diplomat in one of the world's hot-spots might have upset somebody over the years, either real or imagined – and in Colombia, Riley was guessing it might have been real – so it would be reasonable to expect that he would need a level of protection for a while after returning. But how long could it continue? The UK wasn't like the States, where important government officials dragged an army of sun-shaded heavies around with them for life. Over here, she thought cynically, they'd be lucky to get a guide dog on loan for a couple of weeks.

"Isn't it a bit high-risk? For you, I mean. What if some-one takes a pop at him?"

"I doubt it'll happen. They wouldn't leave him unprotected if they were that concerned. The official team signs off in a couple of days, and I'll take over from there. After that, who knows?"

"So you," she surmised casually, suddenly switching tack, "being his protection detail, would be able to get me in to see him, wouldn't you?" It was a rather crude attempt to use him, but one she thought might work.

It didn't.

"Dream on, kiddo," he replied shortly, and gave a brief chuckle. "No way am I going to smuggle you in there. I'd sooner stick a red hot poker in my eye."

"Palmer!" Riley protested. "After all the things I've done for you!"

His eyebrows shot up a notch or two. "Yeah? Name me ten."

"Pig." She scowled at him, but he'd already turned his attention to another scone, which he coated with cream and settled back to enjoy. She let it go and debated what she could say that might penetrate his armour. Not that he'd hold out forever; she'd get to him eventually. The only problem was how long it would take. "I'll have to find out what he's been up to some other way, then." The comment came out before she could stop it. To cover her mistake, she finished her tea and stood up.

"Good luck," he said easily. "Out of interest, what did Rockface say?"

"Rockface?" She stared. "Oh, you mean the butler. Why Rockface? Because he's big and dense?"

Palmer shook his head. "Don't be fooled by appearances. He's good at his job. I'm just interested in how he handled it."

"Basically, he laughed at me and closed the door."

"Was that all? He must have taken a shine to you. He doesn't like the press much. The last reporter who pushed his luck trying to get the story on the wedding got dumped in the fountain." He got ready to take another bite of his scone, then said casually, "Anyway, what makes you think Myburghe's been up to anything?"

Riley bit her lip. Damn – he'd noticed her slip. "I'm not sure I want to tell you now," she said, aware that she sounded like a stroppy teenager throwing a tantrum. As he grinned at her with a show of triumph, she added furiously, "Don't worry - there's bound to be someone who knows why he's been kicked off the diplomatic list."

The effect on Palmer was dramatic: he choked on his scone and sat forward, coughing, his face going red. He waved at her to wait while recovering his composure and wiping crumbs off his shirtfront. Eventually, he stared up at her. "What did you say?"

"Oh, did they forget to mention that?" Riley smiled loftily at his reaction. "Word is, Sir Ken's no longer welcome on the top table at Her Majesty's official bun-fights. Sounds like he's been misbehaving, don't you think?" She touched her cheek, to one side of her mouth. "Cream, Frank – on your face. Wipe it off, there's a good boy."

Then she turned and walked out.

She was tired when she got home, and only half paying attention when she switched on her laptop and called up her emails. The cat was on the sofa cleaning itself, by which she concluded he'd already eaten downstairs courtesy of Mr Grobowski. She just hoped there hadn't been too much cabbage, or he'd be going out for the night.

There was a single message from Tristram, this time placed in the main body of the email. It made her skin go cold.

WHILE GOOD MEN DIED IN THE SOUTH ATLANTIC, ONE BAD ONE WAS SUPPING WITH THE DEVIL. IT'S GOING TO COME BACK TO HAUNT HIM....

7

"Palmer, I need to see you."

Riley had sat on the email from Tristram all night, fearing it was simply a ramping up of his claims to gain a greater reaction from her. It wouldn't be the first time someone had chosen to take out some deeply hidden frustrations on a complete stranger, preferably a person in a position of influence. Stalkers did it all the time, although they were usually content to try and insert themselves into the VIP's life by association, gaining kudos by proximity and implied friendship, a brush-by existence that was ultimately doomed to turn sour.

But the more she thought about this one, the more she felt there was a serious undercurrent at work here. Whatever Tristram was up to, the focus was too specific to be dismissed as the work of a crank. And though it went against the grain to pull someone else in on the story, she felt Palmer had to know. It was only seven in the morning, but she knew he'd be up and about.

"Aw, shucks," he exclaimed yokel-like, when he answered the phone. "You missing me?"

"Frank, I've some information about your protectee. I think you ought to know."

Her use of his first name clinched it. She almost never called him Frank.

"What sort of information?"

"I think I know someone with a grudge against him."

There was a pause. Then he said, "I can't get away until later this morning. The pub in Colebrooke village is called The Armourer. Meet me there at eleven."

"OK." She disconnected before she was tempted to say more, and headed for the door.

Palmer's Saab was already in the small car park behind the pub when Riley arrived in the village, a collection of small, stone-built cottages half a mile from Colebrooke House. She locked the Golf and ducked through the low front door, and found Palmer nursing a fruit juice at a table in one corner. Another glass stood across the table. He looked half asleep, but she wasn't fooled for a minute.

She dropped copies of the earlier emails from Tristram on the table in front of him, and sat down while he read them.

"This is what brought you up here yesterday." His face remained blank, but she felt sure incredulity might be lurking beneath the surface. "Not the wedding. I might have known." He slid the emails back across the table. "It's a crank," he said finally. "Somebody with an overactive imagination. Do you have any proof – any hard details of what Myburghe is supposed to have done?"

She knew Palmer wasn't being as cynical as he sounded. He wasn't stupid, and knew perfectly well that not all the people he worked for were innocent or paranoid. Nor were they all driven to surround themselves with visible protection as a mark of their celebrity status. Some genuinely had reason to fear for their safety – even if merely from the exposure of their family routine by the work of the paparazzi. Where he could, she knew he vetted clients before accepting contracts. Anyone overtly criminal, he left well alone. In other cases, he trod carefully and made his judgements as he progressed.

"I've only got what Tristram tells me," she said. "But there's something about it that has the ring of truth."

He shrugged and said nothing, waiting for her to make out a case for what she was suggesting. He needed to be convinced.

"OK, so it's thin," she admitted. "But we've both worked with less than this before. I know you often go by gut feeling. This is my turn."

"Maybe. But this isn't just anybody."

"That's my point. Even if this Tristram is making this up, why pick Myburghe – unless he's got something against him? He's your protectee or whatever you call them. What if Tristram's driven to do more than send a few cranky emails?" She paused to let that sink in, then asked, "When did Myburghe first go to Colombia?"

Frank pursed his lips. "Years ago. He pretty much made it a career posting. Why?"

"As far back as the eighties?"

"Eighty-one was his first tour." Then he sat up, his antennae twitching. "You've had more emails, haven't you? What did they say?"

Riley took out the latest communication from Tristram and slid it across the table. Palmer read it once, then again, before looking at her and shaking his head. "This could mean anything."

"Come on, Palmer," she protested. "This is getting too close to the core, isn't it? Nineteen eighty-two was the Falklands. Where was Myburghe at that time?"

He sighed deeply and stared at the ceiling, then leaned across the table, one eye on the nearest customers. They were too engrossed in their drinks to be paying any attention.

"OK. I'll tell you what I know. But this isn't for publication, got it? I've only just been briefed about it. In any case, it might not have anything to do with what this Tristram is alleging."

He took a sip of his juice. "Sir Kenneth Myburghe has two daughters, the elder of who, Victoria, is getting married. He also has an eighteen-year-old son named Christian. Sir Kenneth recently returned to the UK after spending most of his life overseas – almost all of it in Latin America. He did it the hard way, working his way up the ladder from consular assistant to vice consul and then up to the plum post of ambassador in the embassy in Bogotá. Four months ago, they pulled him back. The implication was that it was prior to another posting. That hasn't happened."

"Why?"

"No idea. He should have got one by now. But that's by the by. A few weeks ago, he began receiving threats."

"What sort of threats?"

"Phone calls to begin with. Silent calls, nobody there – that kind of thing. He thought it was computerised call centre dialling, but they became too insistent. Occasionally there were a few words whispered down the line before the caller hung up. Nothing specific, just vague threats. Then there were messages on his answer phone saying he was going to die. Three weeks ago he got a stream of letters. Some contained a single black feather, others a crushed spider."

"Yuck. It could be this Tristram."

"It's nasty, whoever it is. Most of the threats arrived by post at his home. Sir Kenneth dismissed them… said he couldn't concern himself with every crank call or letter he received."

"Big of him. What else?"

"Else?"

"You said most of the threats. That means there's an else. The elses are what make your eyes light up."

"Ah. You mean the fake parcel-bomb."

"See? I told you. How fake?"

"Clock, wires, batteries and something called Silly-Putty, which was once big among ten-year-olds, apparently. It arrived before I came on the scene. Myburghe called the bomb squad for that one. They weren't impressed; they only like going out to poke things that really do go bang. Childish pranks annoy them."

"I take it Sir Kenneth doesn't have grandchildren with fertile imaginations?"

"No. The latest threat was last week, just before his son Christian was due back from a trip to the States."

Riley sensed Palmer was about to tell her something nasty.

"Christian didn't come back, did he?"

"No."

"He's probably working his way through all the girls on Venice Beach. He'll turn up when he runs out of money. Or stamina."

Palmer shook his head. "I doubt it. The boy didn't come back, but one of his fingers did."

8

"What the hell could Myburghe have done to deserve that?" Riley asked, her voice low. They had moved in one giant leap from a diplomat receiving threats, to fake parcel bombs and now body parts in the post. How much worse could this get? She was beginning to view the shadowy Tristram in a whole new light.

"Maybe being our man in Colombia was enough."

Riley wasn't sure. In journalistic terms, mentioning Colombia rarely brought thoughts of their coffee or other edible crops. It was more the powdered export that sprang to mind – the kind which doesn't come decaffeinated but has the power to send people to sleep. For good.

"By 'our man', do you mean there was more to his position than Ambassador?" As she knew, the term could mean all manner of things, from the senior embassy position to someone with an altogether more secretive role.

"No, he was just the Ambassador."

"Oh." As brief as her research had been so far, she already had a fund of information about the reality of power and influence in Colombian life. The families running drug production in the hills of Colombia were notoriously brutal in their methods and indiscriminate in their targets, especially when someone threatened their lucrative operations. The British and Americans had been trying for years, with little real success in spite of destroying acres of poppy-producing fields, laboratories and supply-lines. The country was rugged enough and the rewards vast enough to mean that whenever one operation closed down, another sprang up overnight in a new location. That required more teams of soldiers in helicopters to scour more miles of hills and valleys and the use of fires to halt production wherever it was discovered. It made the people running the operations very unpopular among the poverty-stricken locals.

"He'd have still found it easy to make enemies," Palmer said, guessing what she was thinking. "It's one of the reasons why the embassy in Bogotá has a round-the-clock close protection team of Royal Military policemen and some thick armour-plated glass on cars and buildings."

"But we don't know if that's the reason for the threats."

"No."

"Maybe somebody should ask him."

"Somebody could try," he agreed. "Especially after this." He nodded towards the email. Then he looked carefully at her with a serious expression.

"What?" she asked. Palmer was considering something - she could read the signs.

"There's a briefing tomorrow. The wedding is on Friday."

"I know. And?"

"You're included."

"What?" Riley was amazed. After his initial stand against letting her anywhere near Myburghe, here was Palmer saying she was in. "Why the change of heart?"

"Because if it is Tristram behind the threats, we need to find out who he is before he bumps it up a level. So far you're his only contact. It could be useful."

"If he ever opens up to me. He hasn't done so far."

Palmer shrugged. "It's a lead. We could always ask Weller to get his IT boys on to it."

Riley instinctively recoiled from allowing any official snoops near her work or her sources. "Over my dead body," she said firmly.

"Suit yourself. But if anything major happens, you might not have a choice."

Riley subsided a little. He was right. The idea of Tristram progressing from spreading nasty rumours over the internet to something more violent was something she didn't want to contemplate. "All right. But what's my role in this?"

"Well, you're not from the press, for a start. You're working for me. And you give me your word not to publish anything you learn."

"What?" Riley protested. "Hang on, what about my –?"

"Or you don't get in." His tone was uncompromising. "Deal?"

She bit down on her objections. There was an obstinate point about Palmer beyond which it was pointless trying to push him. She'd tried it in the past and knew he wouldn't give way. On the other hand, what choice did she have? She would rather be on the inside getting his help than on the outside going nowhere. "OK, deal. But can we talk about my story later?"

He nodded. "Of course."

"Good. I don't have to go round frisking bridesmaids for hidden weapons, though, do I?"

Palmer allowed a dreamy smile to touch his mouth. "If anyone frisks the bridemaids, it'll be me. As far as you're concerned, this job is strictly no touchy, no feely."

"What if there's a punch up? Weddings always have a punch up." She sighed. "The ones I go to, anyway."

"God, how common. There won't be any punch-ups. The bride's father is a senior diplomat and his wife has connections. The only fighting is likely to be over the bride's corsage."

"You mean she's still got it? How quaint."

"Peasant."

"Just for the record, why? Why include me?"

"Because I need some help," he said candidly.

"I can tell that. Christ, I know you're already over-stretched, even with Man Mountain on the door. But why me – I'm press, remember?"

He rolled his eyes. "Do I have to have a reason? Don't be so suspicious."

"Uh-huh. Tell me."

He blinked, suddenly serious. "What you said earlier – about what you've done for me. You saved my life once. I owe you. And this might help."

Riley felt a stab of guilt. He'd clearly taken her taunt to heart. She wished she'd never uttered the words. "Palmer, that's not what I was talking about. I didn't mean that – I wouldn't do that to you!"

The silence seemed to last a long time. It could have only been seconds, but long enough to stir up unwelcome flashes from two years before, of her hurling a flaming petrol-filled bottle, knowing it might make all the difference between whether Palmer, held hostage inside a warehouse, lived or died.

"Yeah, I know that." He smiled easily, suddenly the old Palmer again, and flapped a weary hand. "I suppose there is another, ulterior reason."

"Go on."

"I thought you could deal with any ruffled feathers of the female variety." He paused and added, "And I trust your judgement better than anyone else I know."

"Oh. Do you? Fair enough." She felt suddenly relieved. The last thing she wanted was for Palmer to feel obligated to her. Their friendship was too valuable for that, and she knew he'd hate her to feel the same way. Besides, he'd more than made up for her saving his skin ever since. "So I'm handling any difficult dames, and you're there for your dark glasses and general air of crude, Neanderthal menace."

"Hey, that hurts. I don't do dark glasses... I think you're confusing me with the US Secret Service."

"Impossible. They're mostly young, pretty and smartly dressed."

"True. They also wear those cute little spiral wire communication thingies. I've been meaning to cut a length off my phone wire and shove one end in my ear. I thought it might impress the punters."

"Has anyone ever told you to get out more?"

"Everyone except my nurse." He fluttered his eyebrows.

"There's one thing," she pointed out seriously. "I'm no bodyguard. Won't it be obvious?"

"Just follow my lead. You've got good instincts, and you've been in this kind of situation before." He knew from previous assignments that Riley was solid and wouldn't go all wobbly over a broken nail. "Just play dumb about your real job. If anyone asks, you do security work with me. But don't talk about it. They won't expect you to, anyway."

"What about Rockface? He knows."

"From what you said about his reaction to you, he probably thought it was a test. Don't worry, I'll deal with him."

"If you say so. Where do we start?"

"Have you ever been on a shoot?"

"As in cameras and anorexic models? Or as in guns, wellies and dead animals?"

"Guns and dead stuff."

"No. I've never seen the point. Although if I was threatened by a large aggressive pheasant, I might change my mind."

Palmer smiled. "The briefing's at eleven in the morning.

I'll pick you up at your place. Bring boots."

"Is that all? No roof-mounted machine-gun? No ground-to-bird missiles? Not even a catapult? It doesn't sound like the usual bit of bird-slaughtering to me."

"God, spare me," he said dryly. "Don't go all animal welfare on me. If you behave yourself, they'll probably let you sit in the car with a bottle of pop and a packet of crisps."

"Oh, goody. I can't wait."

"Let's hope," he added darkly, "they're the only guns we see."

Sir Kenneth Myburghe stared out of the window across the rear gardens of Colebrooke House, to where a team of workmen were putting up a large marquee on the lawn. Normally fastidious about the state of the grass and borders, he found it unusually easy to ignore the damage being done by the influx of men, machinery and equipment he had called in for the celebrations of his daughter's wedding in a few days time.

He turned away and contemplated the letter he had received that morning. On official Home Office paper, it confirmed what he had been quietly fearing all along: that the security team assigned to him in the wake of the threatening letters and fake bomb was being withdrawn and assigned to other, more pressing duties. The apologies were as meaningless as they were sincere, and concluded by suggesting several avenues he might wish to pursue for making alternative security arrangements.

Myburghe flicked the letter away in irritation. What it meant was private security companies, for which he'd have to pay through the nose. The formal missive was almost as chilling as the other, unsigned letters, and ironically meant the same thing: that he was now exposed and his life could be in danger. Fortunately, he'd been expecting it and had already made arrangements via friends. But the confirmation did nothing to ease his anxiety about Friday. He would never forgive himself if anything happened to his family, the most vulnerable of who were Victoria and Annabel.

A knock at the door prevented him dwelling on the situation. It was the reassuring bulk of his butler.

"Sorry to interrupt, sir," the man said. "Mr Keagan called. He confirmed that he'll be briefing Palmer tomorrow."

Myburghe nodded. He was aware of Palmer's capabilities, and that he was good at his job. But Palmer was just one man. What he needed, if the threats were genuine, was a whole team of Palmers.

The butler was hovering, and it was clear there was something else on his mind.

"What is it?" said Myburghe.

"Down at the village pub. The landlord said a man has been asking questions about the wedding."

"A reporter?"

"He said not."

"I expect it was Palmer. Keagan gave him a preliminary assignment to look at the area and report back."

"I don't think so, sir. A foreigner, he said."

Sir Kenneth's shoulders felt suddenly chilled, and he tried instinctively to keep his face blank of any emotion. It didn't do to let anyone know how you felt, even though this man knew him better than most. "Foreign? Not –?"

"Anglo American, sir."

The butler stepped back through the door. As the man turned sideways, Myburghe saw the telltale bulk of the gun in his pocket. Instead of the sense of comfort it should have brought, it merely added to his growing fears.

He turned back to the window. North Americans he could deal with. The man was probably a tourist tout looking for events to sell to his rubbernecking compatriots on their whistle-stop tours of middle England. Show them a few mullioned windows and some oak beams, and they'd be in seventh heaven.

His eyes were drawn towards a clump of trees to one side of the house, where a stable block stood. It had once housed a few horses, but was now deserted. The building was an uncomfortable reminder that any threat to his safety was not as far away as he might imagine.

No, North Americans he could deal with; those further south, however, were a different prospect altogether.

9

By eleven the following morning, Riley and Palmer were turning on to a rutted track leading through a thick belt of trees. Tetbury was five miles away in one direction, the village of Colebrooke three miles behind them. Riley was riding shotgun, which meant holding a map and singing out directions for Palmer to follow. Apart from acknowledging the instructions, Palmer was humming tunelessly and staring out at the greenery. There was a lot to stare at.

They were both clad in rubber boots, although Riley's were Hunter green and fitted properly, whereas Palmer's had come from a self-service station just off the M4. They were black and fitted like canoes. Not that it seemed to bother him.

Riley thought that London seemed far away and was wondering where this particular job was leading them. The idea of a boy's body parts being sent to his father was horrible, especially when set against the backdrop of the shire counties, titled gentry and chinless wonders blasting holes in the sky in the name of sport.

"Who are we meeting?" she asked, as Palmer steered the Saab down a narrow, bumpy back-road bordered by thick hedges.

"A man named Keagan. Major. Ex-military. He's part of the Diplomatic Protection Group and runs the security detail responsible for Myburghe's safety, among others. Sir Kenneth has instructed him to give us a briefing."

"So why out here and not at the house?"

"It's easier this way. There are too many people wandering

around his place – builders, caterers, staff and wedding organisers. Sir Kenneth's holed up indoors and some friends are acting as decoys for the day's shoot."

"Really? Now they'll know what a pheasant feels like. Nice to see they're taking it seriously."

"They are at the moment. Some of Keagan's team are with him, treating it like a training exercise. The rest are at the house." Palmer turned down a track, swinging past a stocky, Lycra-clad cyclist bent over a racing bike. The man didn't bother looking up, intent on tugging at the chain which was hanging loose from the main cog.

Riley was surprised they hadn't sealed up Myburghe's house like a fortress with him inside. If it had been her under threat, she would have found the safest place available and locked herself in with a team of heavies at every access point until it was safe to come out. On the other hand, that was a way to grow old and grey, thereby missing some of life's finer pleasures.

"Thoughts?" Palmer spoke as they cleared a tunnel of trees and turned through a gateway on to a gentle hillside with half of Gloucestershire spread out before them. At least Riley assumed it was still Gloucestershire; her geography was never too good once she was out of London.

"I'm still thinking them," she replied.

Several gleaming 4WDs splattered with mud were parked on the hill, their occupants standing in a group nearby, guns at the ready. They all wore the uniform of Hunter boots, Barbours and peaked caps, and had that air of well-fed leanness which comes from good breeding, money and time spent in the great outdoors.

One or two men turned their way, but nobody moved to greet them. Palmer parked the car facing back the way they'd come. He turned off the engine and they sat waiting for Keagan to come forward. The tree line around them was heavy and dark, full of shifting shadows.

"If you go down to the woods today," Palmer sang quietly. "I counted three."

"Three what?" asked Riley.

"Security men hanging around in the bushes. Four if you include the chunky individual mending his bike near the entrance to the track."

Riley nodded at the men with the guns. "What about them?"

"Strictly local colour. Keagan brought them in to make it look real."

"Risky, isn't it? He could have all manner of collateral damage if anyone lets rip at them."

Palmer grunted as one of the men suddenly swung round with scant regard for his companions and blasted away at a pheasant flying by. The bird didn't even bother to duck and continued on its way, leaving the shooter looking red-faced and the other men laughing. "With shooting like that, any gunman showing up here is in more danger than the birds."

"If the bomb package was a hoax," said Riley, musing out loud about the series of threats, "then why not the finger, too?"

"There was a family ring attached. No hoax."

"Oh." Riley fell silent. The implications weren't good. "In that case, the boy won't be coming back, will he?"

Palmer shook his head. "Unlikely."

"Does Myburghe realise that?"

"I think so."

Riley shivered at the idea. If it was a straight kidnap, even moderate statistics held that most victims died within seventy-two hours of being snatched. In some cases, this was due to inept or simply callous kidnappers; in others it was the fear of being identified if they let the victim go. In a minority there was never any intention of the victim surviving, and few of these made it past the first day.

Then there was the matter of the finger. Getting hold of a spare as a ghastly form of hoax was no simple matter. In spite of the lurid stories turned up by the media about the occasional careless disposal of limbs, it wasn't simply a case of tripping along to the local morgue and buying a spare body part. And grave robbing was a little too public to go unnoticed.

Riley felt sickened at the thought of cutting off a finger. But the cold brutality of the act didn't end there; she was no expert in medical matters, but she figured if the boy wasn't in a proper hospital or at least being cared for by a professional medic when the finger was cut off, he was going to die from shock, infection or blood loss.

She looked up as one of the men left the group and walked towards them, waving a hand. He had a relaxed air of authority and she guessed he must be Keagan. Then she glanced in the rear-view mirror and saw a slight shift of movement in the trees behind the car. No doubt one of his watchers.

She hoped they weren't feeling trigger-happy.

They climbed out to meet the security man. He had a shotgun tucked under his arm and looked as if he'd been born holding it. He was in his early fifties and built like a battletank, with weather-beaten skin and short grey hair beneath a tweed cap. Even without knowing who he was, or seeing the gimlet-like eyes appraising them, there was no mistaking the bearing of a former military man.

"Palmer," he said crisply. His eyes swept across to Riley

and hovered momentarily. "I didn't realise you'd have company."

"My associate," Palmer replied. "Riley Gavin."

The two men exchanged handshakes with wary civility. Riley received a curt nod. The look on Keagan's face said he was unhappy with their presence, but that Palmer had passed muster, so he wasn't about to complain.

"You may have seen my three men on the way in," he said, eyes flicking past them toward the trees.

"Four, actually," Palmer told him. "The man on the bike could lose a bit of weight. That Lycra's deadly with a beer gut."

Keagan's face went tight around the mouth and Riley tried not to laugh. The major had been testing them and had tripped over his own arrogance. He either didn't know or hadn't believed that in Frank Palmer he was dealing with someone experienced in the game of spotting covert surveillance. She decided it didn't augur well for any future working relationship.

"Sir Kenneth wanted you brought in," he huffed, changing the subject, "against my advice and official suggestions."

Palmer looked at Riley. "He means there are lots of hairy-chested ex-Special Forces people out there who are better qualified than me...which is almost true."

"So why not get them in?" Riley asked. It had been puzzling her, too. She assumed that Myburghe, as a former diplomat under threat, would have access to some expert assistance, especially since the threats he was receiving might be coming from his last posting in Colombia. It wouldn't be total cover, but better than nothing.

"Sir Kenneth's personal wishes," Keagan told her. "I've advised him – that's all I can do." His tone indicated he was about to perform a hand-washing exercise, and if Sir

Kenneth wanted to put his trust in a pair of amateurs in mismatched wellies, there was little else the official establishment could do but step back smartly and wish him good luck.

On one level Riley couldn't help but sympathise. Nobody likes having the rug cut from beneath them. But she had no doubts that Palmer would have been checked out carefully first.

"What about your men?" Palmer queried. "How long will they be around?"

"Not long. We're over-stretched as it is with the terrorist situation and we've got more assignments than personnel. The letters and fake bomb here could just be the work of a nutcase. God knows, there are plenty out there."

No mention of the finger, Riley noted. Either he didn't know or it was being kept under wraps like a nasty family secret.

"And the party?" she asked.

"Don't know. We'll be there, but in the background. Unless we're pulled off for something else." His tone indicated that he meant for something more important. "Again, Sir Kenneth's express wishes." He hefted the shotgun to change the conversation. "He's not here this morning, on my advice. But I can give you a briefing. Do you shoot?"

The question was lobbed vaguely between them, but Riley knew it was for Palmer more than her. She shook her head. "Not me. But you boys go and play with your guns. I'll try not to frighten off the birdies."

Palmer followed Keagan across the grass towards the other men. Riley helped herself from a flask of coffee in the car, watching the men shake hands and exchange bonding-type nods and guffaws of laughter. One of them handed Palmer a gun and a handful of cartridges, then they turned towards the open field before them as Keagan signalled to an unseen beater.

Riley wandered along on the fringe of trees near the car, sipping her coffee, turning with a start as a barrage of gun-fire erupted. She watched as Palmer waited for the others to finish shooting, before turning and casually bringing down a pair of shapeless birds without even shouldering his gun. It earned him a startled look from Keagan and a scowl or two from his companions, but Palmer ignored them and re-loaded.

Riley bit down on her distaste at the firepower and the loss of wildlife. She and Palmer had a job to do; throwing a moral snit right now would merely get in the way.

She began to think about what they had taken on between them. At best, they might end up supervising a pleasant party and picking the odd guest out of the ancestral fish-pond. At worst, they might find themselves up to their elbows in something nastier, a situation Palmer had once equated bluntly with having to pick their teeth out of the wallpaper.

If Myburghe was using his daughter's wedding as an exercise in false bravado after admitting to himself that his son wasn't coming home, he might have become blind to the real dangers. And they might surface only when Keagan and his security team disappeared, leaving Palmer and Riley to deal with any opposition.

A flicker of movement drew her attention to a beech tree several yards inside the wood. Riley stopped and sipped her coffee. She was no security expert, but she knew that protection was mostly about setting perimeters: outer ones to deter the half-hearted and to act as a filter; inner ones to catch the badly trained or the inept amateur. Finally – and most critically – there was the very innermost circle of close protection which nobody liked to think would ever be needed if the other two were doing their job.

Was this one of Keagan's men standing close to the shooting party instead of covering the ground further out? Or someone else? An univited guest, perhaps. She scanned the area again in case she'd made a mistake. Maybe what she'd seen was a leaf falling, a swaying branch or even a foraging squirrel. Any or all three, possibly. She was about to move on when she caught her breath and felt the hairs prickle on the back of her neck. A man was standing a few yards away, watching.

10

The man was heavily built and wearing a drab brown jacket and trousers, with a grey baseball cap pulled low over his eyes. He appeared to have streaks of something dark across his face, as if he had rubbed it with a muddy hand. He was watching the shooting party, and Riley thought it odd that if he was a member of the security team, he wasn't facing the other way. His whole body stance and look were too intense, and it was a moment or two before Riley realised that the man was completely unaware of her presence.

She stepped slowly to one side, inching out of his line of vision. Slipping into the trees and avoiding branches at shoulder level and twigs underfoot, she tried not to look too intently at the watcher. Once inside the canopy of trees, it was as quiet as a church, with only a faint breeze stirring the upper branches. The smell in here was green and loamy, with the faint tang of rotting vegetation, and for an instant, Riley was reminded of childhood visits to the countryside, where she had played the tomboy among similar scenery to this. It had all been fun back then, with only imaginary dangers lurking behind every bush and fallen tree trunk, and only friends likely to leap out at her.

This, though, was very different.

She felt something solid against her foot and shortened her step. Looking down, she saw it was a heavy branch, dry and solid, the length of a golf club. She slowly lowered herself until she could reach it, then stood upright again, holding the stick by her side. It felt reassuringly heavy in her grasp.

The man shifted his stance and Riley froze. His head

turned away from the men out in the open, and she saw his eyes shift to the area immediately around him, scanning from right to left.

A bird chirruped overhead, then flew away through the branches with a clatter of wings. Riley held her breath and half-closed her eyes, in case the man looked directly at her. She knew that if you stared too hard at somebody, it might eventually trigger an instinctive response and draw his attention.

Suddenly he was looking right at her, eyes opening wide in surprise. Before she could move, he turned and was gone.

Riley was still holding her cup in her other hand. She dropped it and pulled out her mobile. She could just about see Palmer and the others through the branches, but they were too far away to alert without shouting. It was point-less anyway. If the men around Palmer were just locals, they might panic and start blowing holes in the trees right where she was standing.

"What's up?" Palmer's tone was casual, but he knew there was a problem.

"I'm in the trees, in front of you and slightly to your left," she told him. "There's a man wearing a grey baseball cap and what looks like camouflage cream. I thought it was one of Keagan's men, but when he saw me he legged it."

"Which way?"

"Back towards the road."

"Hold on." She watched him turn and speak to Keagan. The Major snatched a radio from his pocket and began calling names. He repeated one name several times without any response and began to look alarmed, as if all his plans had suddenly come unstuck.

Palmer came back on. "One of his men has gone off-line,"

he said softly. "Stay where you are and watch your back." He began walking towards the trees at an angle away from Riley. He was holding the shotgun in front of him.

Riley felt a cold shiver run down her spine at the thought of all the space behind her, most of it in deep shadow. Two steps sideways were sufficient to disguise anyone dressed in the right colour clothing; four steps rendered them invisible. She tucked her mobile into the top pocket of her jacket, then slid against the comforting bulk of a nearby tree, gripping the stick with both hands. She lowered herself to a crouch, hoping to see some sign of movement nearer the ground, but the thicket was too heavy to see more than a few yards in any direction.

A crashing to her right signalled the man was coming back. She held her breath. Then a darker shape than the background foliage appeared, charging through the thicket but moving with surprising speed.

Riley tensed. If he carried on his path, he'd crash right into her – and she had nowhere to go. She gripped the stick tightly and waited for the impact, hoping she didn't get mown down like a helpless fairy.

But the intruder must have spotted her at the last second. He suddenly veered away with a muttered oath, hurtling at an angle through the trees and leaving behind a whipping frenzy of shaking branches and falling leaves. One of the branches swatted Riley across the mouth and sent her spinning, and by the time she got to her feet, the silent watcher was gone and a tall figure was standing over her with an impassive look on his face.

He was holding a pistol pointed at her head.

"Did you see him?" Riley asked, spitting out bits of bark and clambering to her feet. Her pride was more bruised than her face, and she wondered where this latest man had sprung from. God knows how they taught people like him and Palmer to move, she thought. They were like ghosts.

"See who?" he replied, and before she could protest, he'd spun her round and pushed her against a tree and was running expert hands over her. It was as impersonal and casually expert as it was demeaning, and she wanted to drop-kick him into the undergrowth.

When Palmer appeared, he was no longer carrying the shotgun, but had a furious Keagan in tow, shouting into a small radio. The minder who had searched her waited for a nod from his boss, then stepped back and disappeared among the trees without a word. Riley decided there was nothing wrong with their teamwork, even if their manners sucked.

"You OK?" said Palmer. He spoke automatically, but the look in his eyes showed concern.

"No, I'm bloody not!" Riley muttered. "That ape just treated me like a criminal."

"That was my fault," said Keagan. "I forgot to give him a description." He went back to his radio, clearly not too disturbed by the omission.

Palmer made a signal to Riley to follow him, and they walked back to the car. "We might as well leave," he explained. "Right now, we're in the way. It's still their job."

"They've got four watchers in place, yet someone gets close enough to lob a brick," Riley said angrily, pulling off her boots and replacing them with shoes. Her upper lip was smarting and she had a flash print of the man's eyes in her mind, boring into hers. Not that it would help her recognise him again. The smears of black on his face had done a good job of breaking up his features. "Some protection team."

"Maybe." Palmer nodded, deep in thought. He looked

back towards Keagan, busy organising his men to make a sweep of the woods for their missing colleague.

"You've gone all quiet and moody," she said. "What's up?"

Palmer climbed in the car and started the engine. "Something about this doesn't add up. Keagan told me he's been told to stand down as of tomorrow, ready for re-assignment. That's another way of saying that Myburghe no longer rates a security team."

"So?"

"If Myburghe was still an important member of the diplomatic corps, there's no way they'd leave him exposed – especially if serious threats had been made against him. It would be like telling anyone who cared to listen that it was open season on Her Majesty's Foreign Office staff. They'd have nutcases and terrorists coming out of the woodwork all over the world."

"So they've cut him adrift?"

He nodded. "Looks like it. The only question is why?"

"Maybe Tristram will tell me."

"If you could get him to talk. And if he knows anything."

They drove back to London.

"You were out in Colombia, weren't you?" Riley looked across the table at John Mitcheson, who was staring dreamily back, a happy smile on his face and a glass of wine in his hand. They were in a local Italian restaurant having a late dinner. Mitcheson had completed his latest assignment earlier than he'd thought, but was about to go off on another the next morning. After the excitement of her day in the woods, it was a welcome diversion.

"Uh-huh. For a while."

"What did you do out there?"

"A bit of training, mostly. Their government supplied the anti-drugs units and the British army ran the courses. Why?"

"Bear with me. What's FARC?"

Mitcheson sat up, eyes instantly losing the dreamy look. "FARC? Bloody hell, that's a conversation stopper."

"Sorry. It's a work thing. Palmer told me a bit about them, their fight with the Colombian government. Are they dangerous?"

He nodded. "As snakes. The British and American governments are helping the Colombians wipe out the poppy fields, which is where FARC and the cartels make their money. No poppies, no money, no weapons, no fight. If they can't have a pop at the army or the anti-drugs troops, they take it to the streets and try to knock off anyone they don't like the look of."

"Successfully?"

"When they want to. They've killed some DEA people – the US Drug Enforcement Administration – in the past few years, and a lot of Colombian army and police, along with some judiciary. They don't mess about."

"Is it dangerous being an embassy employee down there?"

"It can be. It's a dangerous place."

"Does FARC ever target them specifically?"

"It's been known. Not so much the Yanks – they're too well guarded, although they've lost some undercover people. But the British are less inclined to use high walls. Other than a team of Redcaps at the embassy, and a few special forces guys helping train the local army and police, embassy staff have to take care of themselves, how they travel, where they go and stuff. But nobody can be protected one hundred percent. On the other hand, FARC know if they go too far, they'll bring down a lot of heat on themselves." He shrugged. "It's a sensitive situation, but so far it's been self-regulating. Why the interest? What's Palmer got involved in?"

She brought him up to date with the events of the past couple of days, finishing with the watcher in the woods.

He listened without interruption, then said gravely, "You should watch your back. The emails don't sound like FARC, but if they are behind the threats, they won't be playing around. It'll come to a head sooner or later."

"What do you mean?"

"They play the odds. If something doesn't pay, they'll leave well alone. And they rarely take the fight outside their own boundaries unless they really get upset." He paused. "And that's what Frank should be asking himself."

"What?"

"If it's FARC or any of the cartels, what the hell could a British Ambassador have done to stir up that kind of hornets' nest?"

11

"Good morning," Palmer murmured. "Rats 'R Us. We've come about the infestation."

Myburghe's butler, whom Palmer referred to as Rockface, answered the door to Colebrooke House. He stared down at Riley and Palmer as if hoping for an excuse to pick them both up and toss them into the fountain, and looked quite capable of doing so. His shoulders seemed to twitch in anticipation of the effort.

"Staff are supposed to use the side door," he growled. The faint sneer he gave Riley clearly indicated that Palmer had explained the reason for her previous visit.

"We're not staff, sunshine," Palmer replied easily. "Now, do we stand out here all day?"

The other man blinked slowly before stepping aside. "I'll tell Sir Kenneth you're here."

The foyer was large and circular, and impressively cool. The floor was marble, as were the columns liberally sprinkled around. The curved walls were covered in fine wooden panels, dotted with tiny paintings, and the effect was completed by elegant pieces of antique furniture at strategic points.

Riley saw a staircase curving upwards, its walls hung with heavy oil paintings of glum faces and owl-eyed family groups staring down in silent resentment. Somehow, she thought it was the only jarring note about the place, as if it had been assembled to create an impression of ancestry.

"Some butler," she commented, as the large man disappeared.

"Bodyguard is closer," Palmer replied.

"At his age?" In spite of his appearance, which would be easily capable of intimidating anyone who might want to do harm to Sir Kenneth Myburghe, it was clear he was in his early fifties. "I thought bodyguards were younger." She smiled at Palmer. "Well, young-ish."

Before Palmer could come back with a snappy reply, Rockface returned and beckoned them across the foyer. He made barely a sound as he walked and Riley checked his feet, half expecting to see him ghosting along on a set of silent rollers.

They were ushered into a room with surprisingly modern furniture, including a plain mahogany desk bearing a PC and printer, and a scattering of nouveau club chairs made of brushed aluminium and leather. The walls were dotted with watercolours, mostly of pastoral scenes, and the whole effect was of functional comfort. It was a startling contrast to the formal austerity of the foyer.

"Sir Kenneth will be with you shortly," said Rockface, before leaving them and closing the door silently behind him.

After the excitement of the previous day, Keagan had put the house and gardens on lockdown while he and his men conducted a rigorous security scan. Palmer and Riley had been advised to stay away until this morning, when they would be needed for a briefing with Sir Kenneth.

They had discussed tactics on the way, and decided that for Riley to be accepted as a security expert on a par with Palmer, she should not remain a dumb follower.

"We need to ask him some questions," Palmer suggested. "So far, all I've had is what Keagan has told me. If anyone knows what's behind the threats and the disappearance of his son, it must be Myburghe. He can't be so naïve as to think he's just been picked on by chance. Anyway, unless

74

there's been a major shift in tactics, kidnappers don't send fake bombs."

Riley was surprised. "You want me to question him?"

"Why not? He might open up more with you. Push him a little. It's for his own good."

"What if he fires me?"

"If he values his life, he won't."

Moments later, a man Riley recognised from the photos on the internet as Sir Kenneth Myburghe opened the door and stepped into the room.

"Palmer. How kind." He shook hands warmly with Frank Palmer, then turned to Riley and gave her a more perfunctory but polite greeting, as if he didn't quite know how to treat her. "Miss Gavin." She thought it was oddly gauche for a man in his position, but decided stress might be playing a part. He nodded towards two of the chairs. "Please. Sit down."

In the flesh, Sir Kenneth was the epitome of the career diplomat: smooth and elegantly dressed in razor-creased slacks, cotton shirt and brogues, he looked comfortable in himself, with a ready smile revealing impeccably white teeth. How much of the smile was genuine, however, was impossible to tell. He wore a faint air of controlled tension, and his face had a gauntness about it that Riley guessed wasn't entirely due to age.

All she could think was that if she had received a body part in the post, purportedly belonging to her teenage son, she would never have smiled again. Diplomats were evidently made of sterner stuff.

"I'm grateful you've agreed to help," he said. He made it sound as if they had been summoned to unclog the drains. Moving over to a small side table, he lifted the stopper off a crystal decanter and raised his eyebrows in a silent offer.

Palmer and Riley shook their heads and waited as Myburghe poured himself a generous helping. Unlike his greeting of Riley, his movements now were practised and smooth, the professional host. He took a sip, lowering the level in his glass by a good third.

Riley glanced at Palmer, who was studying his hands. But she knew he would have seen it, too: beneath the smooth veneer was a man fighting a losing battle with his nerves.

Myburghe sat at the desk and looked at them both in turn. "I gather you're aware of the basic situation?"

Riley nodded, drawing his attention. Barely two minutes in and she was already deciding she didn't much like Sir Kenneth Myburghe. Losing a son was a 'situation'? "I'm sorry to hear about your son."

He frowned and studied his glass. "I still can't believe it."

She glanced at Palmer, who gave her the briefest of nods to carry on. She looked at Myburghe and said, "I know you've been through this already with others, but just in case you've had some ideas: is there anyone you can think of who might wish you harm? Someone who might have made threats – even a while ago?"

"It's not something I can pretend I thought would never happen," Myburghe replied honestly. "There have been threats of one sort or another over the years – more to do with British foreign policies rather than me as an individual. When you work in the diplomatic field, you tend to expect a certain degree of fallout from one group or another. It comes with the job. But you never quite reckon on it being so… personal. A bit like a motor accident, I suppose."

Riley decided that this ability to deal with major catastrophes as if they were minor setbacks must be something they taught in public school, She could almost hear the stiff upper lips clamping shut under pain of God knew what punishment. Here was this man, passing off the possible death of his son as a job-related hazard.

"I gather your last posting was in Colombia?" She almost regretted the choice of words, in view of his evident fall from grace, but he seemed not to notice.

He crossed his legs, now on familiar turf and ready to launch into a lengthy exposé of life at the top. "That's correct. Beautiful country, fantastic scenery and people. But not a nice posting, socially speaking. There are lots of… complications. Too many opposing factions and too many guns. It's a very dangerous place."

"You mean drug traffickers," she interrupted him.

"And others. But, essentially, yes." He looked mildly irritated at having the flow of his talk interrupted. "But there's nothing to indicate this business is anything to do with them, I hope you realise that?" He looked at them in turn, but they didn't react.

Riley asked, "Didn't your security people have some ideas?"

"Some. But nothing concrete." He shifted in his chair. "You have to understand, Miss Gavin, that this job marks you down. Others before me were never quite sure they or their families would be entirely safe." He looked past her. "But that's the price, I suppose, for doing one's duty." He stared off manfully into the distance. The Marlboro Man of the diplomatic corps, thought Riley; this was probably his way of dealing with what had befallen him.

"One thing puzzles me," she said.

"What's that?" He fixed her with a dark look, as if he hadn't expected this level of questioning. What on earth can you be puzzled about? the expression seemed to imply. You, a mere minion. That same facial expression, Riley guessed, had probably had embassy staff running for the hills whenever it appeared.

It reminded her of an old headmistress at high school, who had ceased to hold any fear for Riley after appearing in a pair of giant shorts in the annual teachers versus students hockey match. Somehow a pair of knobbly knees never rated too high in the terror stakes after that.

"If you and your family are such a target, why did you let your son go to the States? He's very young."

For a moment Sir Kenneth looked as if he was about to levitate from his chair. His face coloured a deep red, and he swung his head towards Palmer as if asking why he'd brought this impertinent young female into his house.

Palmer simply stared back at him without expression. "Good point," he conceded.

Sir Kenneth finally spoke when he saw there would be no support from Palmer. "He wanted to see the world... do things – like any other young man. What are you saying?" He looked at them both this time.

"I'm saying," said Riley, "that if he was at risk, I'm surprised he was alone. If you were being watched, they'll have been keeping an eye on Christian, too." What she wanted to say, bluntly, was that Sir Kenneth was being well protected, so why wasn't his son and heir? It was shutting the stable door after the horse had cleared off, but as an example of parental idiocy masquerading as freedom, she thought this one beat them all.

He didn't say anything, and she let it go. It wasn't their place to berate him for letting his son go out into the world unprepared.

"Why us?" She indicated herself and Palmer. "If you've been threatened, surely a man in your position should have first call on some big guns to camp out here. A unit of

Redcaps at least. Failing that, there are plenty of professional companies."

She glanced at Palmer, but he was staring at the ceiling.

"You're quite correct, Miss Gavin." Myburghe gave her a permafrost smile that indicated he was fed up with the questions and wanted to call his butler and have them ejected. Except that he was far too well mannered. "I could call on considerable assistance if I wanted to. I could have my home turned into a fortress and my life become a hermetically-sealed unit for the next six months."

"In the face of threats, it sounds good to me."

"Except that after a time, if there were no further threats to my life, family or well-being, I'd be on my own, or at the very most with a couple of inexperienced men posted in the kitchen and armed with radios. I still wouldn't have my son back."

"Your butler looks very capable."

"Yes, he is. He's been with me for many years. But he's still just one man."

Riley knew he was right. None but a select few at the top of the tree ever got the protection they wanted, and then not even one hundred percent. Everyone else was left out in the cold with a three-point plan security manual and a mirror on a pole for checking under their cars each morning.

"The package," said Palmer. "Where is it?"

Sir Kenneth paled and took another slug of whisky. Palmer the Tactful strikes again, thought Riley. He'd done better than her in fewer words. But it was a question she'd been straining not to ask. Where does one keep a spare finger? she wondered. In the fridge alongside the butter?

"They took it away," he said at last, his voice cracking slightly. It was the first real sign of tension to show beneath the professional veneer. "Keagan took it."

"Was it your son's?" This time it was Riley's turn to lead the charge of the blunt brigade.

He nodded. "I believe so, yes."

"How can you be sure? The bomb was a hoax; this might be, too."

Myburghe pushed back from the desk and opened a drawer. He withdrew a gold signet ring and a framed photograph. He stared at them both for a moment, before sliding them across the desk to Riley.

The ring, which Palmer had mentioned, was heavy and solid and showed an indistinct crest carved into the dull metal.

Myburghe grunted, "It was covered in dried blood when it arrived. I cleaned it off."

Riley passed the ring to Palmer and turned to the photograph. The frame was embossed silver. It held a snapshot of a teenager emerging into young adulthood. He was sitting on an upturned log and smiling easily into the camera, confident and relaxed, the epitome of good breeding. He wore the inevitable uniform of jeans, sweatshirt and trainers, and was the image of his father without the weight of the years behind him. A good-looking boy, thought Riley. Everything in the world to live for. His hands were clasped between his knees.

"You can't see it there," Myburghe said stiffly. "But Christian has a very fine two-inch scar on his thumb. He got it skinning a rabbit when he was fourteen." He watched as Riley passed the photo to Palmer, who glanced at it before passing it back to Myburghe with the ring. The drawer closed on the two objects with a muffled finality.

"The significance being?" said Palmer.

"Practically nobody outside the family knows about the

scar. It's almost invisible. Yet they described it in detail. And the ring bears our family crest. It was designed by my great-grandfather. There's no mistake: it belongs to Christian."

Riley and Palmer exchanged a look. Whoever was making the threats had first-hand knowledge of the boy's physical details, right down to little-known scars. It was about as conclusive as it could get: the kidnappers weren't bluffing.

"That leaves just one thing, then," Palmer said, with what almost amounted to cheerfulness. "What do they want?"

12

Sir Kenneth's eyebrows shot skyward and the silence seemed to reverberate around the room. "Want?" He uttered the word as if he'd never heard it before.

"It's the usual thing, isn't it, with death threats? Pay up or we kill your son. Send us a lot of money or next time it'll be a real bomb. That sort of thing."

Myburghe took another sip of his whisky. His movements were controlled, but in the way a bomb disposal expert might be controlled while sitting on a large amount of Semtex. He was white round the eyes with the effort, and Riley wasn't sure if he was mad at Palmer for the question or at himself for being unable to respond.

"There have been no demands," he said finally, placing the glass on the desk. "No requests, nothing. So far I've absolutely no idea why they're doing these things. Or what they want."

"They?" Riley asked.

He shrugged. "They. He. Whoever is behind this."

"What about the letters? What do they say?"

"Very little. They're crude, aggressive and to the point. My life is in danger and so forth. But no demands."

"Can we see them?" Riley wasn't sure what they could gain from them, but they might provide clues as to the type of people they were dealing with.

"I'm sorry. They were destroyed." Sir Kenneth's eyes flickered with what might have been embarrassment.

"Destroyed?" Riley didn't need to look at Palmer to know that he was as surprised as she was. Whatever evidence there might have been was gone. "What did you do that for?"

"We thought they were crank letters at first, and dismissed them. It's not unknown for a person in my position to receive letters like that."

"Really?" Palmer spoke quietly, his eyes firmly on Myburghe. "In spite of the chance that it might be serious?" His tone was edged with scepticism, and Myburghe picked up on it, twin spots of red flushing his cheeks.

"What are you saying?" he countered.

"I'm suggesting it's odd that Keagan didn't ask the same question. And a man with your experience…" He let the words hang in the silence.

Myburghe finally flapped a vague hand. "It was stupid, yes, and I should have known better. But Keagan shared the view that it was probably the work of a crank. There are plenty of reasons for them – mostly petty. Someone wasn't granted a work visa, or was refused leave to stay here in the UK. Or a trade deal went wrong and someone felt cheated. It's simple enough to take grievances out on the nearest representative – which is usually the embassy staff. Nobody takes them terribly seriously. Anyway, after a while they stopped and I thought that was the end of it. Then the other… things arrived."

"What about the final package?" Palmer asked softly. "Where did that come from?"

"I don't know. There was nothing on the outer wrapping to indicate its origins. It arrived one morning."

"Stamps? Postmark?"

"Nothing. It was left on the doorstep."

Palmer chewed his lip, and Riley thought from his expression that he didn't believe a word Sir Kenneth had said. One thing was certain, however. Whoever had sent the package was close enough to deliver it personally.

Some of this must have communicated itself to Myburghe,

because he said finally, "I think whoever it is, is foreign. The impression I have is, I don't know – colourful, if you know what I mean. Keagan has already been through this with me, anyway. And the Foreign Office assigned investigators." He pulled a bitter face. "Not that they uncovered anything."

"Keagan didn't mention your son," said Palmer. "Or the details of the package."

Myburghe lifted his chin again, as if his collar was too tight. "Because I don't wish my son… my son's fate, to be a subject of general discussion." His eyes burned brightly, and the red flush still glowed beneath the thin skin of his face. It was an indication that the drink he was working his way through might not be his first of the day. "He's not someone to be hauled over some investigator's table and talked about like a statistic. Neither do I wish to have the damned press camped along the drive and dissecting every aspect of our lives in fine detail. I'm sorry."

Riley watched as he finished his drink with a gulp, and wondered what he would say if he realised that one of the damned press was sitting here right in front of him.

They sat in silence, each staring at the walls, until Myburghe stirred and spoke so softly they almost missed it. "There's no point, anyway."

It was as if he was admitting his son was no longer alive. It was possibly the first time he'd been able to do so.

"So why the wedding? Don't you think it's a bit, I don't know… " Riley paused, trawling for the right words.

"Tasteless?" Sir Kenneth's eyes burned and for a moment he looked angry enough to throw his glass at her. Riley wondered why. Surely people closer to him had suggested the same thing already. But then his diplomat's training reasserted itself and his face became a blank canvas once more. "You may be right."

"Actually," Riley said calmly, "I was going to say risky. All those guests milling around. There will be a lot of unknown faces."

"I'm sorry." Myburghe raised a hand in apology. "Please forgive me. I'm afraid this is all a bit much." He took a deep breath. "Both my daughters are well looked after. They have people watching them. Victoria, my elder daughter, wanted to postpone the wedding at first, when Christian didn't come home. She was extremely upset, as you can imagine. She and Christian are – were – very close. But we sat down and talked it through, and felt it would be caving into these… whoever these people are." He looked up at them, misery in his eyes. "It was a family decision."

"And you've absolutely no idea who they could be?" Palmer put in. "None at all?"

"None. I've told you. In a life serving this country all over the globe, I've no doubt there are plenty of crackpots with a grudge who might have picked up my name and address." He gave a bark of disdain tinged with anger. "After all, extortion and brutality are growth industries these days, aren't they? In the end I persuaded Victoria to go ahead. Better to face it rather than knuckle under." His chin jutted out determinedly, reminding Riley of a comic book hero facing up to bad news. "In any case, if I postponed it, there's no guarantee they won't just wait to try again next time."

Nobody said anything, and Riley almost winced at the pompous tones of British Empire bluff and double bluff bouncing around the room. If Myburghe really thought his son's kidnappers had gone to all that trouble and would make no demands, or that they would stand by and watch him marry off his daughter without making some kind of statement, he was either deluded or one teacup short of a set.

"What do you expect us to do?" asked Palmer, returning the talk to business.

Sir Kenneth swung his way with a look of relief, and it was obvious he'd had enough of being made to face up to his shortcomings. "I've heard a lot about you, Palmer," he said at last. The look did not include Riley, but she wasn't surprised. "One or two of your former um, clients, have spoken impressively of your services. Victoria speaks well of you, too, of course."

Palmer took in the name-dropping without a flicker. But when Riley turned and stared at him, wondering about the last comment, he studiously avoided her eye.

She knew almost nothing of Palmer's earlier background, or of the circles he moved in. But the one thing she hadn't been prepared for was that he was acquainted with Victoria Myburghe, the blushing bride-to-be.

Then she became aware that Sir Kenneth had asked her a question.

"Sorry?"

"Your background," he repeated with a tinge of impatience. "Is it the same as Palmer's?"

It put Riley in mind of being interviewed by a headmaster who didn't really want her in his terribly posh school, but was having to accept a quota of rough for the sake of appearances. He'd evidently decided that anyone in the security business was impertinent and rude, with the possible exception of Palmer, and clearly a woman wouldn't be very different.

"Pretty much," she said, with a confidence she didn't feel.

It was evidently sufficient for Myburghe. He made a grunting sound. There was no doubt that, having spent time in Colombia, he would have met more than his fair share of security men and women. Because of the diplomatic and political circumstances in which he'd lived and moved, perhaps he'd managed to do so without having to consider any of the individuals as people before.

"Glad to hear it." He looked doubtful but soldiered on. "Some of Keagan's team have been assigned to cover the church. There are various government and Foreign Office people attending the service, and Keagan thinks the journey between the village and here is a weak spot. I'd like you two to concentrate on the house and grounds, and obviously Victoria and Annabel, when they get here."

"That won't be easy, with just two of us," said Palmer. "They're unlikely to stay together, and in a crowd of any size, that leaves us overexposed. I recommend we get more people in."

"I appreciate that. On the other hand, I know enough about security to realise that I could draft in a small army, and it still wouldn't guarantee their safety. Just do what you can. Please." He looked at his empty glass and put it down on the desk with an expression of regret.

Palmer said nothing, but conceded the point. A large team could never ensure absolute safety. On the other hand, while two focussed professionals blending with the crowd might spot trouble before it happened, it was hardly throwing a wall of steel around them.

"And after the wedding?" Riley asked. "They could still be vulnerable."

Myburghe nodded. "Victoria is delaying her honeymoon, so she won't be travelling for a week or two. Perhaps you have some suggestions?" His eyes slid to Palmer for guidance.

"I'll put a couple of extra people on them," said Palmer, getting to his feet. "I know their addresses. They'll be in place before either of your daughters leaves here." It was as much an instruction to Sir Kenneth as a reassurance. "In the meantime, we'll do a thorough security check of the place. Do you have a list of all staff working here over the next couple of days?"

"Of course," Sir Kenneth nodded. "Good point. I'll see to it."

Myburghe approached the window and watched as Palmer and Gavin crossed the rear garden. They moved comfortably, clearly attuned to their surroundings and each other. He felt a faint rush of comfort at their presence. They seemed to be a good team.

But he knew they weren't enough – they never could be. Not by a long way.

He wondered what was yet to unfold; what barricade would be breached in order to turn the screws on him further? What nameless horror would they mount next to make him do what they wanted?

The door opened and the slender figure of Victoria stepped into the room. She was tall and graceful, and as she leaned forward to greet him with a kiss, he was reminded at once of the huge risk he was taking by going ahead with the wedding. Yet when he had suggested cancelling it in the wake of Christian's disappearance, she, like Annabel, had protested strongly. Thankfully, he pondered, although they knew about the threats, they didn't know the reason for them.

"Is she his girlfriend?" Victoria asked, watching the two figures in the garden.

"I've no idea. I doubt it." Myburghe knew that Victoria and Palmer had once been more than acquaintances. Thrown together by circumstance when Palmer was hired to look after a friend of hers, Victoria had gradually become fascinated by the seemingly nonchalant but watchful ex-military policeman hovering in the background. It had taken solid resolve and the counsel of Susan, his wife, to make him step back and leave them to it, rather than rush in and try to stop the relationship developing. "Have you spoken to him?"

"No. There's no need."

"No regrets?" he queried, and instantly wished he hadn't.

But Victoria smiled and touched his arm, knowing he was concerned for her. "No. Frank's a lovely man. But I wouldn't have figured very much in his life. It was fun, but… " She shrugged. "I'm pleased he'll be around, though. He's solid. I trust him and so does Mummy."

Myburghe grunted, recognising the warning signals against becoming the over-protective father. "Very well. Are you off?"

"Yes. Back to London. I'm having dinner with Annabel and a couple of girlfriends tonight. Perhaps you could make my apologies to Frank?"

He nodded and watched her walk from the room, then turned and looked at a photo of Christian on the wall. His son was smiling into the camera with all the innocence and promise of youth, and Myburghe felt sick and ashamed, the guilt washing over him as it did every waking minute, and even in his dreams.

"Do you believe it?" said Riley, as they made their way back to the car. "That he ditched all the letters and stuff? How dumb is that?"

"People do strange things." Palmer had been quiet as they toured the house, checking exits and stairs, familiarising themselves with the general layout. Now they were off to look at the approaches to the village and the house and grounds. It wasn't giving them much time, but it was essential they got to know their way around in case disaster struck.

"And you're OK with that?"

"No. I'm just trying to figure out why he did it."

"You make it sound as if it was deliberate."

"Maybe it was."

"But that would mean –" Riley stopped and looked at Palmer, who kept walking, but at a slower pace.

"It would mean," he finished for her, "that he didn't want the letters traced."

She caught up with him, digesting the implications of that idea. The only conclusion was astonishing. "He knows who sent them? That's incredible. What makes you think that?"

He stopped. "Most normal people getting threatening letters would go straight to the police. Myburghe's had far worse than letters, but with a hotline right to a close protection unit, he's done nothing about the latest package. I don't think he even told Keagan about the finger. Why not?"

"Palmer, that's a bit wild, isn't it?"

"Depends what he's hiding, doesn't it?" He started walking again and Riley had to scramble to catch up.

"He didn't mention his wife at all."

"Ex-wife," Palmer explained. "They split last year. Lady Myburghe lives in London. She'll be at the wedding, though."

"Does she know about Christian?"

"Yes. He had to tell her in case it hit the headlines."

"You mean he considered not telling her?"

"They don't communicate much."

"Jesus, no kidding!" Riley thought back to the websites

she'd searched. She was certain there had been a photo of Sir Kenneth and his wife taken sometime in the last year or so. Whatever had driven them apart must have been recent. It might be worth taking a closer look.

As they approached the car, she said casually, "So you know Victoria Myburghe."

"Knew her," Palmer corrected her. He held out the keys to the Saab. "Do you want to drive?" The way he said it told her he was hoping it would take Riley's mind off asking awkward questions.

"No, thanks." She climbed in and settled herself down. "She's pretty. Girlfriend, was she? Victoria, I mean."

"No."

"Well, she wasn't a college chum, was she?"

"Hardly. I'd have been arrested for cradle snatching."

"Oh, come off it. She can't be that much younger than you. Anyway, hadn't you heard? Some girls prefer the more mature man."

"Thanks a lot."

"So where did you meet her? Was it at a Young Farmers' ball in Chipping-Cum-Stately? No, of course not. You don't do farms, do you? Or –"

"If you must know," he said with careful precision, taking the car smoothly down the gravel drive at speed, "I met her in London when I was hired to watch over a friend of hers by an over-protective father. They were like Tweedledum and Tweedledee. They went everywhere together. I had to troll along to the same restaurants to keep an eye on them. That's all." He drifted expertly round the fountain, throwing a spray of gravel on to the grass.

That's going to play havoc with the lawn mower, thought Riley. "So you didn't have a relationship, then?"

"No. Could we discuss something else?"

Riley smiled at him. "Not yet. Bear with me – I'm naturally curious about the ruling elite. So no kissy-kissy? No showing her your army tattoos in the summerhouse? Not even once?"

He looked sideways at her and she saw a cool and amused glint in his eye. "We got on while the job lasted. But that was it. Getting hooked on the client or any of their mates doesn't go down well in my business. It makes you both vulnerable."

Riley smiled and nudged his shoulder. "You old dog, you. It worked with Kevin Costner and Whitney Houston. You shouldn't knock it."

He said nothing. But Riley thought she detected the faint edge of a smile on his lips.

13

John Mitcheson waited by a magazine stand and watched three men in army uniform patrolling the concourse of Baranquilla International airport in northern Colombia. They were heavily armed and watchful, and clearly looking for certain faces among the travellers and greeters thronging the airport. As if in unspoken collusion, the crowd opened before them, careful not to walk too close, then closed again behind them like a school of multi-coloured fish around cruising sharks.

Mitcheson was dressed in a pale lightweight suit and white shirt, smart enough to pass as a businessman, but not so smart as to attract the wrong kind of attention, such as these security men or con artists looking for an easy mark. He had earlier bought a copy of a local newspaper and was idly scanning the pages without reading, more intent on watching the tidal flow of the crowd moving through the terminal. He hadn't spent enough time in this country on his last visit to get a real feel for the place or the language, so none of the news really meant anything.

He yawned and felt the grit of a nineteen-hour flight and two stopovers beginning to take effect. The air conditioning in the building seemed to be spasmodic, with occasional welcome downdraughts of cold air alongside pockets of warm, humid fug, heavy with cigarette smoke and the smell of overheated travellers. He needed something to drink but was putting it off until his contact showed up.

After completing his delivery of a packet of documents to a lawyer's office in Panama City – the original reason for his journey – Mitcheson had secured a cheap onward flight aboard a cargo plane to Baranquilla. It meant making the shortest of stopovers before turning round to leave again, but that suited him fine; the last thing he wanted to do was hang around here and come to the attention of the military authorities. Luckily, he'd been able to persuade his local contact to meet him here rather than in Bogotá, avoiding the dangers of entering the capital's airport where security was higher and faces were scanned more rigorously.

He checked his watch, wondering whether to call Riley. He decided not. She had no idea where he was, and would probably blow a fuse if she knew what he was doing. But after what she'd told him about the threats to Myburghe and the possible links to FARC or the cartels, he'd begun to have serious doubts about what she was getting herself into. British diplomats occasionally got on the wrong end of violent protests, but it was rare for the fight to be carried overseas, and rarer still for it to become so personal.

A familiar face appeared among the crowd. The man was middle-aged, stocky and slightly less than medium height, dressed in crumpled slacks and a linen jacket, like so many others here. He was casually wandering along, but there was no disguising the watchfulness in his eyes as he filtered through the bustling throng.

"How's it going, John?" The newcomer smiled and drifted up alongside Mitcheson, deep laughter lines etched in the tan around his eyes and mouth. They shook hands.

Col Pierce was a former British army sergeant who had decided to stay on after leaving the army and make a life as a tourist guide across Colombia and its neighbours to the south. He had been in Bogotá several years before, when Mitcheson had arrived and been escorted out again within weeks, following a violent confrontation with a Colombian army corporal during a drugs raid on a village in the hills.

The corporal had shot a pregnant woman for standing up to him, and Mitcheson, enraged at the callousness of the act, had taken the man into the bush.

Only Mitcheson had returned. It had meant a rapid exit from the country before he could be imprisoned and shot.

"Col. Thanks for coming."

"No sweat. You like living dangerously or are you just bored?"

"I should be OK up here." Mitcheson had never been to Baranquilla before. He'd been counting on the city's remoteness from Bogotá to give him the best odds of getting in and out safely without being recognised.

"I guess so. You were hardly here long enough, were you?" He chuckled. "It's still an all-time record among the lads for short stays. Still, some of their army intelligence boys have got long memories, so let's keep it that way. What brings you back?" He eyed Mitcheson's suit and tie.

"I was making a delivery to Panama City. A friend asked me to do a favour while I was down here."

"Must be a close friend." Col didn't enquire about the nature of the delivery job. He knew how difficult it was for many ex-military men to find employment and that many of them resorted to unconventional means, not all of them legal.

Mitcheson smiled, knowing what his friend was thinking. "It's all legit, I promise. And the friend's close enough. My flight out leaves in an hour."

"Suits me." He led Mitcheson to a bar. "You want coffee or something stronger?"

"Beer would be good."

"OK." Col nodded to a passing busboy and flashed a note. "So, you mentioned Myburghe on the phone. What do you want to know?"

"I know he was here before my time and left recently. Is there anything you can tell me?"

Col gave him a quizzical look. "You mean dirt, don't you? What's going on?"

"He's on somebody's list." Mitcheson explained about the letters, the fake bomb and the delivery of the finger.

"Christ," Col breathed. "Not sure about the letters, but the rest sounds like our old friends down the road." He fell silent as the waiter brought their drinks and scooped up the money. "If it's the cartels, rather him than me. They're not very forgiving."

"Any specific old friends?"

Col laughed without humour. "Hell, name any of them – they'll all send trophies as a warning if they think it'll work." He frowned and scooped some froth off his beer glass with the tip of his finger. "They don't usually go after outsiders, though. Not once they're gone. Mind you, it kind of makes sense, from what I've been able to put together since you rang."

Mitcheson sipped his beer and tried to remain calm. He wasn't as close to this as Riley or Palmer, but he shared their sense of excitement when the balls began to click into place. "Go on."

Col looked at his watch, then flicked his eyes towards two more men in uniform who were loitering and looking their way. These two, Mitcheson noticed, were not as smart as the others he'd seen, nor as well-armed. They were also over-weight and didn't seem too interested in any of the locals, only the more prosperous looking business travellers.

Col said quietly, "Finish up. Something tells me those two jokers are after some easy money. And we don't need that kind of hassle. Let's go get you checked in. I'll tell you what I've got on Myburghe on the way. One thing, though:

you never heard any of this from me. I don't want to get dragged into this end of it."

"It's that bad?"

"If rumours are accurate, it's worse. And if what they say is true, Sir Kenneth Myburghe has got himself into a shit-load of trouble."

14

The first rush of guests began arriving at Colebrooke House just after five. Most were transported in a fleet of gleaming Bentleys, crunching expensively on the gravel drive and spinning round the fountain to form a neat line in front of the house. The occupants stepped out and milled about in the warm evening air, shaking out the stiff formality of the service, which had been held at the village church of St Peter's, half a mile away. Other cars followed in quick succession, forming a line down the drive.

Riley and Palmer were waiting, having made another inspection of the grounds first, while Rockface checked the house and the catering staff. As far as they could tell, Colebrooke House was clear and ready to go.

"It would have been nice to have gone to the service," Riley said wistfully, eyeing the display of elegance emerging from the cars. It looked to her as if half the fashion houses in Europe had been raided to meet the demands of the occasion, and it was clear that, although small by some standards, this was an important date on the wedding calendar.

Palmer, wearing a smart lounge suit – a rare event for him – gave her a sideways look. "Jesus. Women and weddings."

"It's all very well for you," she said curtly. "I feel somewhat underdressed. Make that hugely underdressed." Pressed at short notice to wear something other than her customary jacket and jeans, she had been forced to settle on a lightweight summer suit bought a couple of years ago for a cousin's wedding. It may have been appropriate for that occasion, but she knew it wouldn't match the present level of glamour on display by a long way.

"You look fine," said Palmer, somewhat belatedly.

"Fine?" she hissed, although it was quite a compliment, coming from Palmer. "Fine doesn't cut it. If I'd known it was going to be as glam as this, I'd have held out for a minimum clothing allowance."

"If I'd known you were going to witter on about it," Palmer retorted calmly, "I'd have hired a bloke."

"Philistine." She decided she was wasting her time. Apart from the suit, she was wearing a pair of medium heeled shoes. They didn't enhance the outfit, but she'd already decided that if called on to break into anything approaching a trot beyond the firmer terrain of the paths and terraces around the house, she'd kick them off and to hell with convention. Stumbling about on heels like an idiot while pretending to provide security for the Myburghes would be far more humiliating than going barefoot.

Palmer moved away, shaking his head, and began cruising the gathering crowd, instinctively checking out the men first. They were a mixed group, ranging from fresh-faced young turks in search of a party, slightly older types from the city and the civil service, to a mostly conservative and senior scattering in morning suits and double chins.

Riley hung back, preferring the fringes of the crowds, where it was easier to watch people, and where she felt a little less conspicuous. Palmer seemed unbothered by any such distractions, and seemed to blend in easily, although a couple of very tall ex-cavalry types gave him keen, knowing looks as they strode by. They joined two other men of the same brand, and Riley overheard them reminiscing about people called Neville, Alistair and Jonty, and an evening at the officers' club in Pristina, before they wheeled away with promises to meet up for a game of squash. They smiled briefly at Riley as they passed, too well-schooled to ignore her but probably aware that she wasn't there by the same invitation.

The women were less restrained, given to peals of surprised greetings and much air-kissing. Already fashionably colourful, the amount of jewellery on display was impressive, and the air was soon rent with shrill, catch-up gossip and bursts of laughter as friends and acquaintances spied each other through the crowd.

Uniformed catering staff directed party guests towards the rear gardens, where a large marquee with a service annexe had been set up on the lawns. The atmosphere was balmy and pleasant with only a faint breeze, and most of the arrivals made for a line of champagne-laden white-clothed tables, pausing to scoop up a drink. Then it was on to the lawns in search of fresh air, scenery and some soft grass in which to squish their toes, a sort of sophisticated limbering up before the main event.

Like Clacton beach, thought Riley. Only posher.

Palmer had already checked out the caterers' vans, along with a generator truck to provide extra power for lighting and refrigeration. Each vehicle carried a 'By Royal Appointment' crest. The marquee was a bustle of activity, with trays of food being passed along a line of waiters, and more champagne being packed in ice for later. A manager in a crisp morning suit was directing his troops like a regimental sergeant major, keeping staff in line with a beady eye, calm authority and close attention to his watch. The atmosphere was full of the scent of flowers, with giant floral displays in each corner to add to the sense of colour and glamour.

Riley drifted towards Palmer and nodded towards the roofline, where the silent and deserted scaffolding stuck out like spiky, gelled hair.

"He's pushing the boat out, isn't he?" she said. "With the wedding, it must be quite an outlay, doing up a place this size."

Palmer nodded, strictly neutral. "Lady Myburghe has money, and Sir Kenneth got lucky on the stock market. As for the wedding, Victoria is his eldest daughter. It's traditional."

"So how rich is he?" Riley was wondering how much in real terms Sir Kenneth could put together if and when his son's kidnappers finally made their demands. Judging by the scale of the renovations and the size of this celebration, he evidently wasn't short of funds.

"I've no idea. You thinking about a ransom?"

"Yes."

He stared off into the distance, his face grim. "If he pays up, whatever he has, it'll never be enough. They'll come back for more. Come on, let's take a walk. I want to check the track." He set off with a nod towards a line of trees near the edge of the estate.

Riley followed, still trying to get to grips with the fact that the wedding was going ahead as planned. It was either an attempt by Sir Kenneth to deny the worst, or a brave front against the certain knowledge that Christian would not be coming back. Either way, whenever they had glimpsed the former diplomat, he had seemed brittle, his smile stiff and robotic.

Neither Victoria, nor her young sister, Annabel, had yet put in an appearance at the house. When questioned, Rockface had informed Palmer that they would be travelling directly from London to the church, shadowed by a couple of Keagan's men.

"What's the official explanation for Christian's absence?"

Riley queried. "Surely everyone's expecting him to be here for his sister's wedding?"

"They put the word around that he's down with a stomach bug and too ill to travel," Palmer explained. "It doesn't seem to have raised any eyebrows."

Thoughts of stiff upper lips came to mind, but Riley had to admire their bravado. It was quite a display. If it had been her family under such pressure, she doubted weddings would have figured too highly on the social calendar.

They pushed through a small thicket, Palmer leading the way and Riley treading carefully on the softer ground, until they found themselves overlooking a broad sweep of countryside fading into the distance. A rutted track ran from right to left in front of them, the ground marked by the treads of tractor tyres and horses' hooves. It was evidently a regular exercise route for local riders, as well as an access track for farm workers, and even without Palmer's experience, Riley knew that this point, like the vast amount of open countryside around the house and grounds, was a security team's worst nightmare. It was impossible to keep an eye on all fronts, and the amount of cover provided by shrubs, bushes and several acres of trees could have hidden a small army. Add to that the amount of scaffolding and building materials scattered around the place, and it was a terrorist's dream on a plate.

"This is crazy," she breathed, appalled once more by the size of the task they had taken on. "We couldn't cover all this, even if we had Keagan's entire team with us."

Palmer shrugged. "True. But I've done worse jobs. It's all about being seen to be there."

"I thought security was supposed to be unobtrusive."

"Some is, some isn't. We're both."

"Palmer, are you armed?" Riley had been meaning to ask

him from the outset.

"No. I asked Keagan to get authorisation, but he was blocked. Insufficient need, apparently."

"So what do we do if someone does have a go?"

"We throw champagne bottles."

"Great. I should have stuck to writing about Myburghe – it would have been easier."

Palmer gave her a quick smile. "Well, you insisted on sticking your oar in." He took a small, lightweight Motorola GP radio from his pocket and checked it out. Riley did the same. They were little bigger than a mobile, and Palmer had given Riley and Rockface a quick briefing earlier on how to use them. With so much ground to cover, it would be their only way of summoning each other if needed.

Just then, both radios crackled and Rockface's voice spoke briefly. The bride and groom were on their way.

"Time to trot," said Palmer. "Let's go."

They returned to the main house just as a limousine decked out in ribbons purred up the drive and the newly-weds ducked out amid cheers and flashing cameras. The groom, Simon Biel, who seemed more assured here than the photo Riley had seen on the internet had portrayed, hovered supportively as his bride, Victoria, greeted friends and revelled in her new-found status, her smile outshining by a long way all the other splashes of colour. Every step was recorded by a frenetic photographer, and from his work-rate, it was plain he had been warned that he would have only seconds to record the necessary outdoor shots before the couple were herded inside.

Rockface also danced close attendance, towering over his charges like a large mother hen. As soon as the happy couple were over the threshold, he closed the door. Next, Sir Kenneth appeared and moved through the assembled guests, any signs of nerves no doubt excused as the understandable jitters of a typically proud father. He caught Palmer's eye and nodded briefly. He was accompanied by a slender, elegant woman whom Riley guessed was his ex-wife.

"Lady Myburghe," confirmed Palmer, when she asked him. "Nice woman."

A man with the focussed air of a professional watcher appeared through the crowd. He was dressed in a smart lounge suit, but to expert eyes there was no mistaking his profession. He threw Palmer a brief look, clicked through his mental slides of OK faces, then carried on scanning the people around him before turning to nod to a new arrival in a black Jaguar. The male passenger climbed out and Riley recognised the familiar, burly figure of the Defence Secretary.

"Is that who I think it is?" she said, as the man was ushered inside by the minder.

"Friend of the family," murmured Palmer. "Let's hope he doesn't come to regret today's visit."

They trawled the crowd, picking out a scattering of other public faces. Two peers and couple of back-benchers moved by in easy familiarity; a middle-ranking female opera singer swished past with a party of admirers; an eagle-eyed entrepreneur who had graced the pages of the tabloids the week before was trying hard to be ignored, while two cat-walk models glided past with the grace of gazelles among wildebeest, displaying the hauteur of their trade. A few obviously foreign guests wandered around like confused minnows, no doubt trying to come to grips with the eccentricities of British etiquette and quickly losing the plot.

In between the chatter, the crunch of cars arriving on the gravelled drive continued, interspersed with the thud of doors slamming and cries of greeting. The vehicles were beginning to stack two deep along the drive, some driven on to the grass verge with their noses into the shrubbery. A couple of local youths were trying to maintain order out of this chaos, but whatever system might have been planned beforehand, it was already beginning to break down under the sheer volume of numbers and the exuberance of the occasion.

"We'd better split up," Palmer told her. "It won't make much difference in this crowd, but one of us might spot something. Keep your radio handy." He nodded away from the house. "You do the gardens. I'll check the inside."

Riley walked around the house and through the shrubbery, then drifted towards a collection of brick buildings set back among the trees. The noise dropped appreciably as she walked towards them, and she realised with a sudden chill that she wouldn't have to go far before she was completely alone.

In the fading light, she could just make out some wooden ventilation boxes sitting on the roofs of the buildings, and closer examination revealed she was approaching some stables. From what Palmer had said, Keagan's men had checked these out already, but that was probably two days ago. A cobbled path led all the way from the house and ended in a small yard around which the buildings were set in an open square. She couldn't hear the sound of horses stamping and snuffling, nor any of the associated noises to be found in busy stables. A couple of bulkhead lights shone weakly from high on the walls, revealing the yard to be empty and clean, although dotted with sprouting weeds and coarse grass.

If there had been horses here, she reflected, it must have been a while ago.

The stalls along one side of the open square held an assortment of implements and riding gear. None of it looked clean or fresh and everything was covered in a fine layer of dust. The stalls on the opposite side were also empty save for a scattering of straw and some old, damaged furniture. Over everything hung the dull tang of stale horse manure, and the soft cooing of doves in the rafters added to the sense of rural peacefulness.

She turned to the block in the centre. There were no stable doors to this one, just a single door at one end with a low watt bulb burning in a wrought-iron holder overhead.

The door opened to emit a mixed aroma of stale cigarette smoke, cooking and bodies. Riley reached along the wall near the door and flicked on the light. She was in a small, high-ceilinged anteroom furnished with wooden lockers, a table and chairs. High windows looked out on to a stretch of trees at the rear. She opened a couple of the locker doors, but other than a film of dust and the odd clump of dried mud, they were empty. The whole room had an empty feel of desolation and lack of care, like a small-town railway station waiting room.

Against the rear window wall was a single sink and drainer, with a battered microwave oven standing on one end. Its glass door was open, and the inside was stained with baked-on food remnants. The air around it smelled spicy and peppery.

A cupboard under the sink held a bottle of detergent and a selection of mismatched crockery, chipped and stained with use. The air in the cupboard smelled of damp, and the wall at the back was covered in a dark bloom.

The room had obviously been converted from something else – possibly a tack room, Riley guessed – and turned into a makeshift staff kitchen. The walls had been splashed with white paint but the slabbed floor remained uncarpeted and cold. High on the wall to one side of the sink were two hefty metal brackets, which had probably once held shelves for tackle or other equipment. A metal waste-bin against one wall had been used as an ashtray and the one window was over-painted and firmly shut. With no attempt at creature comforts, it smacked of the purely temporary.

Riley emerged into a corridor that ran the full length of the block, with a number of doors leading off to the rear of the building and two small windows facing out on to the central square. The first door opened with a protesting squeak, the wood swollen in the damp air. The room was simple, about ten feet square, plain and as homely as a coal bunker, with a single bed and one hard-backed chair. A small bedside cabinet was scarred along the front edge by cigarette burns, and any varnish on the top had long been eradicated by the ring-stains of hot mugs and wet glasses. Cheap wire coat hangers bunched along a wooden architrave served as a wardrobe. It could almost have been a prison cell, she thought, and shivered at the thought.

The other rooms were identical. None showed signs of current use, but bore the same lingering odour of recent occupation. The grooms? Or temporary lodgings for some other reason?

As she turned to leave the last room, Riley spotted a small square of printed paper, lying wedged under the edge of the door. She pulled it out and smoothed it flat.

It was a torn scrap from a magazine. The typeface was rough, the paper quality poor. The illustration showed part of a naked breast, the areola tanned and pimpled with goosebumps. The text alongside mentioned the name Licia in bold print and was peppered with vivid exclamation marks. No doubt, Riley assumed, the thinking man's Michelin Guide indicator to soft porn. Unfortunately, whatever the editor was trying to convey about Licia's finer attributes was a mystery to her, as the text was all in Spanish.

As Riley slipped the piece of paper into her pocket, she heard a noise from the far end of the corridor.

Somebody had just entered the anteroom.

15

Riley waited, but there was no further sound above the drumming in her ears. With a rising sense of panic, she realised there was no other way out of here; she was going to have to walk back the way she had come in.

She felt the shape of the radio in her pocket and debated calling Palmer. But that would take him away from what he was doing. Besides, what would he say if it turned out to be an inquisitive guest or a member of the catering staff sneaking away for a cigarette break?

She took a deep breath and retraced her steps along the corridor, her footsteps sounding unnaturally loud in the enclosed space. As she passed each door, she glanced in, but the rooms were empty. As she reached the anteroom, she saw a bulky shadow thrown across the floor.

Rockface.

He looked as welcoming as a fridge-freezer and Riley wondered what he was doing here.

"I thought you were Palmer," she said coolly.

"He's with Sir Kenneth. I said I'd take a tour of the grounds. I saw the lights."

"They were on when I came in. What's this place used for?"

"It's not. Nobody comes here."

Riley nodded and looked around the room. "I'm not surprised. Not very welcoming, is it?"

"It used to be for storage and tack," he explained. "Sir Kenneth had the place done up when he hired some grooms to look after the horses." He eyed the room as if they were discussing soft furnishings, a strange contrast to the surly robot Riley had come to expect. "When Sir Kenneth sold the horses, he didn't need the grooms. They left. That was a good while back." The bare bulb in the ceiling cast a collection of shadows across his face, highlighting the planes and hollows of his eyes and craggy cheekbones. Riley wondered why she was being treated so freely to this information.

"Where did they go?" she asked, edging towards the door. As far as she knew, she had no reason to fear this man, but she would feel a whole lot better once she was out in the open.

He shrugged vaguely and turned to follow her, closing the door behind him and switching off the lights on the outside wall. "No idea. Probably to whatever local stables would give them work. There are plenty in the area, always on the lookout for staff." His tone lacked interest, a matter done and dusted, and Riley sensed he was keen to get her away from here.

She followed him back towards the house. It sounded plausible but she wasn't convinced. The smell of humans and cigarette smoke don't usually last very long, which convinced her that the place had been used recently. And although she knew nothing about grooms and their domestic habits, she couldn't see local lads being into spicy food and Spanish porn.

Behind the house, the party was growing in volume as more guests milled around the entrance to the marquee and the drinks tables. The waiters were toiling like troopers on a gun-carriage race, ferrying supplies of glasses and bottles for thirsty mouths, and from inside came the mellow sound of a sax loosening the mood. A peek through the entrance showed a wall of bodies, some gently swaying to the music, but most talking and drinking.

"You want to check it out?" Rockface nodded towards the marquee.

She shook her head. "Too much noise and too many people. I wouldn't see anything." There was also the danger that if any of them mistook her for an official presence, there might be a stampede as guests with toxic substances charged outside to dispose of the evidence among the rhododendrons and rose bushes.

Rockface nodded and walked away, leaving her to continue her patrol. Seconds later, a drunken male guest spotted Riley and lurched away from his friends in her direction.

"I say – you there!" called the drunk, like a character from a bad stage play. "That single tottie… to heel, I say! Let's have some fun!"

His intentions were spoiled as he tripped over his feet and sprawled to the ground in front of her, a few splashes of wine narrowly missing Riley's legs. He lay there, head rolling, as a gaggle of his friends ambled across in noisy support.

"Thanks," Riley murmured, stepping carefully over him, "but I don't know where you've been."

She completed two tours of the grounds, drifting silently along the edge of the tree line and growing more at ease with the place. She was surprised at how peaceful it was. Somehow it seemed so at odds with the threats Sir Kenneth had received. Or maybe she was growing complacent, allowing the music, the laughter and the balmy evening to get to her.

She passed a few quiet couples here and there, mostly older guests in search of tranquillity away from the noise and pounding music in the marquee. They nodded courteously but kept their distance. Something else to get used to, she reflected: nobody talks to the minders.

She was just approaching the edge of the trees bordering the track which she and Palmer had seen earlier, when the night was blown apart by the sound of a gunshot.

Riley turned and raced back as fast as she could through the trees. Even had she been able to, it was pointless stopping to call Palmer on the radio; he'd have heard the shot, too. It appeared to have come from the direction of the house, and although the sound had been distorted, she was guessing it was a shotgun.

When she finally broke into the open, she saw a crowd milling about in confusion on the lawn between the marquee and the rear of the house. Most of them were looking up at the roof, although apart from one or two shrill demands for an explanation, nobody seemed too bothered by the sound of the shot. She wondered how much of that was down to champagne deadening their instincts for danger.

Riley followed their gaze and saw a gleam of reflected light from what might have been a gun barrel poking out over the balustrade running around the edge of the roof. She felt her stomach tighten with the numb realisation that she and Palmer would now be expected to do something.

Only, with no weapons, what could they do? So much, she thought, for gun control laws. It put all the aces in the hands of the bad guys and left everyone else defenceless.

She was about to call Palmer when she saw Rockface jogging across the lawn from the marquee, a look of consternation on his face when he saw what everyone was looking at. She hurried over to meet him and grabbed his arm.

"Show me the way up," she told him. "Then get Sir Kenneth and the girls somewhere safe." The cabinet minister and other VIP guests would have to fend for themselves.

"It's OK – Palmer's on it," the butler replied, apparently unfazed at receiving orders. He led the way through a side door and up a flight of uncarpeted stairs. They didn't have the same plush feel as the rest of the house, and Riley guessed it was a service staircase. It echoed with emptiness and felt cold and austere – or maybe that was simply a feeling prompted by the knowledge that somewhere above their heads was a man with a gun. She shivered, her light suit suddenly inappropriate for the drop in temperature.

Their footsteps echoed ahead of them as they rounded the first floor stairs and started up the narrow final section. Riley prayed that whoever was up there didn't decide to come down this way.

Rockface must have had the same thought, because he reached under his coat and produced an automatic pistol.

Definitely not your average butler, thought Riley. She wondered if Palmer knew the man was armed.

They came to a low door leading to the roof. It was solid, with a large, square lock holding an ornate iron key with a forged handle. Riley tried the handle and felt the door give a fraction. It was unlocked.

They waited, allowing their breathing to return to normal and straining for sounds of movement on the other side. But it was like being in an echo chamber; Riley couldn't hear a thing above her own heartbeat and Rockface's panting.

"Are you any good with that thing?" she whispered. He was holding the gun in a two-handed grip, the finger alongside the trigger guard. It looked very professional, but she wasn't automatically reassured. Anyone who'd watched a Bond film knew how to hold a gun like an expert.

He nodded. "Among other things, inter-services champion at Bisley. That good enough for you?"

"Fair enough. But remember – it could be some tanked-up chinless wonder up here who simply found the keys to the gun cabinet."

Rockface sneered. "That's his lookout, then, isn't it?"

"True. But assuming he doesn't kill us both by accident, what if you shoot him and he turns out to be the son and heir of Lord Doohickey? You fancy doing time for it?"

He appeared to consider the idea, then gestured at Riley to stand by the door. She realised that he wanted her to open it, so he could go through first. She was happy to let him. Hopefully, he wouldn't get his head blown off.

She leaned over and grasped the handle again. It turned with a faint squeak and the door opened, letting in a cool gust of evening air and the reflected glare of lights from the festivities below. Further across the roof she caught a glimpse of the skeletal framework of scaffolding poking into the sky. The sound of music, although muted up here, was still ongoing as though nothing had happened, and it made Riley wonder what it would have taken to bring the proceedings to a halt.

She opened the door a bit more and held her breath, ready for the squeal of rusty hinges. But the door mechanism was silent. She breathed out very slowly, her chest pounding painfully.

At a final nod from Rockface, she pushed the door all the way back.

16

A man was kneeling by the parapet barely six feet away. He had the butt of a shotgun cradled under one arm, with the barrel poking over the edge. He was dressed like the other guests and seemed to be peering over the top as if searching for someone. An empty champagne bottle lay by his side.

Rockface slipped silently through the door, Riley moving up on one side. The air up here was immediately cooler than at ground level, with a faint breeze skimming the roof. The surface underfoot was flat and faintly ridged, and Riley guessed the area was laid with strips of lead or some other weatherproofing. It should have been the same all over, but as she stepped away from Rockface, she trod on a thin scattering of something brittle, setting off a noise like miniature firecrackers.

The gunman spun round with a start, the barrel of the shotgun lifting towards them. Without thinking, Riley, who was closer, took a quick step forward and kicked the man as hard as she could in the chest.

It wasn't technical or stylish, merely a good, old-fashioned toe punt. But it did the job. There was a muted crack as something gave way, and the shock of contact travelled up Riley's leg. As the man groaned and dropped the shotgun, all she had to do was reach out and catch it before it fell.

As the man flopped over sideways, winded and whey-faced, Rockface stepped past Riley and kicked his hands away from his sides in case he had a backup weapon. There was no attempt at resistance and by the sounds coming from the man's mouth, he was busy trying not to throw up.

Riley peered over Rockface's shoulder as he flipped the

gunman expertly on to his back. He was fresh-faced and looked no more than nineteen, with a slight fuzz across his upper lip.

"Know him?" Riley asked.

Rockface shook his head. "Never seen him before. These kids all look the same to me." He went through the man's pockets and came up with a wallet and a silver hip flask. The wallet held documentation in the name of Charles Justin Clarke, with an address in Mayfair, London, and a folded wedding invitation. "Bloody hell," muttered the butler. "He's a sodding guest!"

"Well, there you go," Riley told him, beginning to feel the surge of adrenalin give way to the shakes. "Lucky you didn't shoot him, aren't you?"

Rockface grunted sourly and gently slapped the man's face. It sounded painful. When he got no response, he went downstairs to tell Sir Kenneth what had happened and arrange for an ambulance. Riley didn't envy him the job. No doubt Myburghe would have something to say about a guest running amok with a gun at his daughter's wedding reception. It certainly wasn't something he'd want splashed all over tomorrow morning's papers while eating his egg soldiers.

Charles Clarke stirred and grunted, his breathing sounding like an old kettle. Riley squatted down and waited for him to come round. He did so by stages, shock and alcohol probably combining to act as a mild sedative.

"What happened?" he croaked. When he saw Riley looming over him, he struggled to move away, but Riley put a hand on his chest to keep him still. Even in the poor light she could see his face was as pale as a fish's belly and covered in an unhealthy sheen of perspiration. Then he flipped over and threw up. When he'd finished, he turned back and sat up, shaking his head.

"Sorry," he said miserably, then gently held his ribcage. "Christ – what did you hit me with?"

"My foot," Riley muttered. "Who were you shooting at?"

"What? Nobody," he muttered groggily and flapped a limp hand towards the darkness. "The treetops... I was tree-cutting."

She looked over the parapet, wondering if he was drunker than he seemed. A group of evergreens showed pale and silver in the light coming up from the ground. Most of them were of the same height, with a uniformity of shape and mass like racked spears pointing skywards. She couldn't be certain, but it looked like the nearest one was missing the top few feet of spindly trunk. Myburghe was going to be even less impressed.

"Where did you get the gun?"

"I found it up here." Clarke retched some more and a thin trickle of bile dribbled from his lips.

Riley smiled unsympathetically. Come morning, apart from a monster hangover, he was going to have a mouth like a mud-wrestler's armpit. And Myburghe's anger to cope with. But at least he was alive.

"You found it." She didn't bother hiding her scepticism. "Not that it makes any difference. Ever been to court on firearms offences? It's a prison term these days."

Charles Clarke looked up as though it had suddenly occurred to him what he'd done, and that firing a gun in a crowded place was very stupid, not to say illegal.

"I did – I promise!" At the thought of prison, Clarke looked horrified. "I came up here – OK, that was out of order, maybe. But I needed a drink – something stronger than bubbly, that's all. The key was in the lock, so I thought, why not? It was boring downstairs, anyway. When I stepped outside, I nearly tripped over the gun. It was lying there. I mean, why should I lie?" His voice was shrill with youthful protest and indignation. He broke off and coughed, and Riley told him to lie still.

She was tempted to explain to him what might have happened if Rockface had come through the door by himself, but that really would have spoiled his night. Instead she stepped across the roof and placed the shotgun out of the way, then peered over the parapet.

The crowd downstairs had already forgotten the fuss and were back to their partying, milling in and around the marquee as if gunfire was a regular wedding day occurrence. No doubt some of them would have concluded it demonstrated supreme sang-froid, a spin-off of good breeding and schooling. Riley preferred to think that with no bodies cluttering up the lawns, the young blue bloods merely figured it was safe to continue drinking and having a good time until someone died.

Her radio crackled. It was Palmer. She told him they'd found what seemed to be a drunken prank gone wrong, and that Sir Kenneth might want to check his gun cabinet. She also mentioned Rockface being armed.

"That figures," he replied, sounding not the least surprised. "See you down here."

Riley clicked off and had another scout round the roof, then went to see how Clarke was doing. He seemed to be on the road to recovery, although not quite fit to trot. Moments later, Rockface returned, and after slinging the youth over his shoulder with no more effort than a pillow, carried him downstairs, oblivious to his groans of pain. Evidently, the possibility of cracked ribs didn't rate highly on the butler's list of medical problems, or if they did, he didn't care.

Riley followed, carrying the shotgun.

"That was quick thinking, what you did up there," Rockface commented as they neared the ground floor. His voice held a faint hint of respect, which was a whole continent away from his earlier displays of mild disregard. "Where'd you learn that?"

"Ballet school," Riley quipped. "He was lucky – if I'd used my entrechat, I'd have probably killed him."

He turned and gave a faint scowl. "Right. Big secret, is it?"

"Something like that." She handed him the shotgun and went in search of Palmer.

She found him by the fountain, halfway down the drive. Someone had switched on a number of large ground lights, illuminating the scene like day. A group of partygoers had congregated, clutching bottles and glasses, most of them in much the same state of drunkenness as the unfortunate Charles Clarke. The women were in strappy dresses and delicate heels, while the men were mostly jacket-less, ties undone to show wads of manly chest hair. They were uniformly blasted and some of them watched the approach of Palmer and Riley with undisguised hostility.

In the centre of the group, a young woman was being propped up by two companions. She was tall, thin and coltish, with long, honey-blonde hair slipping in damp disarray around her face, a girl barely on the edge of womanhood.

"Annabel," Palmer murmured quietly, nodding towards the girl. "I told her to stay close to the house but she went walkabout." He looked closely at Riley. "You OK?"

"No problem. The butler's got the shooter in a stranglehold. I think he's one of the guests. I may have broken one of his ribs."

"Serves him right."

It became clear, the closer they got, that Annabel had been in the fountain. Her thin dress was soaked through and she was shivering in the cooling air, holding a clutch purse close to her chest. Her face was wet and smeared with mascara, as if she'd been given two black eyes, and she was staring around with the vague lack of focus that accompanies the fairly stoned. She didn't look happy.

"Well, well, if it isn't the faithful old bloodhound, Frank Palmer!"

The speaker was a heavy-set man in his thirties. He was clutching a champagne bottle in one meaty fist and had the swagger and sneering expression of someone accustomed to getting his own way. His tone was challenging and sour, and he looked a little too old for this group of mainly younger people, one of whom called him Henry. "I thought you'd given up hanging around the girls, Palmer," he taunted nastily. "Vicks had a narrow escape, in my opinion. No saying what would have happened to the bloodline if you'd got in there, eh?"

Palmer ignored him and stepped up to Annabel. He reached out and gently held her face, peering into her eyes with evident concern. There was little obvious reaction from the girl. "You'd better get her inside and changed," he said calmly to her companions. Then he eased the clutch purse from her hand and opened it, shaking the contents out on to the gravel.

A female voice rose in protest, echoed by a couple of men at the front of the crowd. Riley was about to say something as a powder compact, lipstick, cigarette lighter and a surprising amount of other, normal handbag stuff tumbled to the ground. Then came a trickle of small tablets… and two small plastic envelopes containing white powder.

17

The effect on the crowd was dramatic as they focussed on Palmer and Riley, no doubt trying to gauge how official the two of them might be.

But Henry was less guarded; he stepped forward and grabbed Palmer's arm. "Get your grubby hands off her – and that stuff costs!"

Riley barely saw Palmer move, but suddenly Henry was lying on the floor clutching his wrist, the champagne bottle on the ground beside him, gurgling its contents away into the gravel. As Henry struggled to get up, cursing, his face red with pain and indignation, the rest of the partygoers moved back a few paces.

Riley stepped forward to place herself between the two men. As drunk and aggressive as the man was, she was counting on him not wanting to hit a woman. Some of the other men muttered between themselves, but she couldn't tell whether it was in support of Henry or not.

"Get her inside," Palmer suggested to Riley. "I'll follow in a minute."

As Riley turned to move the girl away, she heard a scrape of movement behind her. Henry was back on his feet and spoiling for a fight, urged on by one or two supporters.

"What the fuck's your problem?" he spat at Palmer, his face beet-red with wounded pride. "Think because you're a minder and you've got your little girlfriend with you, you can act all tough? Much good it'll do you." Behind him, some of the other men were restless with anticipation. They seemed to notice Riley for the first time, and eyed the radio in her hand.

In the total silence that followed, a girl laughed shrilly and a glass fell to the ground and shattered.

Palmer continued to ignore Henry, and stared down at the tablets and the small bags of powder. Then he stepped forward and ground them with careful deliberation into the gravel. Someone protested, but made no move to stop him.

Henry moved towards Palmer in a crouch, hands open and flat, his fingers stiff. His eyes glittered in the reflected lights, and Riley guessed he probably wasn't quite as soft as he seemed. Somewhere in his spare time, he'd learned how to fight – probably karate – and was big enough and sufficiently confident in front of his friends to be dangerous.

Riley almost felt sorry for him. Whatever he thought he knew about Palmer, it wasn't enough.

A spurt of gravel signalled the attack, and Henry seemed about to land on Palmer and crush him under his considerable weight. But he didn't quite make it. Just as they were about to collide, Palmer spun away and executed a savage back-kick into his opponent's mid-section. It was deceptively powerful, and stopped the bigger man in his tracks, eyes bulging with shock and pain.

In the background, somebody moaned softly in sympathy.

Before the big man could recover, Palmer took his wrist and spun him round to face the fountain. Putting his knee behind the man's buttocks, he flipped him over the edge. Henry screamed shrilly and hit the water with a splash.

As Palmer turned and walked back towards the house, Henry began to be noisily sick.

Riley waited for Palmer by the front door. Annabel had been ushered inside by her friends, leaving a wet trail across the foyer towards the staircase. There was no sign of Rockface.

"Any problems?" she asked Palmer. "I'm merely being polite – I know you hate anyone making a fuss after you've been all heroic and hairy-chested."

"The fountain might need cleaning," he replied. "How's Annabel?"

"She'll be fine. I suggested they get a doctor take a look, just in case."

"Good idea. There must be at least half a dozen members of the BMA here."

"Who is Henry?"

Palmer shook his head. "Someone with too much money and ego."

"Sounds like you have history."

"Not really. He was one of the group when I was watching Victoria's friend. Ex-army – guards regiment, I think. He found out that I used to be RMP and made it obvious what he thought. I think he fancied his chances with Victoria. She wasn't interested."

Riley thought she could guess why, but let it go. "Annabel," she reminded him, "was carrying enough drugs to buy a small country."

"I know. Not surprising, though, with the crowd she moves in. I'll deal with it." Palmer looked calm enough but Riley detected a storm brewing. She didn't think she wanted to be in the same room if he decided to tell Annabel's father.

She changed the subject. "Charles Clarke, the kid on the roof, claims he found the gun up there and was just letting fly at the treetops."

"You believe him?"

"I think so. He was too well-oiled to be covering up. He said the key was in the door to the roof. It was in the lock when Rockface and I got up there." She reached into her

123

jacket pocket and took out her hand. She was holding a collection of empty nut shells. "I found these. They were spread on the roof around the door. When I stepped on them, it was like tiny firecrackers going off. It was quiet up there, even with the noise from the party."

Palmer took a moment to absorb what she was telling him. "I think someone left the gun there on purpose. The shells were an alarm. There are bird feeders all over the gardens among the trees. Someone was thinking on their feet."

"But why?"

"To increase the pressure on Myburghe. Whoever it was, probably planned to fire off a couple of shots then disappear. It would be a way of demonstrating how close they could get to his family in spite of the security."

"Except they didn't check if the door was locked. They probably figured nobody ever went up there." Riley pointed towards the scaffolding on the far end of the roof. "I took a walk down the other end. I believe they used the scaffolding to climb up and down. It would have been safer than the risk of being caught using the stairs, which are close to the kitchen."

Palmer nodded. "Makes sense."

"Did you see the shotgun?"

"Not yet."

They went in search of Rockface, who unlocked a steel cabinet in a storeroom behind the kitchen and showed them the gun. Alongside it was a box of spare cartridges.

"I found them in the run-off against the parapet," he explained. He was referring to the recessed channel that ran round the roof and took rainfall to the down-pipes.

Palmer examined the shotgun. It was well used, with signs of rough wear around the butt, but otherwise was

124

clean and well oiled. There was no dust residue or moisture, indicating that it hadn't been out on the roof long enough to gather condensation inside or along the barrel. There were no manufacturer's marks.

"Does it belong to Sir Kenneth?" Palmer asked.

"No. I checked. It's a cheap-jack piece of crap."

"That kid really was lucky," said Palmer, echoing Riley's comment, only for different reasons. "If the person who left this had been up there with it, he'd be as dead as mutton."

They replaced the gun and cartridges and borrowed a flashlight, then walked round the house to where the scaffolding was rooted into the flowerbeds against the building.

In films, Riley mused, it would have been full of useful clues, like footprints with unique sole-patterns sold only in one small shop in Plymouth. But the ground around the base of the framework was a mass of powdered rubble and other builders' mess. If anyone had come down at that point, there were no signs of their passing.

It was nearly three in the morning before the last of the guests departed. After ensuring a stand-in security man was in place for the remainder of the night, Riley and Palmer were able to leave. They both felt wrung out, but spent part of the drive back to London tossing the accumulation of events back and forth, trying to tease out a pattern.

"The gun on the roof was a red herring," Palmer concluded, building on his earlier assessment. "As a sniper's weapon it's a non-starter. OK for bringing down birds or rabbits, and in military terms useful at close quarters for clearing houses. But for long-range accuracy they're as much use as a box of eggs. Anyone hoping to hit a person on the ground from the roof would have sprayed too many other people as well."

When Riley told him about her exploration of the stable block, and Rockface's explanation about the use of the building, he seemed unsurprised.

"It could be true," he commented reasonably. "Lads' quarters aren't exactly the height of luxury. They spend most of their time with the horses, so why splash out on soft furnishings?"

"That place wasn't just austere – it was grim," Riley murmured. "Whoever was sleeping there had time to heat some food and smoke a lot of cigarettes, but that was it. No pictures on the walls, no calendar glossies, no graffiti, no sense of who they were."

"Sounds like a field camp." Palmer changed down and powered through a long bend.

"Meaning?"

"Field camps are functional. You arrive, you eat, you sleep, you get up again when called, and you leave. Personalising your surroundings isn't part of the deal. It leaves too much information."

"So what does that tell us?"

"Either Sir Kenneth is mean to his employees, or whoever was in there had moved in without his knowledge or permission."

Riley leaned her head against the window, finding the darkness outside soothing and almost restful. The thought worrying her, however, was how Rockface had turned up at the stable block so conveniently. The only way he could have known her location was if he'd been watching her. It was an unsettling thought.

Palmer dropped Riley off outside her flat, but declined her offer of coffee and a shower.

"I'll go back to my place for a shower and some kip," he

said. "Then I'd better get back to Colebrooke and see how they're holding up."

Riley waved him off, then went inside to be met by the bulky, grinning figure of Mr Grobowski in the hallway.

"Good mornings, Miss Riley," he boomed, in what he probably thought was a considerate whisper. His accent was as heavy as a tank trundling over scrap iron. "I just getting backs, too. We have a party at the community centre. I feed Lipinski, by the way. He like my dumplings, you bet." His eyes twinkled wickedly as he nodded towards the street. "Was your friend Mr Frank, huh? He's a nice mans."

Riley smiled. For some reason, the elderly Pole was convinced Palmer was her boyfriend. It hadn't occurred to him yet that John Mitcheson had been up and down these stairs more often than a mere friend. "You're right, Mr G," she said. "He's nice."

She bid him goodnight and went upstairs, where she kicked off her shoes with a sigh if relief. The cat was asleep on the sofa, no doubt too full to move, so Riley left him to his dreams and checked her email before going to bed. There was one message. It was from Tristram.

TOMORROW. 34A, ALMONDBURY STREET, BARNSTON, NR HUDDERSFIELD. I HOPE I CAN TRUST YOU.

18

Although described as a part of Huddersfield, Barnston proved to be more of a self-contained satellite suburb, situated on the eastern outskirts.

After a three-hour drive up the M1, Riley found the town centre flush with shoppers, mostly attending a farmer's market in the open square. She located a small car park and strolled along Almondbury Street, which became a pedestrian piazza complete with cast-iron benches and litter bins, and a line of flower tubs gleaming black in the mid-morning sunlight.

She was wondering if she had taken leave of her senses coming here without something more concrete to go on. Maybe she could blame it on lack of sleep after yesterday's excitement at Colebrooke House. But after seeing Tristram's latest message, she had been unable to get more than a brief nap, and had eventually given in to the inner voice telling her she needed to meet this person to hear what he knew and put a face to all the emails.

She located a branch of Boots and looked across the piazza to a line of shop windows with numbers on the fascias. 32 and 34 were easy to see, then came a gap filled by a short stretch of spear-topped, wrought iron railings enclosing a twin set of stairs. Above this stood the signs LADIES and GENTLEMEN.

She walked past the railings and looked up at the next window, which was a charity shop. She frowned and checked the number above the door. 36.

She circled the piazza twice, checking both sides in case she had missed something. But there was no 34A. She checked the printout of Tristram's last email. It definitely said 34A.

She'd been had.

She walked back to the charity shop and pushed through the front door. A woman was writing out price tickets behind the counter.

"Morning, love," the woman said, smiling cheerfully.

Riley returned her greeting. "I'm looking for number 34A," she explained. "But I've a feeling I've got the wrong information. Was there ever a 34A?"

The woman nodded. "Aye, love. Still is, too. You need next door."

Riley stared at the woman. "But there's nothing there apart from –"

"The toilets. That's right." She gave a brief chuckle. "It's our local folly, is that. The council got a grant to build some new public toilets. For some reason, they didn't want to list it on the town plans as a convenience, so some wag called it 34A and the number stuck. Now, when anyone wants to go to the loo, everyone round here calls it doing a 34A." She pulled a face. "A right waste of money if you ask me. Still, you can't argue with bureaucrats, can you, once they make their minds up?" She looked at the paper in Riley's hand. "Who are you looking for, anyway?"

"Somebody called Tristram," Riley replied. "I don't suppose it rings a bell, does it?"

"No, love – sorry." The woman smiled wryly. "That's not a name you'll find much of round here, anyway. Tristram? Sounds a bit southern, does that." She nodded, her good deed done for the day, and went back to her price tickets.

Riley thanked her and walked outside. She glanced sideways at the toilets, then strolled across the piazza to Boots, where she studied the window display. It gave her a reasonably clear reflection of the street behind her, from where she could scan the scene for signs of anyone behaving out of the ordinary. If this was some form of elaborate hoax, the perpetrator might be watching to see if he or she had reeled anyone else in.

After a few minutes, she moved on and did a tour of the piazza. Still nothing.

She thought with distaste about the long drive back and felt a growing sense of annoyance – not least at her own gullibility. All this way on the say-so of a computer prankster!

She spotted a café further along the street and decided a coffee and something sugary might be a source of inspiration – or at least, salve her wounded pride at having been taken in so easily. She walked inside and ordered a latte and a large Danish, and sat down near a collection of elderly people in smart coats and hats, their feet surrounded by bags. Clearly, shopping here was a serious business, and included a stop off at the café afterwards.

"Hello, love. Any luck?" Riley turned. It was the woman from the charity shop, accompanied by another woman who might have been a clone. As if reading her mind, the woman said, "This is my sister, Janice. I'm Eileen, by the way. We're on a coffee break; we need a sugar boost for the energy."

"Good for you," Riley replied. "And no – no luck, I'm afraid."

Eileen relayed Riley's search to her sister in a voice loud enough to catch the ear of several other women, and soon Riley was the centre of attention, with speculation bouncing back and forth about the mysterious name. She didn't explain why she was looking for Tristram, and nobody pressed her for a reason. But nobody could offer anything but shrugs and dubious glances, and soon the café returned to normal. Then an elderly man at the next table caught Riley's eye and leaned across the gap.

"You should ask Jacob Worth," he whispered. He winked, then stood up and collected his coat off the back of the chair. "He's a strange one, that. He might not speak to you. But he's got one of them computers – I've seen him use it. Don't tell him I said so."

"Thanks," said Riley. "Where do I find this Jacob?"

"In the bog, of course." The old man looked at her as if she was slow-witted. "Where else would you find a toilet attendant?" Then he walked out, nodding goodbye to the other customers.

Riley finished her coffee, wondering if this wasn't simply an extension to the hoax. But with the long drive back to look forward to, it seemed worth the extra effort to find out if this Jacob existed, and if he could help. She walked across to the toilet block and down the stairs beneath the sign marked LADIES.

The entrance led to a white-tiled interior lit by fluorescent ceiling lights. A line of cubicles stood on one side, with sinks, hand-dryers and towel dispensers on the other. Everything looked new and shiny. At the end of the room was a wooden door.

She knocked. It felt solid and unyielding. There was no answer, so she tried again. Nothing.

She returned to her car and waited. Council folly or not, whoever heard of a toilet attendant not being in attendance? Maybe he had another block to look after across the other side of town. Or maybe he was deaf and hadn't heard her.

She left the car and returned to the toilets. She debated trying the Gents, but decided that was a step too far. She'd probably find herself being hustled out by a couple of local constables and marched to the nick for questioning.

As she was about to return to her car, a tall, thin man in his fifties crossed the piazza and approached the entrance, walking with a pronounced limp. He was dressed in smart trousers and blue shirt, with a dark blue anorak and matching tie. He eyed her warily but didn't speak. In his hand was a small paper bag. Printed on the outside was the name of an office supplies company.

Without knowing why, Riley's instincts told her that this was the man she was looking for.

"Jacob?" She spoke quickly before he could disappear down the stairs. "Can I speak to you?"

The man paused, then shook his head. "It's not a complaint, is it? Only you have to address complaints to the council offices. I'm only the attendant here." With that, he turned away and hurried down the steps, clutching his bag.

"Wait!" Riley followed him, but stopped at the entrance, not quite ready to cross the threshold. "Jacob? Please – I need to talk to you." There was no answer. She heard a door being unlocked and closed very quietly, the sounds echoing clearly over the hiss of water. "Jacob," she called. "It's about Tristram."

She waited, but there was no response. She was about to leave when she heard a noise at the entrance and the man re-appeared. He looked pale, his chin trembling, and was holding on to the wall to keep his balance. He was still clutching the paper bag in his hand.

"What?" he asked softly, blinking in the light. "How do you know about him?" His eyes glowed with an inner fire and Riley could feel a furious energy coming off him in waves.

She took out the email and held it up so he could see it.

"Because Tristram sent me this," she explained. "And others like it."

"To you? No." Jacob shook his head and began to back away. "No, that's not possible."

Riley stepped after him. At least he hadn't denied the name Tristram.

"Don't go. My name's Riley Gavin. You – Tristram's been emailing me about Sir Kenneth Myburghe." She paused as his eyes darted from the email to her face. He showed all the signs of being about to bolt back inside. "I think I can help you."

"No. Can't do it," he muttered defensively, and turned away like a child guarding a secret. "See Barbara. The library. She'll tell you." Then he was gone, scurrying back inside. Seconds later, the inner door slammed shut.

19

"Jacob?" The middle-aged woman stacking books on a wheeled trolley frowned at her. "What would you want with my Jacob?" She looked pointedly at her watch. The library was about to close.

After leaving 34A, Riley had asked for directions to the local library, and been directed past a half-timbered pub to a stone-built, almost austere Victorian building. The inside, by contrast, was bright and cheerful, with the welcoming glow of lights and the warm, musty smell of books.

Riley shrugged. "To be honest, I'm not sure. He told me to come and speak to you. Barbara at the library, he said. You know who I mean, then?"

The woman gave a wry smile. "I should do – I've been married to him long enough." She looked around at two remaining readers and another woman stacking a trolley on the other side of the room, then said quietly, "What's he been doing now? He's not well, I'm afraid. You're not the police, are you?" Her eyes opened in alarm at the thought.

Riley was quick to reassure her, sensing that it wouldn't take much for this woman to shut down, just like Jacob. "Nothing like that," she said soothingly. "It's this." She took out the emails and showed them to the woman, and explained how they had directed her to number 34A.

Barbara read the text, her face draining of colour. Then she handed the emails back, her hand darting to an elegant cameo brooch at her breast. "It's silliness, is that," she whispered. "It's so long ago – he doesn't mean anything by it, not really. I'd forget about it, if I were you. It's nonsense." She turned away, busying herself, hoping her visitor might give up and go away.

"Wait. Please." Riley touched her arm. She had to find some way of bringing this to a conclusion. If this was just 'silliness' as Barbara described it, then so be it. She could simply chalk it up to experience. Maybe Jacob, the woman's husband, was unwell. But having seen her reaction to the emails, Riley wasn't so sure. There was clearly something going on here, lurking beneath the surface, and Barbara knew what it was. "He must have wanted someone to know what he knew about Sir Kenneth Myburghe, or why send me the emails?"

Barbara didn't respond, although she stayed where she was, no longer intent on flight.

"Why Tristram?" Riley urged her. "Is that name important to him?" It occurred to her that without confirmation that Jacob Worth and Tristram were one and the same person, she was still at square one.

"What happens," Riley continued, "if he sends these emails to someone else – maybe one of the tabloids? They won't be put off so easily. And they won't be subtle about it, either. If they smell a story, they'll come looking for him in droves."

It was this point which seemed to penetrate the woman's mind. She nodded and sighed deeply, as if reaching a decision she had been considering for a long time. She led Riley over to the deserted reference section and invited her to sit.

"He won't speak to you," she explained softly. "He doesn't – speak to women, I mean. It's part of…what happened to him."

"How do you mean?" Riley leaned in close, intrigued. "Part of what?"

"I can't tell you much… that's up to him if he wants to.

But Jacob was… in the Falklands – in the Navy." Barbara spoke concisely. She seemed calmer now, as if unburdening herself was helping. "He was with the Defence Intelligence Group, working in Latin America. He never says much, but I know he was working with the British embassies down there, trying to get support against the Argentinians. This was in nineteen eighty-two. He'd been over there for a couple of weeks, travelling about. Then on the fourth of May, he was told to join some other officers on HMS Sheffield. There was to be a conference of some sort and Jacob and a friend named Tom Elliott were to brief the meeting about what they'd found."

"The Sheffield?" Riley trawled her memory for details with a sense of foreboding. "But wasn't that –?"

"She was hit by an Exocet. It didn't explode, but the ship caught fire. Jacob and Tom were in a wardroom for the conference when the missile struck. A bulkhead door was blown off by the impact and entered the wardroom. It broke Jacob's leg, but… Tom was crushed. He was taken off the ship with Jacob, but he died of his wounds. There was nothing they could do. It was such a waste."

Riley waited, saying nothing.

Barbara took a small handkerchief from her sleeve and dabbed at her eyes. "You asked about Tristram earlier. He uses the name after one of the other ships. He said it's safer than using his own name. It's useless telling the man, but he blames himself for not saving Tom's life. The Navy told me he couldn't have done anything – that the door was too heavy for one man to lift, and the damage was too severe – but he won't listen. In the end, what with the wounds and that, it all got too much; he had a breakdown." She shrugged. "He's been like it ever since. Bouts of depression, anger, insomnia – guilt, too, which is worse, poor man. But there's no getting to him. God knows, we've all tried."

"Is that why he's working where he is?" Riley tried to be tactful, knowing this must be difficult for Barbara to talk about.

"Yes. He tried other jobs. I mean, his career in the Navy was over, but he did try. Securicor was one place, but when they asked him to do night shifts, he couldn't sleep properly in the day and it began to tell on him. Tom's son, Ben – he's a policeman – helped by taking him out for drives and suchlike. But it didn't last. Then he saw the attendant position advertised down at the Job Centre and applied." She shook her head slowly, eyes somewhere in the distance.

"That must have been very hard."

"Harder for him than me, love." Barbara looked up with a touch of fire in her eyes, and Riley saw the pride that Jacob's wife still felt for him, in spite of his problems. "Much harder. Especially when friends asked why – knowing his background in the navy, I mean. But he said that's what he wants." She shrugged. "And that's where he's been ever since. It suits, him, you see. He feels safe down there. Removed. A bit like being on board ship, I think. He's on his own for the most part, but there's always people he knows who pop in for a chat. They never stay long because they know it's not needed, but it's enough. He likes to read, and he does puzzles and such, like Sudoku. He draws, too – people, mostly – and makes model ships and stuff. He was always good with his hands like that."

Riley nodded and felt an unbidden thought creep into her mind. Would that include putting together a fake bomb? "But why all this stuff about Myburghe? He wasn't on board the Sheffield, was he?"

"Not him, dear. That's the whole point, isn't it?" Riley was about to ask her what she meant, but Barbara twisted her fingers together and continued, "What you said about other people… the tabloids. I couldn't have that happen. It would destroy him. Could you get someone to talk to him? A man, I mean. He won't talk to you – not alone, anyhow."

"But he contacted me," Riley pointed out.

"I know, love. He probably thought…" She paused and looked embarrassed, and Riley thought she knew why.

"He thought Riley was a man?"

"Yes. Sorry." Barbara took a deep breath. "He's not good around women these days. I don't know why. He used to be so confident – a bit of a charmer, actually." She stared off into the distance, a faint smile bringing a light to her face as the memories came flooding in. Then she shook herself and continued, "I don't want him talking to others about it. He could get into trouble, couldn't he, saying things like that? And the tabloids don't care who gets hurt, do they? Myburghe is important, after all."

"You know who he is, then?"

Barbara nodded, eyes flickering beyond Riley as if she didn't want to make contact. "Oh, yes. I know who he is." She dropped her head, but not before Riley saw a flash of something deep in her eyes. It might have been anger, but it was too brief to tell.

"Did Jacob talk about him?"

"Sometimes." She waved vaguely. "He talks about…things, now and then. Things he remembers. I'm not sure he knows what he's saying most of the time. But he mentions Myburghe more than most things."

Riley held her breath, her heart thudding. This time, while Barbara was talking, she'd seen something more in her face, and heard something in her tone of voice when she talked about Myburghe.

Was it contempt?

When Barbara didn't speak, Riley urged her, "Go on."

"Well, he's the man who got so friendly with those lords, wasn't he?"

"Lords?" Riley leaned forward and touched the woman's arm. Instinct told her this was important. "What lords, Barbara?"

"Well, they're not real lords, are they?" Barbara said dismissively. "Not like ours, anyway. Except to their own kind, probably. What is it they call those people in Colombia? Those awful cartels... the drug lords."

Riley made the return trip to London in a daze. She'd been on the brink of dismissing Jacob Worth as a certified head-case, a man living under massive delusions, when suddenly she'd been snapped back to basics by Barbara Worth's revelations about her husband's background and his connection with Sir Kenneth Myburghe. Whatever she'd hinted about the former ambassador had been fuelled by her husband's ramblings and would have to be verified. Unfortunately, the only person who could do that – apart from Myburghe, and she wasn't about to ask him – was Jacob.

And Jacob either couldn't or wouldn't talk to a woman.

She was still chewing it over when she got home. Tired from the drive, she was about to turn in for an early night when her phone rang. It was Weller.

"We picked up an interesting visitor yesterday," the senior policeman announced breezily. "From the States. Used to be one of your lot."

"My lot?" Already with a head like cotton wool, Riley was having trouble deciding what Weller was after. "Have you been harassing single women again, Weller? There are laws against that."

"Journalist. Hack. Whatever they call 'em over there." She heard the rustle of paper followed by a crunch as he chomped on a sweet. "Toby Henzigger. You know him?"

"No. Should I?"

"He was freelance, like you. Covering international crime stories for rags like the Washington Post, New York Times, Chicago Tribune… he moved around a lot, mostly in the southern hemisphere."

Riley desperately wanted to say so what, but she knew Weller wouldn't have called without good reason. She picked up on the past tense. "Was?"

"He got sucked into a story about drug shipments from Latin America. Rumours put Henzigger a little too close to the action to have survived without having his head shot off – unless he had friends in murky places looking out for him."

"That doesn't mean anything," she said bluntly. "We all have to share space with some unpalatable characters from time to time."

Weller chuckled appreciatively. "Touché, Miss Gavin. But Henzigger's upset a lot of people over the years. This could have been their way of getting even. Anyway, the story ran for a while before everyone involved suddenly developed collective amnesia. But the damage was done."

"What does Henzigger say?"

"He claimed his assignment had been set up by a freelance news agency, and he was working alone to keep his profile low because of the circumstances of the story. That should have been enough to get the wolves off his back. Then a photo surfaced showing him head-to-head with a close aide of one of the main Colombian narcotics producers, a man high on the DEA 'Wanted' list. That about did it for him."

Colombia. Riley managed to keep her mouth shut, but

the word was enough to send a buzz through her. "What happened to him?"

"By then, they figured where there's smoke there's usually somebody with a blowtorch. Bad enough nasty foreigners are shipping drugs to innocent American teenagers, let alone someone from the Fourth Estate being involved. It was enough to cost him his job."

Riley frowned. Why was Weller telling her all this? He was unlikely to be trying to give her a career boost by tipping her the wink on dubious former journalists coming into the country. "What's he doing over here – lecturing to London's finest?"

"How droll," muttered Weller. "But not such a bad idea, now you mention it. I'm sure there's plenty we could learn from him. Actually, he claimed he's here on holiday. He made the mistake of coming in under false papers, but he was recognised at immigration by one of their embassy spotters. They thought we should know, so we picked him up."

"Kind of them. And this affects me how?"

"Ah. Yes." Another crunch echoed down the line. "Among his various personal bits and pieces was a piece of paper with your name on it. Now why would that be?"

Riley was astonished. "I've no idea. I've never heard of the man. Did you ask him?"

"Of course. He wouldn't say. Said it was just a name he'd picked up out of professional interest. Must be nice having fans out there."

Riley ignored the dig. "Where is he now?"

"No idea. The Yanks finally admitted they didn't have any objection to him being here, and he was found to be carrying his legitimate passport, anyway. He reckoned it was all a mix-up. In the interests of the so-called special relationship, we slapped his wrist and let him go. Personally, I'd have slung him on the next flight home. The man's clearly unhinged. Still, what can you do, eh?"

"Well, thanks for telling me. I'll look out for him."

"Do that. You might also warn your friend Palmer when you see him next."

"Why?"

"Henzigger had another piece of paper in his wallet. It had Palmer's name and the name of someone we've all heard of."

"Who?"

"Sir Kenneth Myburghe."

The phone clicked off, leaving Riley with a hollow feeling in the pit of her stomach.

Myburghe again?

The more she heard from Weller, the more uneasy she felt about his tactics. Why had he chosen to call her, a member of the press? Why not one of his other contacts – of which he must have many? Was it really just to check Henzigger's story? Or had he decided to set some cats loose and see what came scurrying out of the wood pile?

20

Next morning, Riley forced herself out of bed and into a brisk walk through Holland Park. She needed the exercise to blow the kinks out of her system after the previous day's drive, and the fresh air to get her brain into some sense of order. She collected a croissant and coffee on the way and chewed as she walked, sharing space with mothers and strollers, joggers and children.

So far, she told herself, she had a man hinting at some sort of scandal surrounding a senior British diplomat with a service record in Colombia; Frank Palmer guarding the very same diplomat; a senior cop from the Met taking an interest in Palmer, and now a disgraced American journalist with a background in South America taking an interest in all of them.

Whatever was going on involved too many people she couldn't get to. Palmer because he was…well, Palmer, although that might be less of a problem if she could collar him long enough to wear him down; Myburghe because he was out of bounds; Weller because he was playing puppet-master; and Tristram AKA Jacob Worth, who claimed to know something, if only he would part with the information.

She threw the remainder of her croissant to a couple of pigeons, then strolled on, sipping her coffee, until she found herself at the southern edge of the park on Kensington High Street. She was about to turn back when a man fell in alongside her, matching her pace.

"You're Gavin, right?" said the man genially. He was tall and solid, with tired eyes set in a swarthy face beneath short-cut grey-flecked hair. He could have been a business-man looking for directions, but not too many businessmen sidle up to women on the street and use their name.

Riley readied herself for a seedy proposition and checked her coffee mug, but there wasn't enough to do more than stain his shirt.

"You're Riley Gavin," he repeated quickly, sensing her wariness. He had an American accent, although with some of the edges smoothed off, as if he'd been out of his home country a lot. "I know it's you because I got your picture from a piece you did a while back. And I've already seen you with your pal, Palmer. I need to talk with you."

Riley stopped and turned to face the man. "Where did you see us?" There were plenty of pedestrians about, so she wasn't alarmed. But one thing she didn't want was to have this stranger following her back to her flat.

"You were at that shoot near Colebrooke. I saw you watching. Palmer was off killing stuff." He grinned without humour. "I had to leave in a hurry, remember?"

Then she realised: the man in the woods. He looked bigger here, somehow, as if being surrounded by trees and undergrowth had diminished him.

Seeing that she had placed him, he said, "Yeah, that was me. What do we get for trespassing on private land in this country – slammed in the stocks or hung from a tree?"

"You're out of date," she told him. "We stopped hanging people when you lot started lynching cattle rustlers. It got so tacky. Who are you and what do you want?"

"My name's Toby Henzigger," he said neutrally. "I'm in the same line of business as you." He held out his hand.

Riley ignored it, her thoughts flashing back to Weller's phone call of the previous day. This was getting spooky.

Henzigger shrugged and stuck his hand back in his pocket.

"Can we go somewhere and talk? This is a bit public for my tastes."

Riley was concerned about how he'd found her. She wasn't in the phone book and she didn't give out her home address, having learned from colleagues long ago that unhappy subjects of the criminal kind had a knack of finding out where journalists lived, and might choose to make late calls to protest their innocence or anger.

"Here's fine," she said. "Talk about what?"

"I've been looking for you. I know you're an investigative reporter – I've read some of your stuff. You heard what they said about me?" His right eye flickered slightly as he spoke. It was an almost imperceptible movement, which Riley guessed wouldn't have been visible if he hadn't been standing so close.

Riley didn't want to spoil his day by telling him that he hadn't been nationwide news, but said anyway, "Well, I heard you were almost a guest of Her Majesty. False passport, wasn't it? Bit unwise, in view of the current state of things."

Henzigger looked sour. "It was a mistake," he muttered. "It was all a mistake. Did you know I've never been charged? They let me sweat it out for over a year, then dropped the case." She had to think hard about that, before guessing that he wasn't talking about being pulled in by Immigration, but his problems before that.

"Isn't that a relief?"

"Oh, sure." It came out with a hint of sarcasm, and he wiped a hand across his face. It was a big hand and looked as if it could do a lot of damage. The nails were clean, but the skin was rough and deeply tanned, suggesting Henzigger spent a lot of time outdoors. "Look, I know you don't have any reason to trust me. But I need to talk. Can we get a coffee somewhere? Somewhere public – you choose."

Riley nodded. In spite of herself, how could she not be intrigued? Part of it was professional, wanting to know Henzigger's story. The other part was a growing sense that this man might know something important about Sir Kenneth Myburghe. Otherwise, why had he been there?

"This way," she said, and led him along the street to a café where they could talk safely without being isolated. She let him place the order and sat down at a corner table. When he joined her, she didn't waste time in small talk. "What do you want from me?"

He tasted his coffee, then reached for more sugars, tearing off the paper ends with a jerk and pouring the contents into his cup. He flicked the paper fragments away. "I was set up, you know? That stuff about unauthorised contacts and me being too close to the cartel was pure crap." He looked sour, as if he was bubbling with suppressed rage. "You know how it is. Over the years I could've taken back-handers to kill stories, and cut into some deals big enough to pay off the Bolivian national debt. And nobody would've known. Not Washington, not Congress, not the Department of Justice – nobody. But I didn't. You wanna know why? Because it didn't interest me. I didn't become a newsman because I liked the retirement plan or I figured the industry had a good ethics programme. I did it because a college buddy killed himself on coke – and that was before it got fashionable. He fell in with a bad crowd on campus who liked to 'experiment'. Only they didn't know what they were getting into and they got sold some shit cut with face powder. His first shot and he dies in agony. And he wasn't the only one. I figured right then that it was going to get worse and maybe I could help make a difference by working my way up and exposing some of the underbelly of the drugs market." A little bubble had formed on his lip with this impassioned claim, and it popped when he clamped his mouth shut.

"So how come you're still walking around?"

"Because they couldn't prove anything. They listened to the rumours, they tracked down everyone I ever met and they talked to every junkie who had a deal to cut. It's no surprise they got the story they wanted to hear."

"But?"

"In the end they decided to drop it. And you know why? Because it never would have stood up in court. Trouble is, shit sticks. After that I couldn't get hired to write page numbers." His look of disgust deepened at the memory of how he'd been treated and Riley felt a flicker of sympathy. But it didn't explain why he'd been in the woods at the shoot in Gloucestershire, or why he was now sitting in front of her. Nor how he'd tracked her down.

"How did you find me?"

He took his time answering, as if he was marshalling his words to make sure they came out right. "I need your help. I need someone I can trust. To be honest, I'd never heard of you until I picked up the name of your military cop pal, Palmer."

"In relation to what?"

He gave a thin smile. "Sir Kenneth Myburghe. Who else?" When Riley remained blank-faced, he continued, "I took a drive in the country and followed the shooting party Myburghe was supposed to be in. I knew straight away he wasn't there, though, and figured it was a decoy set-up. That's where I saw you and Palmer."

"How did you get our names?" Weller had told her that Henzigger had Palmer's name in his wallet at Immigration, suggesting he knew the name before entering the country. But that didn't explain how he'd got hold of it.

He seemed to read her mind. "I still got friends, don't worry. They found out Palmer was running protection on Myburghe and got his name through the licence plate number. Then they hooked on to you. The rest was easy."

"What's your interest in Myburghe?"

"It's because of him that I was set up." He sat back suddenly, looking tired, as if he'd been harbouring the words for a long time and it had cost him a great deal to get them out. He shook his head. "That sounds lame, right?"

Riley agreed. It did. It also sounded like every crook who'd ever been caught with his nose in the trough, making excuses. Criminals were always innocent and crooked cops were victims of a frame-up. It was an old song.

"How could he have been involved? He's a British diplomat."

He looked away. "Oh, he's involved, believe me. It's why I came over here. I fouled up coming in on false papers, but it gets to be a habit in my line of work. By the time I realised, I was in line at Immigration and couldn't get to my real ID. I figured, what the hell, it was nothing that couldn't be sorted out." He shrugged fatalistically. "I was wrong. In the end someone at the embassy made a call and they let me go. I guess they knew it wasn't worth the hassle."

He made it sound so simple, Riley almost found herself believing him. She had never used a false ID, so had to take it on trust that if you did so all the time, you might reach for the wrong one under stress. But would Immigration really allow someone who'd used false papers to go free on the say-so of the US Embassy?

"How does this affect me?"

"You were out near Myburghe's place in – where is it, Gloucestershire." He pronounced it the American way, with staccato syllables. "At the shoot. Are you doing a piece on him? You should – it'd make your hair curl."

She waited for him to elaborate, but he didn't. She guessed he was referring to Colombia. As a journalist, Henzigger would have made it his business to know all the key players in the area he was covering, putting names to faces, sorting out the friendly from the hostile. It was a subtle balancing-act, having to mix and meet on one hand with people from embassies and trade missions, and then going off to rub shoulders with men and women who wouldn't know a canapé from a can of beans.

"What were you doing in the woods?" she asked.

He smiled crookedly, a thin sliver of charm breaking through the angry veneer. "That wasn't my finest hour, was it? I'm getting too old for all that backwoods stuff. They nearly had me." The expression dropped away just as quickly as it had come. "I was just doing some ground-work. I got past the guards but I didn't expect you and your partner to roll up. Is he for real? That was some fancy gun-play. I thought there was strict etiquette to hunting over here."

"There is. But Palmer doesn't play by the rules. It's why they don't invite him very often."

"I guess not. He any good?"

"Yes. So what was this groundwork for?" She was getting irritated by the way he was constantly wandering away from the subject, as if reluctant to approach it head-on.

"You ever heard of a guy called Walter Asner?" When she shook her head, he continued, "He was a trade secretary at the US embassy in Bogotá. Career diplomat, like Myburghe, only lower down on the totem. He'd moved around a bit, the way those guys do – Europe, Middle East, Far East, places like that. Then he learned Spanish and moved to South America. He was out there a long time." He tapped his fingers on the tabletop, a nervous reaction. "Just over a year ago he returned Stateside. He'd done his time, put in the hours, and he wanted out."

"Early retirement?"

"Uh-huh. Supposed to be, anyway. He was in his fifties. Good time to go. Still a lot of years left to kick back and watch the flowers grow." He traced a line through a puddle of moisture on the table top, and Riley suddenly knew he was going to tell her something unpleasant.

"Go on."

"He never made it. One evening he pulled into his garage, closed the door behind him and blew out his brains."

21

Riley waited, not quite sure where this was leading.

"Walter Asner," Henzigger continued after a few heart-beats, "wasn't what everyone thought." The way he said 'Walter' produced a faint softening of his features – at least, for a moment. "By that I mean he wasn't the embassy suit he pretended to be."

"Not a diplomat?"

He shook his head. "Walt was special... part of a unique programme. He came from a family of career administrators. He was smart, well educated and knew pretty much what made the world tick. But he wanted to join a team that made a difference. He wasn't prepared to simply push paper around the way his father had done. The administration recognised that. But they knew he had other skills, too. Skills they could use. They put him through training with the DEA – Drug Enforcement – and once he'd finished he was dropped out and fed into the embassy circuit under deep cover. Not even the staff he worked with knew what he was really doing."

"Why the secrecy?"

"It was a programme set up about twenty years ago. A focus group in the Department of Justice decided it would be a neat idea if they had some special agents who knew how to hold a knife and fork, to blend into the embassy circuit. Their job would be to work the corridors, mix with the foreign mucky-mucks and look for sources, contacts, that sort of stuff. But they weren't to get involved with the day-to-day anti-drugs war. They'd concentrate on the people at the top, their aides and secretaries, while the rest of the DEA troops would work the streets. It was a good plan, too. It brought in great intelligence from both ends, some of it top grade. You'd be amazed what those stiff collars hear at some of those fancy trade gatherings. And Walt knew how to work 'em. He was good."

Riley saw where he was going. "But somebody found out what his true function was?"

"Must have. He was way too experienced after all those years to have let it slip. Hell, I'm not even sure his wife knew."

Riley shrugged. Maybe, after all the years working under such circumstances, Walter Asner had simply become careless. "Could it have been suicide?"

Henzigger shook his head with measured emphasis. "Not a chance. Walt and I went back a long way. He wasn't the type." He held up a quick hand to forestall argument. "I know, the shrinks say everyone's got it in them; that everyone's got their breaking point. I hadn't seen Walt for months, but I spoke to him before he quit. He wanted to enjoy life, not end it. He had lots of plans, all of them involving his wife Margie and their boat."

"This still doesn't explain why you've come to me after all this time. Are you saying Myburghe was involved?"

"Myburghe," Henzigger said, appearing to have only heard part of what she'd said. His eyes glinted sharply. "I hear he's been getting some letters and stuff."

Riley was surprised. She wasn't sure how much Henzigger knew or how much was guesswork, but by 'stuff', did he mean the fake bomb, or his son's finger and ring?

"There's been some crank mail. How did you hear about it?"

He showed his teeth, ignoring the question. "Crank mail? Is that what you call it over here? Jesus." He sniffed and added, "What's it about?"

"I don't follow."

"What do they want? What're the demands?"

She shrugged. "There haven't been any – at least, not yet." She wondered if he knew about the fake bomb. If he was as well informed as he claimed, he probably did. But she decided to try it out. "Apart from the bomb, anyway."

He looked stunned. "Bomb?" He dropped his voice and hissed, "What freaking bomb?"

Got you, she thought. So you're not as well informed as you think. "It was a fake. The police think it was a disgruntled former worker."

"And no follow-up note?"

"No."

He raised an eyebrow. "Kinda strange, don't you think? If someone sent me a fake ticker through the post, I'd expect I'd have to pay out, in case they sent a real one."

"Perhaps whoever's behind it is playing a waiting game."

"Sure. And in the meantime, you and your buddy have been hired to watch his back?"

Riley frowned. Pinning this man down was like dealing with a hyperactive kid. "Are you saying this business with Myburghe is connected to your friend Walter?"

He gave her a sour look. "Damn right. If there's one thing I learned after all the years I put in this business, it's that connections to Colombia always rise to the surface sooner or later like dead fish in a pool. Walt died after working there, my career and reputation went down the can, and now Myburghe is being threatened – and he was there longer than most. Even money says the common thread must be Colombia."

"And you want to find out to clear your name."

"You got it."

Riley wasn't sure how much to believe. Yet she couldn't argue with his logic. Looking for a common link to all three men, the most obvious conclusion was the place they had last worked. Except that each case appeared to be different. It wasn't what anyone would have called a definite pattern.

"What do you expect me to do?"

"Work with me," he replied bluntly. "I'm trying at my end, through contacts at the embassy and a couple of DEA offices here in Europe." He smiled coolly. "I've still got friends who don't believe all the mud they threw at me. I'm trying to find out what Walt was working on before he retired. I know what I was working on before I got shafted, so it's a matter of seeing where the connections are."

Riley stifled a feeling of anger at his arrogance. "And you're hoping I'll investigate Myburghe for you? Why should I do that?"

"I came over to do it myself... but I'm open to any help I can get. I know you're smart and capable, and you're pretty tough." The look behind his eyes had suddenly become wild and unsettling, and Riley noticed that where his hands were gripping the table, the skin was white with tension. It made her want to move her chair back and put distance between them.

"You expect me to spy on him for you?"

"You're in a position to keep an eye on him. See what he does, who he meets, that's all. OK?"

The way he said the final word was like fingernails down a blackboard. Was he taking it for granted that she would help, as if she had rolled over, easily seduced by his hard luck story? Or was it the hard edge of desperation that she could hear in his voice? Either way, she heeded the instinctive alarm bells and said vaguely, "I'll think about it."

"Sure." As if throwing a switch, he was suddenly reasonable

and calm again. "You're being cautious. I guessed you would be." He slipped a hand in his shirt pocket and took out a slip of paper. It held a phone number. "You can get me on that number anytime. You could be a big help, you know – and get yourself a mega-bucks story."

With that, he stood up and walked away.

22

When Riley returned to her flat she found Weller strolling along the pavement outside. He had loosened his tie and seemed to be enjoying the air. She looked round for a snatch-squad of burly coppers, but he was alone.

She stared hard at him. "What do you want, Weller? This is getting annoying."

"Just passing," he replied breezily, and looked round at the buildings. "Nice neighbourhood, this. Bit outside my bracket, though."

"I doubt that." She thought the idea of Weller just passing was as likely as Father Christmas in July. Besides, she was convinced he would have already been here to ascertain where she lived before buttonholing her in Caffé Nero a few days ago.

"Relax," he said, fingering a luxuriant bay tree in a wooden tub. The old lady next door had placed it there with Mr Grobowski's approval, and was now watching Weller like a hawk through a side window. By the scowl on her face, Riley reckoned that if Weller so much as bent one of the leaves, she'd be out with a broken chair leg to beat him to a pulp. "I wanted to ask if you'd seen Henzigger yet?"

Riley almost admitted she had. Then she thought better of it. Let Weller do his own dirty work. "Should I?"

"Well, he did have your name on him. It seems an odd thing to carry if he had no intention of contacting you."

"You said you had no interest in Henzigger."

"We didn't. Then we found out a bit more about him. Seems the Yanks fibbed a bit. He's got history."

Riley worked hard at keeping her face straight. Did Weller know she'd just been talking to Henzigger? Was this chat some sort of test? "What kind of history?"

"Classified stuff. Goes back years. Panama, Nicaragua, Chile... he's knocked around a bit, mostly in the southern hemisphere. One thing's sure, he wasn't just a journalist."

"What?" Riley felt her face drain of colour and thought about the line of chat Henzigger had fed her not twenty minutes ago. How could anyone be so convincing? What the hell else had he lied about?

"We think he was DEA," Weller continued, unaware of her inner turmoil. "Might still be for all we know. But if the Yanks don't want him, why should we get stuck with him? We've got enough undesirables of our own."

"Good point," Riley agreed, recovering quickly. "So why not pick him up and put him on the next plane?"

"I'd love to. Trouble is, we can't find him. I thought he might have contacted you."

Riley smiled. If she were to believe this man, the Met couldn't locate Frank Palmer when he was with Sir Kenneth Myburghe, and now they'd lost an unwelcome American with a dodgy past who'd come into the country on a false passport. "Sorry. I can't help."

"No matter." He rocked back on his heels and sniffed the air as if he was on the sea front at Brighton, then said carefully, "I'm probably wasting my time, but I'd hate to think you were getting into something nasty, Miss Gavin."

"What's this, Weller? Fatherly concern for my well-being?"

He shrugged. "No skin off my nose," he said. "But if you're being too adventurous, I'd rather know about it before I have to come along and scrape you up with a shovel. This thing with Myburghe, for example." This time there was no title. "A little birdy tells me you're on the team now."

Riley had been wondering how long it would be before he mentioned that. No doubt he was plugged into the same information network as Keagan.

"He's been receiving hate mail," she said truthfully. "He wanted someone to watch his family during the wedding. He employed Palmer, who asked me to help out."

"Mmm… I heard about the mail. A fake bomb, too. Pity he didn't keep any of the evidence. I thought that was a bit careless for a man with his background." He made it sound as if he didn't believe it possible. "Probably a disgruntled servant, I imagine, trying to put the frighteners on him. What do they call it – below-stairs friction? Paying you well, is he?"

Riley was ready for the sudden switch in questions. "Yes, actually. Why, are you jealous?"

Weller snorted gently. "Not me," he said amiably. "But a word of advice: if you haven't been paid yet, I'd get it quick if I were you."

"What do you mean?"

"The last I heard, which was just the other day, so it's still hot news, is that Sir Kenneth Myburghe is as flat, financially speaking, as one of Gandhi's flip-flops."

Riley thought about the building works and the wedding. Could it be true? Had Myburghe over-extended himself? "Doesn't his wife have money?"

"Did have, years ago. She divorced him last year, cutting off any funds at source."

"Why the divorce?"

"No idea. Gossip says his gambling. But it could be the fact that he's no longer being considered for foreign postings. I'm surprised he hasn't had to sell the country pile by now. Still, I suppose he could always offer it to the nation in perpetuity. A rehab centre for heroin addicts –

now that would be useful, don't you think?" He gave her a shark-like display of teeth, then turned and walked away, whistling softly and leaving Riley to speculate on how much he hadn't told her.

And why the reference to drugs?

Riley went inside and typed up some notes, always useful therapy when she felt pressured about a job. The pounding of the keys was oddly soothing, the end result often producing clarity where none had existed before. When she had reached a hiatus, she brewed coffee and ruminated, before calling Palmer and telling him all about her visit to Barnston, the sudden appearance of Toby Henzigger and ending with Weller's latest information.

"Hellfire," he commented dryly. "It's like moths to a flame with you, isn't it? Does anyone insure you?"

"Very funny, Palmer. Don't you see where all this is leading? We – you – need to talk to Jacob to find out what he knows."

"Possibly. He sounds like a case of post-traumatic stress to me. What then?"

"After that," she said carefully, "it might be useful talking to Lady Myburghe."

There was a long silence before Palmer replied. "I don't think I'd recommend that."

It wasn't a definite no, but a long way from yes. "It's important," said Riley.

"Why? Because wives know their husbands best?"

"Partly. I think she might have information about Sir Kenneth that we won't get from any other source."

"How does that affect our current situation?"

Riley sighed. She wasn't sure if it was Palmer's instinctive code of in-built discretion, but he seemed determined not to make this easy. She told him what Weller had said about Myburghe's finances. He listened without interrupting.

"Even without that," said Riley, "I'd be interested to know why Lady Myburghe left him after all those years of marriage. And exactly how is he funding the wedding and the renovations at Colebrooke House when, according to Weller, he's flat broke."

The line ticked and hissed, and for an instant she thought of Weller, and men with electronic boxes running a tap on her telephone line. She dismissed it as burgeoning paranoia and waited for a reply.

"Palmer?"

Eventually he said, "Do you believe Weller's being straight?"

"I can't see why he'd lie about something like this. What would he have to gain? You've met him – what do you think?"

Palmer didn't bother denying that he knew Weller. "Maybe. I only met him once. He seemed OK, but he's bound to have an agenda of some sort."

"I agree." The fact was, the more she saw of Weller, the more she was certain that he was using her and – by association – Palmer, to stir up whatever pot he'd got bubbling before him. But that was tactics.

Another long pause, then Palmer said, "I'll call you back." He rang off.

Riley sat and waited, partly because she wasn't sure what to do next. She was worried that her friendship with Palmer was approaching a watershed, and was beginning to regret having pressured him to take sides. True, he was quite capable of making decisions for himself, but clearly he was also fighting his own moral code about making judgements on the people he worked for. And having Riley pushing him with information he wouldn't normally have been privy to was plainly clouding his deep-seated issues of loyalty.

He called back after twenty minutes. "One hour's time," he said briefly, and gave her an address in Belgravia. "Don't be late."

"Will you be there?" she asked.

"No." He disconnected.

23

Fifty-five minutes later, Riley arrived outside a splendid town house in a smart white-stucco terrace, with an imposing portico and a shiny black front door not unlike the one at Colebrooke House. The litter-free street was lined with cars, all gleaming as if in testimony to their owners' status, and she felt a frisson of nervousness as she mounted the steps and rang the bell.

She was half expecting to see another version of Rockface, stiffly formal in a suit and tie. But the door was opened by a tiny Filipino woman in a smart royal-blue dress, who didn't look as if she could throw a fit, much less a punch. She smiled and invited Riley in with a timid gesture, and it was obvious she had been told about the appointment.

Riley stepped past her into a large hallway furnished with a deep pile carpet and several impressive pieces of antique furniture. The walls were exquisitely decorated in soft shades of sage and oatmeal, and she felt relieved at having changed into a smart skirt and decent shoes before coming here.

"Please go through to the drawing room," the maid asked her, indicating a door to the right. Then she turned and walked away with tiny, elegant steps.

Susan, Lady Myburghe was flicking through a glossy magazine and sipping at a porcelain cup of colourless liquid. She wore a beautiful silk dress of burgundy and black, off-set by a string of black pearls, yet her feet were encased in a pair of fluffy pink bedroom slippers with frayed toes, a startling contrast in colour and style. It was only when she looked up that Riley saw her eyes bore a deep sadness and her skin lacked lustre, like faded parchment.

She felt a twinge of guilt for coming here with what she had in mind, but reminded herself that this woman had been her husband's close companion for many years, and consequently should know more about him than anyone on the planet.

"Sit down, Miss Gavin." The invitation was crisp and authoritative, promptly shooting down in flames any thoughts Riley might have had about sweet, defenceless old ladies. And up close, she judged her to be somewhere in her late fifties. This was a woman accustomed to being in charge, no matter how saddened by the hand that fate had decided to deal her. She reminded Riley of Nancy Reagan, without the former First Lady's brittle outer casing. She gave a signal to the maid, who had slipped into the room without a sound. "You'll take tea?"

"Yes, please," Riley agreed, since it didn't seem to be in any doubt, and sat on a hard, low-backed couch which must have been reserved for short-stay visitors. She hoped she didn't tumble over the back and disgrace herself.

Lady Myburghe went back to her reading and sipping, which Riley decided meant she wasn't supposed to speak until tea was poured. She thought about Palmer and what he would have done if he'd been here. No doubt he'd have had this old biddy eating out of his hand.

After an age, the maid returned and poured tea, including one for herself. Then she sat in a chair by the window and studiously ignored them both.

"Don't mind Jenny," said Lady Myburghe. "She barely understands English and acts as my chaperone. So. Frank Palmer speaks very highly of you. He says I should help you." A faint softening of her features made Riley wonder if there was a member of the Myburghe clan that Frank

Palmer hadn't made a good impression on.

"Frank and I sometimes work together," she explained. "As we are at the moment."

"But you're a journalist." The statement came out with a faint crackle of accusation, and even Jenny turned and stared at her, no doubt the word a familiar one.

"Yes." Frank must have decided to tell her the truth.

The older woman's eyes were like twin points of jet, and Riley wondered how many times Sir Kenneth had been fixed with them for some transgression or another, before he finally developed an impenetrable outer casing.

"Very well. Palmer said I should trust you. What do you wish to know?"

"It's about your husband," she said, trying not to clink her cup and saucer together.

"Ex-husband." Lady Myburghe dropped the magazine on the floor as if signifying what she thought of him. "What has he done now?" Her tone was of the much-put-upon wife waiting for the latest piece of bad news about her husband's drunken debauchery.

"I was wondering why… why you left him?"

Just for a second, Lady Myburghe looked as if she'd swallowed a live frog, and the maid jumped as if Riley had made an obscene suggestion. So much, thought Riley, for the maid not having much English. A large carriage clock on the mantelpiece ticked quietly away, as if counting down the seconds until she was hung, drawn and quartered and thrown into the gutter to rot for having breached a clear rule of etiquette.

"Jenny. Go and see to dinner, will you? I think I might dine early this evening." She sat and watched her maid depart, then looked at Riley with an expression of cool distaste. "That's a highly personal question."

Riley nodded. "I agree. It is."

Surprisingly, the other woman almost smiled, and sat back in her chair. "You were at the wedding reception, weren't you – with Palmer?"

"Yes."

"You may well have formed the opinion that my ex-husband is a very capable person. He's a good diplomat and administrator. He's also extremely clever, articulate and astute at dealing with awkward situations – especially political ones. An ideal person, in fact, for the posts he has held."

Riley nodded and sipped her tea. It was fragrant, light and very refreshing. Darjeeling? Earl Grey? Definitely not Tesco's Finest. What was this line of talk building up to? She immediately had her answer.

"Unfortunately, he's also a fool and a gambler. The two rarely mix well." Lady Myburghe plucked a hair from her lap and flicked it away. "I could tolerate the foolishness, but not the gambling." She swivelled her eyes towards her guest. "You know what I mean by foolishness."

"Umm… I suppose." Riley could hazard a guess, but she didn't think uttering the words 'other women' was necessary.

"Good."

"So you divorced him because he gambled?"

"No. I divorced him because he lost."

"Oh." Riley felt an urge to laugh outright at the directness of this statement, but decided it might be misinterpreted.

"Do you gamble, Miss Gavin?"

The look accompanying the question would have melted Riley into the carpet if she'd said yes, so she shook her head and thanked the stars for never having picked up the habit. She was sure the other woman would have seen through a lie. "No. It's never been my thing. Didn't he try to change your mind?"

"Miss Gavin, after all the years… it was too late." She smiled for the first time with what looked like genuine humour. "Besides, when I make up my mind, it would take far more than anything Kenneth could do to change it." She shrugged slim shoulders. "He was too involved in his work, anyway. I knew what it would be like right from the start, but instead of improving, it got worse. It became a vital form of release for him, I suppose." She suddenly looked at Riley and said, "Why am I telling you this?" The idea seemed to genuinely surprise her.

"Perhaps because you needed to?"

She smiled. "Yes. Maybe you're right."

"When you said he lost, was it a lot?"

The older woman's eyes dimmed and she looked away, as if trying to decide whether to answer or not. When she spoke it was with a sigh. "In the beginning, when we were first in Colombia, not too much. He'd lose some, which depressed him. Then he'd have a big win and everything would be rosy. Then another loss, followed by others, then a win or two. It's hardly a unique story. The wins, of course, never quite matched the losses, and in the end he lost a great deal. Far too much." She looked directly at Riley, but didn't elaborate, and Riley guessed she had probably never spoken about this before. It must have taken her a great deal of effort to do so now.

"He must have won recently, though. The work on the house… the wedding."

"Palmer warned me you might ask about that. He said I should help you if I could, but that the outcome might not be pleasant. Is that what you think – that it won't be pleasant?"

"To be honest, I don't know." Riley was surprised, both by

166

Palmer speaking for her and at Lady Myburghe's evident regard for his opinion.

"Palmer's a strange man," the other woman continued, as if Riley had spoken out loud. "Very tough to those who don't know him, but not so much to those who do. He was close to my daughter, at one time." She took a deep breath and her next words came out in a rush. "My family has no money, Miss Gavin. Not a bean. This house is held in trust, and will go to my daughters when I die. I can't sell, if that's what you're wondering, but I can't afford to live elsewhere, either. A stately prison is, let me tell you, still a prison. Ask the royal family."

There was no mention of her son, Riley noted immediately. She was tempted to jump in and ask why, but decided to leave it for the time being. There were other things to find out. "What about Colebrooke?"

"A rotting pile of stones into which Kenneth is pouring money at a demented rate." She raised a perceptive eyebrow. "And you're wondering how can he afford it if he gambles so unsuccessfully. Well, I wish I knew." She put down her cup and rearranged the folds of her dress. "I've never told anyone else, but it's one of the other reasons I decided to leave him."

"You don't know where the money comes from?" Riley asked softly. She felt her mouth go dry and asked herself how far this was going. For some reason, she still hadn't been thrown out on her ear and Lady Myburghe was still talking about matters she must have found deeply upsetting, not to say humiliating. Yet there was an almost rehearsed manner in which she was speaking, as if the words didn't quite match the emotion she must have been feeling.

"No. I don't." She stood up and looked through the window into the street, and Riley stood, too, feeling the interview was over. But Lady Myburghe hadn't finished. "To be frank, that's why I agreed to talk to you – talk to someone, anyway. I'm terrified it may have something to do with Christian's death."

"I'm sorry?" Riley was stunned. Death?

"I'm not stupid, Miss Gavin. My son is dead, I know that." Her lower lip trembled, then became firm as her chin lifted again. When she spoke, it was as if she was alone in the room, her voice as soft as velvet but as cold as permafrost, the rehearsed tone absent. "We had our children late in life. Christian was the youngest. He should never have gone to America in the first place. There were lots of other places he could have visited. But Kenneth knew best. It would make a man of him, he insisted; broaden his horizons and show him the real world." Her words dripped with a coating of bitter sadness. "As if Kenneth had ever experienced the real world himself."

"But the trip was Christian's idea, wasn't it?"

Lady Myburghe turned with a faint frown. "Is that what Kenneth told you? I suppose it was, really. At first, anyway. Christian hated Colebrooke, said it was like a mausoleum for old things and old people. I quite agreed with him. He desperately wanted to travel, to see the world just as his friends were doing. But he was concerned about me and decided to stay here with me in London and get a job. Kenneth objected most strongly. He felt spending a year away would be good for Christian. A year away from me, is what he meant, foolish man. Not that he ever understood our son." She turned away again and a tremor ran through her slim frame. "I'll forgive him for many things, but never that."

There was nothing more to say and Riley couldn't ask any more questions without feeling that she was turning the knife in an already open wound. She wanted to ask if she was aware that her ex-husband had now lost his position in the diplomatic corps, but decided against it. Maybe she knew about it anyway, along with all the other indignities he'd heaped on her during the marriage.

She quietly left Lady Myburghe to her sadness.

"He's some hero, that Sir Kenneth," she told Palmer later.

They were waiting in Palmer's office in Uxbridge. After leaving Lady Myburghe, Riley had received a brief call from Mitcheson. He was on his way from the airport, and suggested she might like to get together with Palmer, to hear some interesting information. He had ended the call without saying why, but he'd sounded serious. She had immediately called Palmer and arranged to meet him at the office.

It was small and lacking in light, and bore the wear and tear of the years. But Palmer had demonstrated his dislike of innovation by using ancient furniture and never moving anything, not even the dust. That included pot plants, desk, chairs and filing cabinets, all of which were probably welded to the carpet by the passing of time.

Pride of place on Palmer's scarred desk was a Rolodex, a present from Riley, who thought that all private detectives should have one, and a flat-screen computer monitor, with an impressively flashy power unit tucked away on the floor underneath. When he wasn't out working, this was where he could usually be found, playing games and surfing the internet as if he had all the time in the world.

"How so?" Mention of Myburghe made him check his watch. The former ambassador had gone to ground in London with his butler/bodyguard, and told Palmer to take some time off. Palmer was plainly expecting a call any time soon to get back on the job at Colebrooke House.

"He cheats on his wife, gambles away her family fortune, lets her go without a fight, then kicks his son out into the world where someone kidnaps him and chops off his finger. And all the time he's maintaining his image of probity and spending money like his balls were on fire. Money his wife claims he doesn't have. Can't have. Doesn't that strike you as unusual?"

Palmer said nothing but stared at the desk top as if he was half asleep. He hadn't said a word since Riley had begun talking. After a few seconds, he sat up and spun the Rolodex with a dry clatter. "We need to find out more about Colombia, and what happened over there. That's where it started."

"What about your mate Charlie in Whitehall?" she suggested. Charlie was a records man deep in the bowels of the Ministry of Defence who knew all manner of useful people and secrets. He had been very helpful in the past, when she and Palmer had needed information available only through official MOD channels.

"I already asked him. Whatever is out there won't be on any of his records. We need information of the other kind. Preferably inside information – even gossip."

"Where are we going to get that?"

Before Palmer could answer, the office door swung open and John Mitcheson walked in.

24

"Well, it's not FARC you've got to worry about." Mitcheson dumped his flight bag on the floor and dropped into a chair. "The Fuerzas Armadas Revolucionarios de Colombia are too busy fighting off a government crack-down at the moment to send nasty surprises to foreign diplomats." He sounded tired, but the sombre tone in his voice wasn't entirely due to jetlag. He leaned across and kissed Riley, then nodded at Palmer.

"Jeez," Palmer breathed. "I'm glad you got that the right way round."

Riley stared at Mitcheson, then craned her neck to study the baggage reclaim ticket affixed to his bag. "Me, too. Where have you been?"

"I had a delivery job to do down in old Panama. After what you told me, it seemed a waste to go all that way and not do some digging." He looked at Palmer. "You wouldn't have some tea in this place, would you? I've had enough bad coffee to kill a wombat and if I drink anything alcoholic, I'll fall over."

Palmer swung his feet from behind his desk. "Breakfast or Green?" He walked over and poured hot water from a kettle into a mug. "Actually, make it Typhoo – the mice like the Green." He turned back and bent to examine the luggage tag, peeling off the top layer to reveal another ticket underneath. "I see you've been to Colombia."

"What?" Riley was stunned. Apart from the surprise of hearing where he'd been, she knew how dangerous it was for Mitcheson to go anywhere near the country he'd once been flown out of in such a hurry. "What the hell did you go there for?"

"For you, of course." He smiled back at her. "It's OK, I was there less than an hour." He stretched out his legs and yawned. "I know a tour guide down there who used to be with the British army. He knows as much as anyone about what goes on, so I asked him to sound out some people for me." He nodded as Palmer handed him a mug. "Turns out he didn't have to do much. He did a tour with the Close Protection unit guarding Sir Kenneth Myburghe."

"What did he say?" asked Riley.

"Nothing too electric to begin with. There had been vague threats because the British were trying to persuade the hill farmers to grow other cash crops instead of poppies and coca. Unfortunately, the farmers weren't happy because the price of alternative crops like fruit, coffee or exotic flowers didn't match what they could get for poppy cultivation. Neither could they harvest more than one crop a year. Some of them became very militant and that's when FARC got involved."

"Hell of a sandwich," commented Palmer. "Cartels on one side, FARC on the other."

"Right. Because of the tension, the CP team on the embassy was strengthened, which is when Col, my contact, joined them. They accompanied Sir Kenneth everywhere in armoured vehicles. Government meetings, briefings, embassy bashes, foreign trade events – you name it, they went there. In between they scouted routes, searched buildings and vehicles, briefed embassy and military contacts, checked anyone and everyone likely to come anywhere near him. The team before them said it was pressured and frantic, and they'd soon wish they could get out of there. They'd had three attempts on the previous ambassador's life, several attempts on other officials, especially the military attaché, and discovered plans to bomb the embassy and set off explosions in culverts on the route from the embassy to the airport. Even their families were targets."

Riley thought back to her talk with Lady Myburghe. Had that been the reason for her getting out of the marriage? Living in an embassy compound couldn't have been much fun, especially knowing her husband had been targeted by the local drug lords. But was it enough after all this time?

"Col was on the team for quite a while," continued Mitcheson. "He accompanied Sir Kenneth pretty much everywhere he went. The timetable was changed every day, as were routes in and out of the embassy area, the cars involved and even the drivers, in case details were leaked. It became standard practice. But each time there was a change, it was an official one; there was always a briefing at the last minute, then they'd switch cars or venues, change their clothes, keep full radio contact, that sort of thing. Everything was as tight as a drum. It had to be."

Riley sensed something was coming. It was in Mitcheson's face. "Until?"

"A few weeks after Col joined the CP team, Sir Kenneth arranged a meeting at a country club outside Bogotá. The team had just left the embassy compound, supposedly on their way to a trade meeting, when Sir Kenneth gave them a new set of directions. They did as he ordered and arrived at a large, fancy building in the country. Sir Kenneth went in with one man, a guy who'd been with him for years, and told the rest of them to stay outside."

"Unusual?"

"Bloody suicidal, according to Col. They should never have been there without notifying the embassy first and having full backup from the local police or army. The team

173

leader went apeshit because they couldn't check out the building or the approach routes first. But the ambassador always had the last call."

Palmer stirred. "He pulled rank."

"That's right. The meeting lasted just over an hour, everything was civilised and they all went home safe and sound."

"So no problem."

"Not at first. He had three more meetings in the same place over the next two months. Each time they were unannounced until the day. And always Sir Kenneth went in with the same one man. After the third meeting, the team leader decided to check out the place for himself, to make sure they weren't being set up to take a hit. What he saw made his hair stand on end. The place was a fully-fledged casino. No house limits and any game you cared to try – including a few I shouldn't talk about in polite company. He counted twelve gunmen around the place, and a bunch of known cartel women."

"Women?" said Riley.

"Girls. He got out of there fast and relayed the information to the embassy. They sat on it. Told him it was all OK and not to worry."

"Did they go there again?"

"Yes. There were other meetings in remote locations, sometimes late at night. Each time Sir Kenneth had his man with him, but not always the full CP team. On a couple of occasions he met with an American. The team leader didn't get a name."

"Always the same man?"

"Yes. Then one day the team leader insisted on going in, too. It was a new place they hadn't been to before. They had a stand-up row. Sir Kenneth eventually gave in, but only on the understanding that the leader stayed in the lobby. There wasn't much more he could do. Sir Kenneth and his usual man went upstairs, and when they hadn't come down after an hour or so, the leader went for a look-see. He was just in time to see Myburghe and his guard coming out of a suite. They were accompanied by the American... and a man he recognised as Jesus Rocario. Rocario's a senior cartel member and wanted on several counts of murder and drug trafficking."

"That's insane."

"I'll say. The cartels are scary people – and Rocario is one of the nastiest. Col couldn't believe Sir Kenneth or any other member of the British establishment would have anything to do with them outside a court of law."

Palmer rested his feet on the edge of a desk drawer. "Could the meetings have been officially sanctioned?"

Mitcheson shrugged fatalistically. "He didn't think so. But look at Northern Ireland; the government had meetings with the IRA throughout the eighties and nineties. I'd say it wasn't, though."

Riley stood up and walked to the window. "So Jacob was right." The news that he hadn't been spinning a tale built out of guilt and ill-feeling left a nasty taste in her mouth.

"Who was the American?" Palmer asked, still intent on what Mitcheson had learned.

"No idea. He could have been US Drugs Enforcement Administration working undercover, maybe even a shipper." Mitcheson put down his mug and yawned. "All Col knew was, it smelled wrong. The lack of normal activity, the changes of programme, the subterfuge... it wasn't right."

"The bodyguard who went to these meetings with Sir Kenneth," said Riley. "You said it was the same man every time? Could we trace him and see what he knows?"

Mitcheson nodded. "That's where it gets interesting. Col couldn't remember the guy's name, but said the man wasn't Military Police. All he knew was, he'd been recruited from a British army training programme in Belize some years before, and stayed on with Myburghe."

Palmer shifted in his chair. "Special Forces?"

"Col didn't think so. He knew most of the Special Forces guys down there. He was very capable, apparently, knew all the right moves and never put a foot wrong. But he didn't really fit in. Didn't speak much and when he wasn't on the job he kept to himself."

Palmer gave a half smile and looked at the ceiling. "Did he describe him?"

"Yeah. Big, tall, and a face like the back of a tank."

Rockface.

25

The road to Colebrooke House was quiet save for the occasional vehicle, and Riley was happy to sit back and leave it to Palmer to get them to their destination in one piece. He drove efficiently and silently, absorbed in his thoughts. Apart from the occasional glance in the mirror and toying with an unlit cigarette, he had said very little since leaving London.

His reaction to the news of Sir Kenneth's activities in Colombia had been muted. With the information coming from a source as close to unimpeachable as it was possible to get, he'd moved from surprise to a mood approaching simmering anger.

"And this Col bloke," was all he had said when Mitcheson finished talking, "he's on the level?"

"I'd stake my life on him." Mitcheson had stood up and nodded goodbye before heading home to catch up on some sleep. Riley had accompanied him downstairs, then returned to join Palmer.

"What do you want to do now?" she asked, after a few moments of silence.

Palmer pulled on his jacket and dug out his car keys. "First, we eat," he replied. "Then we go walkies in the country. You game?"

Riley nodded cautiously and glanced at her watch. It was nearly four o'clock. She hadn't been aware of time passing so quickly. She had no idea what Palmer had in mind, but if he was planning on eating now, it had to mean they'd be out late tonight. "I'm game. Only if we're going to get down and dirty, I need to change my clothes." She gestured at her skirt and heels. While they may have been suitable for tea in Belgravia, they wouldn't match jeans and boots for the sort of location she suspected Palmer might have in mind.

"No problem. We've got time. We'll swing by your place now."

"What are you expecting to find?" she asked before they left London. "He's unlikely to have anything incriminating at his home."

"Maybe. Maybe not," he replied. But he knew Riley was correct. If they did find anything, it would be a miracle. Crooks – even upper-class crooks with cut-glass accents – rarely leave evidence lying around for others to trip over. On the other hand, every now and then, even clever crooks got careless.

"Sir Kenneth is getting substantial sums of money from somewhere – he has to be. We know it isn't gambling because his wife says he's hopeless at it."

"I'd go along with that," Palmer confirmed. "I've known a few high rollers. Sir Kenneth isn't the type."

"OK. So how is he doing it?"

"He's taking money from the cartels." It was a notion that had occurred to Riley as well, in spite of all her instincts. It stunned her that a British Ambassador might be in hock to some of the most heinous purveyors of misery in the world.

"Where does Rockface fit in?"

"An opportunist," Palmer theorised. "From squaddie in Belize to bodyguard and butler. But always managing to be in on the action. We should talk to him, too, but I don't think he'll play ball."

By the time they coasted through the village of Colebrooke, everything was quiet, the huddle of houses wrapped in sleep. It had been hard watching the clock tick away earlier, but Palmer had insisted there was no point in coming here before dark. He drove past the entrance to the house. The gates were closed. If Sir Kenneth had arranged for anyone new to watch the place, they were keeping a low profile.

They followed the lanes in a gradual winding gradient behind the estate, every bend bringing a narrowing in the width of road. With no signs of houses or lights, they could have been driving across the far side of the moon. As they neared the top, they could just make out a sweep of fields on one side, falling away into a valley, while on the other was a dense black nothingness. The headlights occasionally caught flashes of white from a herd of cows, or the smaller shape of sheep nestling against a hedge, and Palmer eventually switched off the main beams and relied on the sidelights.

"Where are we going?" Riley queried as they rounded another bend and edged up a bumpy incline.

"Back entrance," said Palmer shortly. "I know another way in."

Riley didn't bother asking how.

He turned off the lane and took the Saab through a gap and up a pot-holed track burrowing like a tunnel through the trees. They bumped and lurched for about two hundred yards, the sides of the car scraping gently against overhanging foliage, before reaching a small clearing.

Palmer stopped and switched off the lights and engine. "From here, we're on foot."

They climbed out and stood in the dark, listening to the cooling engine ticking and the soft creaking and groaning of the trees. Overhead, a few stars were visible through the canopy of leaves, and in the distance a fox barked shrilly, a haunting cry in the still of the night. The air was

179

surprisingly pleasant, holding a residue of warmth from the day.

"Tell me," Riley said softly, when Palmer materialised alongside her, "there are no creatures in these woods I should be frightened of."

"This is England," Palmer reminded her, hand-locking the car doors. "The most dangerous creature in this wood is you." He handed her a small torch. "Only use that when you really have to."

"Have a heart. I'm a city girl. I don't normally do forests – they make me nervous."

"Then you've led a sheltered life. This is a wood. Forests are bigger. Come on."

His voice faded into the gloom and Riley realised she was suddenly alone in the dark. She scuttled after him, glad of the torch.

The going was tougher than it looked, with uneven surfaces, tree roots snaking across their path and thick undergrowth impeding their way. Even using the torch in brief bursts, the vegetation was so thick it was easy to lose track of where Palmer was.

"We're about a hundred yards from the house," he whispered, stopping at the edge of the tree line. "The back sweep of lawn is directly ahead of us over a wire fence. From there on, it's open ground apart from a few bushes."

"Can't we walk round the edges? We could move in along that track we saw the other day."

"It would take too long. And on an estate this size, there might be poachers about."

They reached the wire fence at the edge of the trees and huddled down to watch, studying the open slope leading to the garden and house. Everything around them was silent, as if someone had switched off the volume and even the wildlife was safely hunkered in cover holding its breath. And waiting.

As Palmer had warned her, there was a lot of open ground in front of them, with only a few bushes for cover, darker masses set against the uniform backdrop of grass. They could just make out the shape of the house and a gleam of glass from one of the windows, and slightly to one side a ghostly expanse of white: the marquee, yet to be dismantled after the wedding party. High above all this and standing out against the night sky was the parapet where Riley and Rockface had discovered the man with the shotgun.

Palmer led the way through the wire fence, then sat watching the house for a couple of minutes. Riley studied him, amazed by his ability to concentrate, his outer demeanour calm and controlled when all she wanted to do was walk straight up to the house and hammer on the door.

Satisfied there was nobody about, Palmer set off across the grass with Riley close behind, keeping as much of the bushes as he could manage between themselves and the windows. Their approach forced them at an angle towards the side of the house, and they eventually dropped into a lengthy section of dry ditch bordered by an ancient stone wall. Palmer had earlier described it as a ha-ha. He'd also warned Riley it might be wet in places.

She stopped beside him and cursed fluently under her breath.

"Water?" he queried.

"Sheep shit," she replied, and wiped her hand on the grass.

A trip along the rear and sides of the house using the cover of the ha-ha revealed everything was locked tight. There were no lights on in the building and the curtains were pulled across the windows. They stayed away from the revealing expanse of the white marquee, keeping a healthy distance from the main building where they knew intruder lamps were scattered along the walls, tripped by motion detectors.

As they came level with the front right corner of the building, Palmer veered away from the tree cover. A few strides later, they were standing close to the door where Rockface and Riley had accessed the stairs to the roof. A faint glow came from lights placed along the front face of the house, but these were low-wattage and more for effect than security.

Palmer fiddled with the lock. Seconds later they were inside. He closed the door behind him and switched on his torch. They were in the lobby, which was bare and cold, with the echoing emptiness of the stairs vanishing up into the dark towards the roof. To their left was a door leading into the house proper, and the kitchen storeroom where Rockface had locked the shotgun.

"How did you do that?" Riley queried, referring to the ease with which he'd got through the door. She decided that one of the skills she'd have to ask him to teach her one day was picking locks. It could come in useful if ever she locked herself out one night.

"I nicked a key," he replied shortly. "How else? Come on."

They had already decided on the drive down that if Myburghe kept information about his former activities anywhere, it would most likely be in the office where he'd briefed them on their initial visit. There was a PC and a desk, and both would have to be checked to see what they might yield.

Palmer opened the door and led the way through the darkened kitchen and a utility room, and out into the foyer, which was lit by a small night-light in an alcove. A clock mechanism clacked away noisily nearby, effectively muffling the noise of anyone approaching, and Riley kept close to Palmer, aware of the hostile stare of the portraits looking down from the walls.

Palmer barely hesitated before crossing the foyer to the office door. He tried the handle. The door opened without hindrance. He stepped inside and cursed softly.

The room was a wreck. Papers were scattered everywhere, the PC monitor was humming but tilted crazily to one side, and the drawers to the mahogany desk were lying on the carpet, their contents spread across the floor like confetti.

Riley checked the pictures on the wall for signs of a wall safe. In her experience, even the blindingly obvious sometimes worked. She gave up after the third one when she noticed that it was slightly out of kilter. Whoever had been here before them had already looked.

"There." Palmer pointed with his torch to the side of the desk. There was a dark streak of something down one corner of the polished wood. Riley touched it with her fingertip. It was sticky.

Blood.

Palmer moved towards the door. "I'll check upstairs, you do the ground floor. Don't go outside."

Riley nodded without comment and waited for Palmer to disappear. She made a quick search of the ground floor, room by room, using the torch sparingly to avoid tripping over fragile furniture. But there were no further signs of an intruder and no disturbance to indicate a search had been made. She went back through the kitchen to the lobby, and stared out into the garden.

Palmer's warning not to go outside was reverberating in her mind like a challenge. She knew he was the expert in these circumstances, but she felt an automatic resistance at being told what to do, even by him. If she followed the tree line round the house, she figured she would have a better view of the windows and of anyone skulking around where they shouldn't be, while keeping safely out of sight. She opened the door and slipped outside, then hurried across the grass to the nearest belt of trees.

The smell of pine was powerful out here, with an underlying aroma of rotting vegetation. She trod carefully, wary of dry twigs and rabbit holes, wary, too, of a sudden attack from out of the darkness. She stopped and listened every few yards, trying to distinguish normal night sounds from the not so normal. It wasn't easy.

The wind in the trees didn't help. Even a slight breeze sounded like rushing water, effectively cutting off any potential man-made noises such as snapping branches, the scrape of clothing or an involuntary cough. In contrast, it also threw up imagined sounds, such as the ticking of branches translating into a weapon loading, and the falling of a dried leaf like the scrape of a shoe. It wasn't a venue for the faint-hearted or the over-imaginative.

Riley reached the corner of the stable block, and was about to turn and check the house, when she froze.

The stable block lights were on.

She flattened herself against the wall, her mouth as dry as sand. Walking into a trap couldn't have been simpler; she would have to enter the open square formed by the buildings, with no sure escape if anyone was waiting for her. If they were and made themselves known before she entered the central block, turning and heading back into the woods would only be an option if she could run faster than her pursuer. Entering the building made even that a non-starter.

She glanced back at the house and saw several lights burning along the top floor. She knew instinctively what Palmer was doing: he was drawing attention to himself, trying to lure anyone in the grounds back to the house. It was all the opportunity she was going to get, so she stepped round the corner of the first stall and through the open door.

The air was as she recalled previously: musty and smelling of straw. She put her fingers over the lens of her torch and flicked it on. In the restricted glow, she saw the same pile of discarded tackle covered in dust. But no horses. And no baddies with big guns or knives.

Someone had left a pitchfork against one wall, the tines spotted with rust and the handle worn smooth with use and broken off halfway down. Riley picked it up and held it like a lance. It might not be much, but if the person who had ransacked Myburghe's office was here, it was better than going in empty-handed.

She sneaked a look around the door towards the central building where she'd seen the anteroom and sleeping quarters. Bright light spilled out from the door and a couple of small windows, but she couldn't hear a sound. She ghosted past the other stalls, a faint swish of weeds and grass sprouting from the cobblestones brushing her ankles. She checked each stall, her relief growing as each one proved empty. Then she was outside the anteroom.

She sniffed. There was a strange smell in the air; one that hadn't been here before. It was almost sweet, slightly heavy, and the explanation for it lurked in the back of her mind, just out of reach.

She shook her head, refusing to be spooked by the unknown. After all, what could there be here that she hadn't seen the other day? Bracing herself, she stepped through the doorway into the light.

What she saw was like a slap in the face, and her every instinct was to scream and not stop.

Rockface was staring down at her from the far wall, a giant, grotesque gargoyle, his bloodless face frozen in agony.

26

Riley felt a surge of something bitter rise up and threaten to spill out across the floor. She swallowed hard. Not that it would have made things any worse; what she was looking at was beyond anything she could think of. Against every fibre of her being, she forced herself to look again.

Rockface was hanging on the wall like a side of beef.

He had been stripped naked, his wrists tied by orange baling string to the two heavy brackets Riley had noticed the first time she came in here. Even with his height, they were positioned a good two feet above his head, and the weight of his body bearing down had made the string bite deeply into the flesh of his arms. A couple of lengths of the same string had been looped beneath his chin to keep his head up, so that at first glance he seemed to be watching the doorway, his face distorted into a lopsided grimace. If he had been standing at any time while tied up, his strength had long given out and he had slumped downwards, his knees now bent and giving his trunk a curiously elongated appearance, like a reflection in a fairground hall of mirrors. He had lost some of his impressive build, making him seem thinner and less awesome; shrunken, even, as if starved over a long period of time.

Riley was torn between the instinct to check for life signs and the scalp-tingling desire to run from this awful place and get help. But even as she overcame her fear and stepped closer, she realised that the former bodyguard was beyond any assistance she or anyone else could give him.

His blood had splashed on the wall behind him, vivid and glossy, like dark lipstick. More had run in sticky streams down his torso and legs. The hair on his chest was matted with it, as was the area around his groin, and more was puddled thickly on the floor beneath his feet. A heavy globular trail led to the sink, beneath which lay a wide pool of water. On it, a collection of soap bubbles floated silent and still, like little boats on a lake.

The analytical part of Riley's brain kicked in. She was no expert, but the blood was coagulating, which meant this must have happened within the past few hours. Long enough for whoever had done this to have slipped away. She realised that the killers – surely it would have taken more than one man to do this – would have had to wash themselves afterwards. She forced herself to cross the room and look into the basin. Just visible beneath the surface of the reddened water was a large kitchen knife, the blade heavy with streaks of red clinging to the shiny metal.

She concentrated on maintaining her breathing and backed away, then turned and walked out of the anteroom and down the corridor. Gone was any idea of stealth; instead she used speed and intent to overcome the fear brought on by the horror of what she'd just seen. She kicked open each door with a crash, the pitchfork held out in front of her, half expecting at any moment for someone to come rushing out. But nobody did.

The rooms were the same as before: cold, unoccupied and soul-less. Just rooms. She went back to the anteroom and stared at the body. She was tempted to do something, to cut it down. But she couldn't bring herself to go near, telling herself that it was evidence, like the knife, and that she shouldn't touch.

She rang Palmer and told him.

"Two minutes," was all he said.

While she waited, she busied herself searching for the

dead man's clothing. It had to be here somewhere, unless his attacker had stripped him before bringing him to this place. She couldn't imagine the big man coming in here willingly unless he had known his attacker, or unless he'd arrived by chance and had been overcome before being stripped and mutilated.

She found his things bundled inside one of the lockers. Black shoes and socks, dark pants, light blue shirt and t-shirt. But whoever killed him had already searched the clothes; the pockets were turned inside out, the hems and cuffs rolled back and checked. Whatever Rockface had carried on him – if anything – was gone.

Riley replaced the clothes in the locker, wondering why they had taken the trouble of putting the clothes out of sight in the first place. Why bother – after this? Then she realised: shock value. In this white room, they wanted nothing to detract from the horror of seeing the body against the stark background.

Palmer whistled a warning before stepping through the door. He looked up at the body, his jaw muscles clenching, then took in the rest of the room at a glance. He eyed the pitchfork in Riley's hands.

"You OK?"

"Why would anyone torture him like this?" Riley muttered thickly.

"More than one," Palmer said quietly, echoing her earlier assumption. "It would have taken at least two men to get him up there." He nodded at the brackets, then moved closer to study the string looped under Rockface's chin. It had been tied tight across the top of his head. It looked painful, even in death. "It wasn't torture," Palmer concluded. "This was punishment. He wasn't meant to speak."

Riley's throat felt as if it was stuffed with cotton wool.

189

She needed a distraction. "Was there anything in the house?" It was going to take a long time to wipe this sight out of her mind, and she didn't want to think about the agony Rockface must have suffered or why he had been killed in such a horrific manner.

"Nothing useful," Palmer replied. He moved across to the microwave and sniffed at the door. "And no sign of Myburghe." He sounded puzzled. "If he was away, why was Rockface here? Bodyguards never, ever leave their charges."

"Unless whoever killed Rockface took Myburghe."

"Possibly." He didn't sound convinced. "His name's David Hilary, by the way. I found a bedroom with his stuff in it – papers and couple of ID cards."

At least, Riley reflected, the dead man now had a name. Funny how she'd never thought to ask what it was before. It made her feel guilty.

Palmer bent and touched a spot of blood with his fingertip and held it up. "This was fairly recent," he said. He led the way outside and they stood for a few moments in a pool of shadow, watching and listening. The killers were probably long gone, but neither of them was anxious to go rushing back across the gardens and discover the hard way how wrong they might be.

"What do we do?" said Riley. She felt somehow disconnected, as if she had stumbled into a nightmare and hadn't the strength to pull herself out.

"We leave," said Palmer. "Now. There's nothing we can do here."

They made their way by a circuitous route through the perimeter trees and out across the lawns at the back, Riley allowing Palmer to lead her by the arm. There was no sign of life other than a couple of owls and the sinuous outline of a fox slinking unhurriedly into the bushes. The sight of the animal, natural and free, merely served to heighten the contrast with what they had just seen in the stable block.

The walk back to the car was quicker than the trip in, and Palmer wasted no time getting back out on to the road. After a few miles, he stopped at a public phone to call the police, leaving a brief, anonymous message, then hanging up and wiping the phone before getting back in the car.

"What are you thinking?" said Riley eventually, as they entered the glow of lights along the Western Avenue on the outskirts of London. She was relieved to be back in civilisation. The regular strobing of overhead lights should have been making her sleepy, but she hardly noticed. She wasn't sure if she would ever be able to sleep again.

"Myburghe," said Palmer, muttering beneath his breath. "Where the hell is he?"

It was obvious that if a bodyguard went down, the principal was immediately at greater risk. No bodyguard, no shield. Only they'd found no trace of Myburghe, which was odd. He should have been screaming from the rooftops, or at the very least summoning help by phone. Unless he was unable to.

Palmer dug out his phone and dialled a number. "Sir Kenneth's mobile," he explained. They listened to a recorded message telling them that the subscriber was unavailable. He dialled another, but it rang several times with no response. He switched off. "I'll drop you off and we'll meet up in the morning. There's nothing more we can do tonight."

"OK."

He looked keenly at her. "You all right?"

"I'm fine," she lied.

The truth was, she felt anything but.

27

Whenever sleep evaded her, Riley got up and drank tea and ate biscuits. It usually worked a treat, but this time there were too many vivid images floating about in her head. The cat wandered in and sat close by her leg, purring softly and allowing her to reach down and pet him. He seemed to be acknowledging for once that it was Riley who needed the consolation of quiet companionship.

Succumbing just before five in the morning, she slept fitfully for three hours, then showered and dragged herself round to Nero's. Although the images of the anteroom were beginning to recede, she needed normal sights and sounds to help the process along.

She found Palmer lounging in a chair by the back wall, nursing a large mug of coffee and eating a croissant. If he had any remnants of nightmares, he was dealing with them in his own way. With Palmer, she reflected, you couldn't always tell.

"Didn't you sleep either?"

He shook his head. "Not much."

"Any news?"

"Of Myburghe?" He shook his head. "Nothing yet."

They deliberated on the events of the previous evening. There had been nothing in the tabloids, which was hardly surprising. By the time Palmer's anonymous tip-off had been acted on, it would have been too late for the morning editions. The evening editions and broadcast media, however, would probably have a field day, and Colebrooke would be awash with reporters and film crews for days.

"Something's bothering me," said Palmer finally, as if

he'd been tapping into her thoughts, "about the stable block."

"Is that all?" The whole place had bothered Riley, especially the bit with the body in it.

"The microwave – it smelled odd. Did you notice?"

"Spicy food, you mean?"

"Yes. I thought the place was abandoned weeks ago. It smelled fresher, somehow."

Riley shrugged. "Rockf- sorry – Hilary said the place was used by the grooms." She was having trouble thinking of the man by his proper name. Not that it mattered any more. "They must have cast iron constitutions, all those early mornings and cold saddles." She remembered the piece of magazine paper she had found on the floor, and rummaged in her pocket. She'd stored it away without giving it further thought. "I found this in one of the stable block rooms, the night of the wedding party." She handed it to him.

Palmer studied the few words of text. "Could be nothing," he commented. He stood up. "But you never know. I'll just be a minute." He drifted out, tapping into his mobile as he went.

It gave Riley time to think about what to do next. Tracking down Myburghe was a priority, but for that, they needed somewhere to begin – a jumping-off point. And without a single clue as to where he could have gone, the world was far too big a place. She found her thoughts drawn towards Weller, and whether he would even give them the time of day once he found out what had happened at Colebrooke House.

When Palmer came back he was looking pensive. "The grooms employed by her father," he said, "spoke Spanish."

"Her?"

"Victoria Myburghe." He gave her a sideways look as if to forestall any further comment.

"Isn't that what we thought?"

"True. Except Victoria says they arrived after the horses had been sold."

"Oh."

"So what were they there for?"

"Sir Kenneth would know," Riley said. Stating the blindingly obvious may not have been original, but it filled a gap in their line of thought. But where the hell was he? The unsettling thought was that they hadn't had time to look around the rest of the estate, and he could still be there somewhere lying dead or seriously hurt. On the other hand, if the place was besieged by reporters, it wouldn't be long before one of them stumbled over the body.

Hell of a way, she thought, to get an exclusive.

"What about Myburghe's daughters? Do you think they know where he is?"

Palmer shook his head. "I asked. They don't. Anyway, he'd be dragging them further into his troubles, and I can't see him risking it." He stood up and stared at the ceiling, eyes narrowed in thought.

"You've thought of something," Riley said, seeing the signs.

"There's one person who might know," he said at last. "Come on."

"Palmer," Lady Myburghe greeted him with a faint smile as they were ushered into the sitting room by the diminutive Jenny. "How nice to see you. And Miss Gavin." In spite of her courtesy, the dullness in her eyes seemed more pronounced than ever, leaving her drained of colour.

When Jenny finished serving tea, Palmer looked pointedly

at Riley.

She caught the signal and said, "Lady Myburghe, your husband once kept horses at Colebrooke House."

"Yes. He bought them years ago, when he was in funds for once. God knows why – his interest in horses was and still is limited to how long they take to run round a race track. I doubt he's ridden one in fifteen years. I'm sure he only kept them because it was the thing to do. Why do you ask?"

"Did he hire some Spanish grooms to look after them?"

She frowned. "Hardly. He had a couple of local lads from the village. Until the wedding, I hadn't been there for months, of course – not since… well, since returning from South America. But Victoria and Annabel told me about some men he'd brought in with some silly explanation about giving work to people who needed it. It was just a few weeks ago, I believe. But he no longer had the horses – he'd sold them all – and he'd got the local lads work in other stables. So what he was doing bringing in foreign grooms, I've no idea. They left, too, in the end." She looked at them in turn, lingering on Palmer the longest. "Why?"

"We were puzzled, that's all," said Palmer. "It seemed… odd to us, too. Do you know who they were?"

"No idea. But according to Annabel, they weren't Spanish." She had developed a sudden gleam in her eye as if pleased at being able to get something off her chest.

"What made her think that?" Riley was developing a faint throb of confusion.

"Like Victoria, she spent some time in South America with us, before coming back here to boarding school. Then there were holidays, of course. Being younger, she picked up the language remarkably quickly – especially the local slang, which is particular to the region where it's used. Annabel said the three men spoke Spanish, but like born-and-bred Colombians, most probably from the countryside around Bogotá. She didn't like them. She found them rather crude."

Palmer and Riley exchanged a look. Why hadn't Lady Myburghe made any kind of connection between the country her husband used to work in, and the nationality of the men who had been staying in his stables? Or was it that she hadn't wanted to? Fortunately, she had gone back to staring into the distance and didn't appear to notice the silent questions bouncing back and forth over her head.

Questions like, if the 'grooms' were Colombians, where were they now?

"Do you have any idea," Riley said hesitantly, feeling a knot forming in her stomach, "where your husband might be?"

"No, I don't." The older woman stared down at her hands. Had she been anyone else, Riley would have accused her of lying, but she held herself in check.

Palmer wasn't quite so tactful.

"Really?" His tone was gentle, but it was clear he didn't believe her, either. If she had any doubts, the look on his face was confirmation.

"I do not," she insisted firmly. But her eyes told a different story.

"David Hilary," Riley asked, choosing her words with care. "He's been with your husband a long time, hasn't he?"

"That's right. When Kenneth was promoted, he was advised to take protection for the family. There weren't always official people available, and someone recommended David... I don't recall who." Then her aura of rigid self-control seemed to collapse in on itself, and she sank back into her chair like an elegant beach ball slowly deflating.

"I… I'm sorry. I'd like to be alone for a while – would you mind?" She closed her eyes and touched a hand to her cheek.

Riley frowned. If the older woman was feeling faint, it had come on rather suddenly – and conveniently. Then, as she stood up to join Palmer, the realisation came to her: Lady Myburghe still loved her husband. The split was all an act.

Jenny appeared as if by magic, before Riley could say anything, and they left, leaving behind them a host of unanswered questions.

"That wasn't so good," Palmer observed as the front door closed behind them. They walked down the steps and stood on the pavement. "She's hiding something. Those grooms have been around fairly recently – I'd bet money on it."

Before Riley could mention her thoughts about Lady Myburghe's cover-up, a car pulled in at the kerb alongside them. The rear door opened to disgorge a familiar figure.

"Well, well." Weller stepped across the pavement, straightening his cuffs. "Two of London's finest busy-bodies. Been anywhere near Colebrooke House in the last twelve hours, have we?" A uniformed constable emerged from behind him and stood to one side, waiting.

"You really must stop following me around like this, Weller," Riley told him. "People are beginning to talk." She spread her smile to include the constable, but he stared back with a cold expression.

"That's truer than you know," Weller replied, eyeing her with a touch of flint. "And it's pointless making eyes at PC Hennings. He's on duty." He threw a studied look at Palmer, who stared back with an expression of boredom. Palmer's way of dealing with officialdom was to pretend it wasn't there.

"Dead bodies turning up always worry me," Weller continued enigmatically. "Where were you two last night?"

"Out walking," said Riley.

"Together?" He glanced at Palmer, who shrugged and said nothing.

Weller didn't seem offended or surprised by the silence. He glanced up at the windows of the house behind them. "Don't tell me," he said. "Myburghe's ex-missus lives here, doesn't she? Nice place. Must be worth a packet. Are they in?"

Riley caught Palmer's look and instinctively shook her head. His meaning was clear: the last thing they needed right now was Weller talking to Lady Myburghe. In her fragile state she might let on that they had been asking questions about the Spanish 'grooms' and the stable block, a subject a little too close to home, given what Weller had just intimated. "You were right about the money thing, Weller," she said. "But he's out. What bodies are you talking about?"

Weller ignored Riley and stepped up close to Palmer. "Last night at Colebrooke House," he explained, "an ex-squaddie named David Hilary was murdered. Seems someone didn't like him. He was Sir Kenneth Myburghe's butler and bodyguard. You probably knew him."

"Of course," Palmer replied, and exchanged a look of feigned surprise with Riley. "What about Sir Kenneth – is he OK?"

"No idea. But two phone calls were made late last night, alerting the police, both within half an hour of each other and both by male callers. Unfortunately, the local plods couldn't undo the padlocks on their bicycles and weren't able to get there for an hour after the calls. Now I know you two wouldn't do the sort of things that were done to Hilary, but something tells me you might be able to help me with my enquiries. Care to make my life a little easier?"

Riley reminded herself that Weller hadn't risen high in the police force without having something between his ears. Two phone calls? Palmer had made one; so who had made the second? And was it before Palmer's call or after? If after, it meant someone had been watching the house and had seen Palmer and Riley enter and leave. The idea was unsettling, and her thoughts switched to Toby Henzigger. Had he also been roaming about in the wilds of Gloucestershire last night?

"Sorry. Can't help you," she said truthfully. "We knew Hilary, of course – he was around Myburghe all the time. But that's all."

Weller sighed and stepped towards the house, followed by the uniformed officer, then turned and came back. "Two things," he said, lowering his voice. "One, you haven't asked how Hilary died, which I find a little odd in two people with noses for trouble – and one of you a hack. Answer: he was tortured and bled to death, in case you're interested. Two: there were actually two deaths reported last night, both connected with Sir Kenneth Myburghe. The second was in the States."

Riley guessed what he was going to say. She glanced at Palmer. From his stillness, he also knew what was coming.

"Who else?"

"The body of a young man was washed up on a beach in Florida yesterday afternoon," continued Weller grimly. "It was identified as Christian Myburghe."

28

"How did it happen?" The stark image in Riley's mind was of a pale corpse lying on wet sand, one finger missing. It was accompanied by vivid flashes of David Hilary's abused body hanging on the wall of the stable block.

"Drowning. The local police think he went swimming fully clothed while under the influence of alcohol, and got caught in a riptide. Happens all the time, I'm told. Kids get down on the beach for parties and barbecues, drink too much, smoke wacky backy or snort snazzle dust and get carried away. Literally, as it happens."

"How did they find him?"

"A couple of fishermen got him tangled in their nets off-shore. They didn't stick around long enough to say where. Fortunately, there was a wallet and a blood donor card, so the local cops didn't have to rely on prints to confirm his identity. He'd been dead several days. It wasn't nice."

Riley almost felt the question rising in Palmer's mind and beat him to it; she figured it would sound better coming from her. "Was he intact?"

Weller stood back and stared at her, eyes narrowing. "That's a bloody odd question. But since you ask, no. There were some fingers missing and other injuries – probably caused by a boat propeller." He straightened up and gestured PC Henning to move towards the house. "Now, if you'll excuse us, we have an unpleasant duty to perform."

"Florida," said Palmer quietly, as the two policemen disappeared inside. "Not quite where I expected. But maybe not surprising."

Riley agreed. She had been expecting somewhere like

Mexico or the Caribbean – locations occasionally tinged with a shade of darkness that might reflect what was happening here. But Florida, especially around Miami, with its long-established assortment of underworld gangs incorporating the mafia and Cuban exiles, more than fitted the bill.

"Do you want to go back in?" she asked, nodding towards the house.

He shook his head. "No. I don't do grief. Let's get some exercise."

"Suits me." She walked alongside him, comfortable in the silence, aware that they both needed time to chew over what they knew and come up with a course of action.

The main problem was, the one thing they needed to know – the whereabouts of Sir Kenneth Myburghe – still eluded them.

"Christian wasn't meant to come back, was he?" she said eventually.

Palmer shook his head. "Unlikely. Unless he tried to escape and died in the process. My guess is, it was an arranged hit all along."

"But why?"

"For something Sir Kenneth did. Or something he didn't." He stopped and lit a cigarette. "The finger was a last warning; the body was to be the pay-off."

Palmer went on to explain what he meant. If Sir Kenneth Myburghe had been under some kind of ultimatum, the price of delay might have been the reason for his son's finger being sent to him in a bag. A clear warning that they were not playing games. The discovery of the youth's body, however, took it into a different league; it meant Myburghe had refused to comply. The question was, by doing so, had he automatically signed his son's death warrant?

Palmer threw the cigarette away. "Damn. There's something I still don't get."

"What?"

"The threat levels: they're too irrational. One minute they're sending nasty letters and fake bombs made of silly putty and wires. The next it's a finger, gutting a bodyguard and killing Myburghe's son. They don't match. Why bother with crank letters if they were going to kill the kid in the end, anyway?"

Riley saw where he was leading. "Two different people at work?" Then she had a flash of inspiration. "Jacob Worth! He could have sent the letters and the fake bomb. And he wouldn't have needed to step outside Barnston to do it."

Palmer nodded. "From what you say, he had the motive – he hates Myburghe enough to send malicious emails about him – although we still don't know why."

"You need to ask him," said Riley. "He won't talk to me."

Palmer nodded in agreement. "Can you set it up for tomorrow?"

The storeroom in 34A was cramped, hot and claustrophobic, and smelled strongly of soap overlaid with the acrid bite of industrial bleach. Palmer was amazed anyone could stand it. Yet for someone apparently suffering a form of battle stress, Jacob Worth seemed strangely at ease among the clutter of cleaning materials, boxes of paper towels and other unlabelled equipment stacked around the walls.

"I'm sorry about Miss Gavin," Jacob said politely, when Palmer explained who he was. He tugged at his blue work shirt and straightened his tie. "I didn't realise…" He shrugged and looked around as if checking everything in his subterranean domain was present and correct. "She wasn't angry, was she? Only she should have said she was…

you know. Or had a photo above the articles, the way some journalists do. That way I'd have known."

"Don't worry about it," said Palmer easily. He hesitated, wary of starting out too quickly and sending this man scurrying into whatever safe haven he might have built around himself. "She's sorry she upset you."

"No worries." Jacob reached across his desk and picked up a blue paper towel. It was ridged and creased from being folded many times, and he proceeded to fold it again and again, concentrating on the task, his fingers moving quickly and firmly until the oblong of paper was reduced to a solid block. "No worries." He peered at Palmer and paused. "You want some tea? I can do tea if you'd like."

Palmer nodded. It had been a long drive and he was feeling jaded. "Tea would be great."

"Grand. Grand." Jacob leapt up and busied himself with a kettle, mugs and teabags. As he did so, a faint buzzing began in the room, and it took Palmer a few seconds to realise that the sound was coming from the former Intelligence officer.

"What were you, then?" Jacob turned away from the kettle as it boiled. "You weren't Navy, were you? I'd know if you were Navy. Army, I bet." He turned back and made the tea, his movements economical and practised. He placed two mugs on the table with a bag of sugar and pushed one of the mugs in front of Palmer. The tea looked like gravy.

"RMP," said Palmer. "Special Investigations Branch. You?"

"Defence Intelligence Group." Jacob spoke proudly, quietly, and pulled his mug towards him. "A small department, self-contained... but we did good work." He pointed to a photo on the wall. It showed a group of men in tropical whites, smiling at the camera. The detail was too small to make out faces, but Palmer thought he recognised Jacob in the centre of the group. He looked less shy, smiling happily out at the world.

Jacob blinked a few times, then cleared his throat and said, "We tried, you know… to get all the Latin American countries not to take sides. Not many people know that. They probably think it was the politicians or the Foreign Office who did everything. But it wasn't." He nodded and sipped his tea. "There wasn't much time, you see. It all blew up, the Falklands did, and suddenly we had to hit the ground running and start talking to our opposite numbers and others to get them on-side." He smiled almost slyly. "Getting them not to be on-side with the Argies, is what it really amounted to. Stepping back from the line. All the same thing, really, I suppose."

"Important task," said Palmer. "It seems to have worked."

"Absolutely. Absolutely." Jacob's response was intense, and he nodded eagerly several times. "Absolutely. Vital, in fact."

The words seemed to jump out as if on impulse, and Palmer decided to bring the conversation back in line before Jacob sank into more reminiscing. "Where did you meet Sir Kenneth Myburghe?"

Mention of the ambassador's name seemed to make the man shrink. He peered into his tea, then looked away and flicked on a small television monitor on one side of his desk as if he hadn't heard. The blue-grey image showed the men's room taken from high on the wall. Palmer guessed the camera lens was situated in one corner where it would command a panoramic view.

"Jacob?"

"Bloody perverts," Jacob muttered, although nobody was there. "I have to keep an eye on them, you know. Damned nuisance, they are. Talk to you while you're peeing – it's not right. Puts people off coming here." He flicked off the monitor and looked at Palmer as if the interruption hadn't happened. "I was in the north for ten days," he said, his voice more businesslike, "dodging between Bogotá in Colombia and Quito in Ecuador. Had to use shite little planes flown by madmen. I was working on their military people, trying to get them not to side with Galtieri. It wasn't a matter of taking our side, nothing like that; we just didn't want them interfering and sending Galtieri any hardware."

"Did Myburghe help?" Palmer desperately wanted to focus the man's mind, but knew it wasn't going to be easy; he had too many memories jostling for position, ready to come pouring out, each one another form of distraction.

"He should have. But he was always too busy, wasn't he?" Jacob pulled a sour face. "I asked him... I needed him to get me some introductions, like the others. We had orders to get names of relevant personnel from the embassies. But Colombia was difficult, they said. Sensitive. There had been problems with agreements on the control of the drugs trade. I was told to tread carefully. Even Myburghe said I shouldn't go blundering in without his say-so."

"So you waited."

"I had no choice. It wasn't right, though." He pulled another paper towel from a box and began folding it. Then he stopped. "I wasted days while he ponced about. And all the time things were threatening to go pear-shaped down in the South Atlantic. In the end, I decided to follow him." The words were said softly, as if he didn't want anyone but Palmer to hear him.

"You did what?"

"Well, it was the only thing I could think of. I'd had help from everyone else. So did Tom. There were four of us to begin with, but two went sick. Tom Elliott and me, we divvied up the countries left, those that we knew we could approach, which wasn't many at the end of the day, but what could we do, eh?"

"OK. What happened?"

"I'd been trained in surveillance and undercover work." Jacob grinned, displaying an almost childlike delight at possessing a valued and secret skill. "And a few other bits and bobs. The embassy pen pushers didn't know that. Thought I was just some pretend-spook filling in for the real ones. But I knew my tradecraft. Was good at it, too. Followed Sir Kenneth right to his meetings. Him and his protector."

"Did this protector have a name?" Palmer kept the questions short. There wasn't much he could do about Jacob's rambling approach but try to keep him on track.

"Hilary. David Hilary. Stood out like a hairy mammoth at a tea party. There were others on the protection detail, but they weren't close, not like Hilary. Him and Myburghe were tight. Big feller, good at his work. He didn't see me, though." He chuckled proudly and pushed his mug away. "They needed eyes in the back of their heads to see me. Tom was my best mate, you know. Solid. Nice bloke." His face softened and Palmer said nothing, waiting for the moment of distraction to pass. Then: "I got nowhere with Myburghe, of course. It didn't take a genius to see he was up to no good. You don't meet up with the cartels unless you're stupid or you have official sanction. And he didn't."

"How do you know that?"

Jacob scowled, then smiled, his expression changing like traffic lights. "I checked. You think we went down there without knowing what was what? No way. They gave us open access to Intel material, human and signals, verifiable by the desk controllers in London. We had to know everything that was going on, see, so we didn't trip over any ops or tricky situations. Who was talking to who, who was with us, who wasn't. But there was nothing logged. Nothing."

"Where were these meetings?"

"Posh places, like country clubs and golf courses. Most of them were on the outskirts of the city. As far as I could make out, most were fronts for gambling and stuff – places people like Myburghe shouldn't have been seen dead in."

It confirmed what Mitcheson's friend Col had described, almost to the letter. Palmer didn't want to ask the next question, but he had to. They couldn't move forward without it. "What do you think he was up to at these places?"

"It was obvious, wasn't it?" muttered Jacob. "He was getting himself in with these people. Why else would a British Ambassador meet known drug gangs?"

29

"Can you be sure?" Palmer felt his own certainty begin to drain away. There had been the faintest note of doubt in Jacob's voice, right at the end. This wasn't what he or Riley had wanted to hear.

Jacob grew defensive. "I couldn't get that close, could I? But I hung around after one of his meetings, and heard some men talking as they went to their cars. They owned the place, see, so they got careless about security. After all, who was going to threaten them? They had the whole country in their pockets. Pathetic."

"Go on."

"They were bragging about having a British Ambassador on the hook. Like it was a big achievement. One of them mentioned an IOU – a big one – and said maybe one day they could get a 'By Appointment' crest put on their letterhead. It was obvious what that meant, wasn't it? I didn't need to know any more. Myburghe was selling out to get himself out of debt."

Palmer was surprised. "You speak Spanish?"

"Yes. I did a three-month exchange stint with the Spanish Navy. I was a quick learner."

Palmer nodded. The words 'on the hook' could only be interpreted one way: Myburghe was a big fish and the cartel wasn't about to let him go. And the 'By Appointment' reference could only have been meant in a supply of goods context. It didn't take a genius to guess what the goods were, or what they had planned for Myburghe's future. The simplicity and nerve of it was breathtaking.

"Why didn't you go to your bosses with your suspicions?"

Jacob's expression tightened and Palmer guessed at a mix of emotions, including guilt, anger and sorrow. His next words confirmed it. "I was going to. Had a report ready, with times, places, people, all that. But everything had blown up at Port Stanley by then and we were summoned to HMS Sheffield for an urgent briefing. I didn't have time to file the report."

"Did you tell anyone?"

He nodded. "I told Tom on the way down. He said I should be careful because if there was no proof Myburghe was dirty, I'd lose my job. But I knew I was right." He paused, took a deep breath. "We were just starting the briefing when the Exocet struck. It didn't explode, but the impact blew off one of the bulkhead doors. Tom got hit. I couldn't help him. Next thing I knew there was smoke, oil and flames everywhere and I was being carried off the ship." He rubbed furiously at his face, then bent and slapped his bad leg. "Got this for my troubles."

Palmer allowed the silence to lengthen, but the former Intelligence man appeared to have run out of things to say. He stood up and stretched his legs while Jacob fiddled with his paper towels. As he went to sit down, he saw a newspaper cutting sticking out from under a pile of magazines on a chair. It was yellowed and creased and dated from several weeks ago.

It mentioned the forthcoming marriage of Victoria Myburghe.

"You started writing to him," Palmer said softly. "Why, after all this time?"

Jacob dropped the towel and crossed his arms tightly, like a defensive child. "I couldn't stand it. For years I swallowed it, not thinking about him and what he did. Good lads were dying while he was meeting with those…

bastards. Lads like Tom." He stared up at Palmer with fierce intensity. "Tom had a son, you know. Ben's his name – he's a DS in the West Yorkshire Police. A good kid, but he should have had his dad. Then I saw the piece about the wedding and… I had to do something."

"You could have told Ben."

"No." Jacob shook his head. "It wouldn't have done his career any good. Still got my file, but it's old now, like the names in it. I wanted to unsettle him – Myburghe, that is." He smiled that sly smile again. "Used a bit of the old psy-ops – psychology – letting him know it hadn't been forgotten. It hadn't gone away."

"And the fake bomb?"

"Shouldn't have done that. It was nonsense. A moment of stupidity."

"And the rest?" Palmer found he was holding his breath, waiting for the final answer.

"Rest?" Jacob looked puzzled. "What rest? There wasn't anything else. I lost my bottle after that." He stared down at the table. "I started emailing that Gavin reporter instead, hoping he might be interested. She, as it turned out."

"You were right," said Palmer. "She was interested." He wondered if he'd been told everything, or whether there was still something secreted away in the darker recesses of this man's damaged mind. If there was, he wasn't sure if it would change the way things looked. Even now, after listening to what Jacob had said, he couldn't shift the man's own words from his mind.

"I'd been trained… in surveillance… undercover work. And a few other bits and bobs."

He questioned whether, deep down, those 'other bits and bobs' had prepared the man to kidnap and maim or kill another man's son. Somehow he doubted it.

A thought occurred to him. It was a loose connection, and probably meant nothing, but he knew he had to ask. "Have you ever heard of a Toby Henzigger?"

Riley was fast losing patience. She'd agreed to wait outside only because she knew Jacob Worth wouldn't talk otherwise. But she didn't like being left out, especially when the initial contact had been with her. Now she was having to do what she hated most: kick her heels and wait for someone else to get the details.

Her feelings were approaching boiling point by the time Palmer emerged from the toilets and walked up the steps into sunlight. He had a tight look on his face. He paused to light a cigarette, then led the way back to the car.

"Palmer!" Riley felt like punching him on the shoulder. "Come on – give. What did he tell you?"

"He sent the letters and the fake bomb," he told her. "But that was all."

"That's it? You were in there nearly an hour. What were you doing – playing Scrabble?"

Palmer eased out of the car park and headed for the motorway. On the way, he related everything Jacob had told him. By the time they hit the M1 southbound, they were reduced to silence while trying to figure out where to go next.

"This Henzigger," said Palmer, as they drove down the slip road. "He's been in there right from the beginning. Now he pops up again. I wonder why."

Riley nodded. "What made you think of him?"

"Jacob spotted him on two separate occasions, both of them at meetings with Myburghe and cartel members. He's either DEA working undercover, or he's something else."

"If he was DEA," said Riley, "surely they'd have moved in

on Myburghe ages ago? This has been going on long enough."

Palmer squeezed the Saab between two trucks. "Is there any chance you could speak to him?"

"Henzigger?" It wasn't something Riley was keen to do, especially with the latest developments. But she agreed with Palmer; Henzigger was involved. All they had to do was find out to what degree. "Maybe," she said cautiously, and remembered the number the American had given her. She dialled and heard it ring a dozen times before it was picked up.

"Yeah, can I help?" The voice was American, with a faint southern twang. It wasn't Henzigger.

"Is Toby there?" Riley asked.

"Uh… this is his cellphone, but he's in a meeting right now, ma'am." In the background somebody was pounding on a keyboard and a computer bleeped, followed by the slamming of a drawer and a burst of laughter. Office sounds. "May I take a message?"

"No, thanks, I'll call back." Riley risked a question. "Can you tell me where you're speaking from?"

"Sure, ma'am," the voice replied unhesitatingly. "This is the United States Embassy, London."

30

Riley gave it fifteen minutes before calling again. In the meantime, she and Palmer tried to make sense of what Henzigger was doing at the US Embassy. The man who'd answered his mobile had sounded hesitant, the way you would if picking up someone else's phone. Perhaps Henzigger had left it outside the meeting room by request.

"He might have been called in," Palmer reasoned, floating theories. "Easier to keep an eye on him that way."

"But? There's a but in there."

"It sounds like he's not exactly a stranger there. Interesting."

When she re-dialled the number, Henzigger answered.

"Riley. How are you?" He sounded wary, and she guessed he'd been told about her call.

"I need to see you," she told him. "Something's come up. I think you might like to know about it."

"Sure thing," he said readily. "No problem. But, uh… you want to give me some idea, as a taster?"

"I'd rather not. It's sensitive."

There was a lengthy pause and she thought he'd gone. Then she heard a hollow sound and realised he'd placed his hand over the phone. "OK," he said at last. "I can do that. When?"

"How about tomorrow?"

"No. I've got stuff to do all day. After that, I might be out of here."

He was leaving? "This evening, then."

"OK. Make it seven. Where?"

Riley named a spot on Chelsea Embankment. It was cheap psychology; familiar turf for her, but a bit off-territory for Henzigger. She wasn't overjoyed about the timing, though. She'd have preferred bright sunlight and lots of people.

"I'll find it. See you there." He cut the connection.

Palmer looked concerned. "Is this wise?"

"It's the best I could think of," said Riley. "I don't think going to Grosvenor Square will accomplish much. If he's not meant to be on the books, they'll simply deny any knowledge of him."

"True. What are you going to tell him?"

"I don't know yet. I'll think of something."

Palmer sighed and glanced at his watch. "I'll get there early."

But Riley had other ideas. "You'd be better trying to find Myburghe or keeping an eye on his daughters." She smiled with more confidence than she felt and asked herself whether she was walking into something she couldn't handle. Only time would tell.

Palmer dropped her at her flat, fighting her idea all the way. But as soon as he left, Riley got on the phone. It took her half an hour and a combination of cheap lies and silky persuasion, but she was finally put through to a number and asked to wait. Weller was in a meeting but when he came on, he sounded relieved to have an excuse to get out of it.

"If anyone asks," he told her, "you're a high-grade informant with important information."

"A snitch? Thanks, Weller."

"Don't let it go to your head. And you don't have to go round speaking out of the corner of your mouth or calling me guv'nor. What can I do for you?"

214

"Is Toby Henzigger on the side of the angels?"

"I doubt it, after what the Yanks told us. He's got a sticky reputation and is still under suspicion. As for us, we don't like people coming in on false plates, no matter who they are. Why?"

"He came to see me." She didn't mention that it had been the previous day; she wasn't sure Weller would understand the time lapse. Neither did she want to tell him yet about her meeting the American by the river, unless she had to. "He wants my help clearing his name."

"Can you turn water into wine? Why you?"

"I've no idea," Riley said honestly. "Maybe he thinks because I'm a journalist I'll listen to him."

"And will you?"

"I'm reserving judgement. I was hoping you could shed some light."

Weller gave a snort. "Do me a favour. Why do you think I came round to pick your brains?"

"So how come he was released and allowed to stay in the country?"

There was a silence while Weller digested the question, deciding how much he could tell her. "My superiors had a call from the Home Office," he said finally. "They'd had a call from Grosvenor Square. The US Embassy claim Henzigger's false plates thing was a mistake. He'd got his papers mixed up and by the time he discovered the fact, it was too late. A favour for a favour, the message went. It's all bullshit, of course. What's going on? Is this tied in with Myburghe?"

Riley ignored him. "Is Henzigger with the DEA?"

Weller's reply was loaded with caution. "He might be. Why?"

"Is that yes or no?"

"It means I don't know. And the so-called 'Special Relationship' doesn't include that sort of information. What else did he say?"

"Nothing much."

Weller gave a noncommittal grunt. "Have you seen Myburghe yet?"

It was a sudden switch, but Riley was expecting it. "No."

"Pity. If you do, tell him to get in touch." He ended the call.

The main thrust of outbound traffic was dying as Riley made her way down Flood Street towards the river. Daylight was fading quickly, leaving small pockets of shadow between emerging street lights like clusters of dark cotton wool. In the windows, she caught glimpses of people preparing for the evening, safe and secure behind their double-glazing and solid front doors. It made the outside world suddenly all the less appealing.

As she turned the corner into Cheyne Walk, she was greeted by a strong smell of stale Thames water and the clatter of a boat pounding up river. Lights twinkled on the far bank and a siren sounded mournfully from further east, bouncing off the water like a stone skipping across a lake. A line of cars was caught at the lights by the Albert Bridge, the fumes heavy on the air.

Between the embankment and Cheyne Walk lies a small garden, open to the road, but backed by a spread of thin trees and bushes. In spite of the proximity of so many passing vehicles, and the noise and fumes in the air, it is a popular spot for local residents and tired walkers.

An ideal place for a meeting.

Riley crossed the road and walked through a gap in the trees. She found Toby Henzigger standing by a wooden bench, hands thrust into his pockets. Other benches were placed every twenty yards or so, empty of the little old ladies who usually sat there, feeding the birds and watching the cars go by. Henzigger seemed to be alone.

He turned and watched her approach, rocking back and forth on his toes. He looked slightly greyer and thinner than the last time she'd seen him, but it might have been the light.

She walked past him and stopped at the statue of Boy David. The figure was of a stick-thin child in memory of the Machine Gun Corps in World War 1. Somebody had balanced an empty cigarette carton on one of the statue's shoulders. Riley plucked it off and dropped it in a waste bin.

Henzigger was wearing a sports jacket, slacks and white shirt. It made him seem oddly at home in this peculiarly English setting. He turned to face her. The move seemed deliberate, and put the nearest street light at his back. She felt her nerves tighten. She was hardly a threat, even if she was a good thirty something years younger.

She sat down on the bench and looked up at him. From her position, the light formed a halo around his head, throwing his face into shadow. The move seemed to confuse him momentarily, as if she had managed to undermine him with her show of composure.

"Thanks for coming," Riley said politely, and saw a flicker of movement near the street corner she had just passed. She forced herself to look away.

"What do you have for me?" he asked impatiently.

Riley allowed the seconds to tick away, watching the passing traffic. She didn't want to get the discussion under way too quickly, and it wouldn't hurt for Henzigger to sweat a bit. Just as she opened her mouth to speak, a faint noise came from the gloom beyond the bushes. She relaxed and smiled.

Henzigger threw her a dark scowl. "Did I say something funny?"

"No," she said. "Sorry – just a random thought."

From across the way came another dull noise. Two down, thought Riley, and wondered how many there were. Henzigger didn't seem to have heard anything, but he was capable of moving quickly, as he had demonstrated in the trees near the shoot.

"Are you alone?"

The American shifted impatiently. "Of course. Look, you said you had something."

Riley wasn't sure whether to feign being helpful, hoping to draw something out of him that way, or to try and rattle his cage and shock him into saying more than he'd intended. Being nice wasn't going to cut it; Henzigger wasn't here for pleasantries, nor was he interested in London's quainter locations.

And he hadn't brought company because he was scared of the dark.

"A body was found at Myburghe's house last night," she told him.

"So what?" He stared down at her, his stance as tense as a steel hawser.

"Don't you want to know who?"

"Like I should care." His voice was a growl, dismissive. "Who was it – your ex-military cop pal, Palmer? He shoulda stuck to divorce cases and construction sites."

"Not quite." Henzigger had clearly checked Palmer's background, and in spite of seeing him at the shoot, had dismissed him as little more than a security guard playing out of his league. A big mistake.

"So who then?"

"You know him. A man named David Hilary."

"Never heard of him." The denial was automatic.

"He was Sir Kenneth Myburghe's bodyguard in Colombia. Big man, face like Mount Rushmore?"

"Oh. Yeah, I remember." The admission was grudging. "He's dead? Shame. How'd it happen?"

"He was cut to pieces."

He didn't say anything.

"The thing is, Toby," she continued, "the police are interested in three men who'd been staying in the stable block where Hilary was found. They moved out not long ago. The locals, who notice these things, thought they were Spanish grooms brought in to school Sir Kenneth's horses. That's rubbish, of course, because he doesn't have any horses."

"So?"

"Someone recognised the men's dialect. Where was it from? Oh, yes, Bogotá."

"Wow. Sounds like you got illegal immigrants. Tough shit."

"Not these. A trundle through immigration records will probably show who they were – and where they came from. Put that together with the fingerprints and Bob's your uncle."

"Hunh?"

"Never mind. They left a porn magazine behind. Colombian porn. I'm told the pages of glossy magazines are what the DNA and fingerprint boys call 'high yield'. Must be all those sweaty fingers on that nice, shiny paper."

While Henzigger digested that, which she hoped was even ten percent true, she turned her head to follow a speeding ambulance heading west, and caught a glimpse of a tall figure standing near the corner of Flood Street.

John Mitcheson.

Even as she spotted him, he stepped back into the gloom and disappeared.

"You're still not telling me anything I want to know," Henzigger muttered, but he no longer sounded so sure of himself. He glanced to one side, then quickly back at Riley.

"But I thought you wanted to clear your name?" she said.

"I do. So?"

"I did some checking of my own. I had a friend speak to a friend in Bogotá. He said you regularly attended meetings with members of a middle-ranking cartel. One of the places you used was a country club just outside the city."

"That's a lie!" Henzigger was quivering like a bowstring. But his voice gave him away. Riley had hit a nerve and Henzigger was shaken. "Who the hell told you that?"

"You were being watched, Toby." She turned the screw a bit tighter. "You weren't aware of it, but a British Intelligence officer was logging your every move. You and Myburghe."

"Jesus, you're dreaming." His voice was a whisper.

"What are you really doing here, Toby? And why come to me? It certainly wasn't to clear your name. That would have been a neat trick, seeing as my influence with the authorities is less than zero. Was it a smokescreen while you got close to your old friend... and business partner?"

He said nothing. But Riley guessed his brain was working at fever pitch, planning an argument out of this place. With his background, he'd spent all his life saying only as much as he needed, relying on deception and cover stories to protect himself. Now it was beginning to wear thin under pressure.

"Come on, Toby. You can tell me." She was taunting him,

hoping to make him lose his temper. If there was one thing people like Henzigger hated, it was not having the upper hand. "Has Sir Kenneth let the side down?"

"I don't have time for this." He began to turn away.

"Are you still DEA? I called your mobile number. You were speaking from the US embassy."

"I was there on business."

As the automatic evasion left his mouth, she saw him hesitate. He hadn't denied it. Then he looked around again and seemed rattled. If he was waiting for his Colombian friends to come and help him out, thought Riley, he'd be a long time waiting.

Riley stood up and walked away. It wasn't what Henzigger was expecting. But he didn't let her go without a parting shot.

"That wasn't smart, Riley," he called, his voice cutting across the traffic noise. "Not smart at all. There are other ways of getting Myburghe to co-operate."

The threat was plain and chilling. Any pretence of wanting to clear his name was now gone. It could only mean one thing. The daughters.

She took out her phone and called Palmer.

"You should check on Victoria and her sister," she suggested, and told him what Henzigger had said.

Palmer grunted. "Already done. I had them moved, just in case."

"How did they take it?"

"They hissed a bit. But they're safe. I'm going down to Colebrooke later to check the place out."

Riley breathed a sigh of relief. Henzigger would hiss, too, when he found his 'leverage' had been spirited right out from under his nose. She told Palmer to be careful and rang off.

221

As she walked back up Flood Street, Mitcheson stepped out from the shadows and joined her, slipping his arm through hers.

"Was it worth it?"

"Too early to tell," she replied. "You were busy." She clutched his arm, the impact of Henzigger's threat suddenly catching up with her. If Mitcheson noticed, he pretended otherwise. "Thanks for your help."

"My pleasure." As they passed beneath a streetlight, she caught the expression on his face. It was times like this when Mitcheson worried her; when the look in his eyes went beyond the merely threatening and entered another realm altogether.

"Were there any survivors?" She just about managed to keep her voice level. In spite of knowing a little of Mitcheson's background, the idea of him calmly disposing of any opposition, even for her sake, was something she didn't want to contemplate. It represented a darker side to him, a side she wasn't entirely sure of.

"Of course. They'll be OK. Eventually."

"Really?" The last thing they needed was Weller calling round with awkward questions about dead Colombians littering the embankment. She'd seen what Mitcheson could do when danger threatened.

"Scout's honour." He looked at her with complete innocence, but it still left her wondering how far he would go if push came to shove. She hoped she never found out.

The phone was shrill, dragging Riley out of a deep sleep. She rolled away from the comforting warmth of Mitcheson's arm and picked up the handset. She was surprised to see the time was just approaching midnight.

"Sorry to spoil your beauty sleep." It was Weller, sounding

not the least bit apologetic. He crunched a mint and continued, "Can you come to the US Embassy? Ask for Portius. I'll meet you inside."

Riley snapped awake. "What, now?"

"My, you're quick. We're having a meeting with a State Department suit named Henry Portius. He's got some information he wants to share about Henzigger."

Riley didn't bother hiding her surprise. "Why me? I'd have thought you'd want to keep the press as far away as possible. I mean, don't get me wrong, I'm –"

"Because you're a material witness," Weller interrupted. "At least, that's what I'm calling you. As such, you might be able to help. And right now, I need all the help I can get." He rang off and Riley slumped back on to the pillow for a moment before hauling herself out of bed.

31

Riley was met in the security lodge at the side of the embassy by a square-jawed US marine in a uniform with mathematically-precise creases. He kept calling her 'Ma'am' and looked as if he ate nails for breakfast. Other than a couple of armed policemen patrolling the pavement, and the glow of lights from inside the embassy building, there was little sign of activity.

The marine marched over to a phone and stabbed out a number, and spoke softly with someone on the other end. He managed to move without crimping his shirt or spoiling the mirror-gloss shine of his shoes.

By comparison, Riley felt a mess, having thrown on jeans and a blue cotton shirt, and a sports jacket which she figured gave her at least an element of respectability for this time of night and the place she was going.

The marine ended his call and returned smartly to the counter.

"Ma'am? Could I have your cellphone, please?" Riley handed it over, and he placed it in a box. "It will be here to collect when you leave, ma'am. This way, please, ma'am." He snapped into an about-turn and set off at a brisk pace, looking back to make sure Riley hadn't got waylaid in his slipstream.

They entered the main building and negotiated the security screens, climbing to the first floor and passing several closed doors at speed. There were no overt signs of staff other than her square-jawed escort, and she wondered what would happen if she broke into a run.

The marine gave her no time to find out. He skidded to

a stop by a plain door, knocked once and showed her inside, then departed at a gallop. Maybe, thought Riley, he was on a time-trial.

She was in a plain meeting room, with a long table, a twin line of chairs and a large US flag mounted on the wall at one end. The air smelled vaguely of mints. Then Riley saw why: Weller sat at one end of the table, nursing a cup of coffee.

The man across from him had his back to the window. He was stocky, with carefully trimmed brown hair and eyes the same colour. He looked neat and contained in his conservative grey suit, and looked to be in his early forties. He didn't seem pleased to see Riley, but stepped round the end of the table and shook hands cordially enough.

"Miss Gavin. Henry L Portius. Nice to meet you." At least, Riley noted, when he took his hand back he didn't wipe it on his jacket.

She nodded at Weller, who indicated a chair next to him and sat forward in a businesslike manner.

"Henry agreed to this late meeting," Weller announced, as if he was in his own office, "after I lodged a request for the DEA's input." He flashed a smile at Portius and received a cool look in return. Riley took it to mean that the 'request' had been a forceful one. It was an indication of Weller's clout and how high this matter must have gone to get their agreement.

"I'm still not sure we have an interest here," Portius said carefully. He jerked his chin up from his shirt collar and looked hard at Weller. Riley wondered if the meeting was being recorded.

"Don't be an arse, Henry," Weller said genially. "One of yours is off the rails and causing mayhem. Of course you've got an interest." He paused a heartbeat. "At least, I take it Henzigger is no longer an agent?"

"Of course not. I hope you understand that." His eyes swivelled Riley's way and blinked once, the following stare cold and unfriendly. Riley took it to mean that he knew what she did for a living and was trying to intimidate her to silence. It probably worked a treat in the States and sent their journalists scurrying for cover. Right here and now it came across as the cheap bullying trick that it was.

"We'll see, shall we?"

Weller coughed quietly and tapped on the desk. "Riley, I've already given Henry a summary of the situation as far as I know it, and he's agreed to help." He fixed her with a look that said don't wind Portius up because he's come a long way, and technically speaking, we're both on foreign soil. "He assures me that Henzigger is no longer an active agent with any branch of the US government. I believe him."

"If you say so. But why was he here?"

"He was required to check in," Portius said, "following his little problem with your Immigration department."

Riley stared at him. Little problem? The man had come into the country on false plates! She wondered if 'checking in' was the reason Henzigger had been in the embassy just hours ago when she rang him, and whether Portius was aware of that fact. "Where is he now?"

"I don't have that information."

"But you have been keeping a watch on him?"

"Correct." Portius's confirmation was supported by Weller's nod.

"May I ask why?"

"It was routine procedure. He caused a problem. We like to make sure he won't cause more before leaving." He smiled thinly.

Riley looked at both men. This was going nowhere. "What do you want from me?"

"How about filling her in on the background stuff first?" said Weller.

Portius sighed, clearly reluctant but no doubt under orders. "Just over a year ago there was a drugs operation involving a shipment of cocaine and heroin from somewhere south of the Caribbean. It was tracked to the UK, and the operation was co-ordinated through a senior DEA officer named Quinn, who followed the shipment all the way to London." He stared past Riley with a wooden face. "Unfortunately, the operation was compromised as the boat was docking."

"The general consensus is that Agent Quinn was recognised by a member of the gang," Weller supplied casually. "He's something of a media figure, apparently… for a law enforcement official." He avoided looking at Portius, who looked as if he wanted to explode at the obvious taunt.

"Quinn wasn't that high-profile," he muttered coldly.

Riley tapped her fingernail on the table before they came to blows. "How does this involve Henzigger?"

Portius nodded, throwing a final resentful glare at Weller before continuing. "The control centre was set up in the harbour master's office, where they could observe the ship right to the berth. We were also watching the water, making sure no other vessels approached the ship offshore. Once it was in close, Mr Quinn decided he wanted to join the men down in the Customs shed, for a closer look."

"Just for the record," said Weller, "Henry here advised against it. Didn't you?"

"Yes." Portius puffed his cheeks out. "I did."

Riley sensed a subtle bit of blame-shifting going on and asked, "But he didn't listen?"

"That's right. He insisted on going. Maybe he'd been behind a desk too long and needed the action. We gave him the harbour master's yellow coat and a hard hat, and made him carry a box of files, for cover. That was all."

"And?"

"He got part way across the yard and the men on the boat spotted him."

"They must have had damned good eyesight, from that distance," Weller muttered sourly, turning the screw. "A hard hat, a yellow coat and carrying a box – yet he was still recognised? Who were the men on the boat - janitors from the Washington office?"

Portius opened his mouth but said nothing. Riley realised he wasn't entirely convinced about what had happened, either. Take any group of men on a construction site, all wearing coats and hard hats, and you'd have to get close to distinguish one from another.

"So what are you saying?" she asked finally.

"I'm saying Quinn was made by somebody who knew him. Somebody who'd worked with him and would recognise him at a distance." The admission was grudging, and she realised that Portius must be under some powerful pressure to admit such information to a British policeman and a member of the British press. What she didn't know was why.

"Sounds reasonable to me," said Weller. His smile dared Portius to contradict.

"Did you find out who the person was?" asked Riley. She knew what he was going to say; he just didn't like admitting to foreigners that they had a bad apple in the barrel, a concept that was anathema to their whole way of thinking.

"There's evidence to suggest," Portius's voice sounded strangled, as if he was trying to expel a nasty object lodged in his throat, "that it was Toby Henzigger."

32

"More than a bloody suggestion," Weller put in dryly. "Our information puts Henzigger in London when the bust was blown, but he'd left notes with friends to say was travelling in Europe."

"So what?" Portius looked close to bursting, his face growing red with a mixture of emotions. Clearly embarrassment was high on the list. "Last time I heard, England was in Europe, too. And there's no rule to say he couldn't come here if he wanted."

"OK." Riley broke in on the threatening feud. "But how does Henzigger know Quinn?"

Portius seemed relieved by the interruption. "They both went through the DEA training programme together. They were even roomies for a while. In those circumstances, you get to know people like your own family." He scowled as if reluctantly acknowledging that every family has a black sheep.

Riley couldn't blame him. Nobody liked the idea that a former colleague was batting for the opposition. "So he was working with the drug shippers," she said. "What made him do it?"

Portius shrugged and looked depressed. "We don't know. Maybe he was exposed for too long. If so, we should have spotted it sooner. Maybe he was compromised and got in too deep. The fact is, he's been under suspicion for unauthorised activities in Latin America, but all our investigations so far have revealed nothing. Nothing we can use, anyway."

"Did he have the ability to mount the shipment? It's hardly

like shopping at B & Q, is it?"

Portius looked puzzled by the reference but shrugged it off. "Sure. He had the contacts, the sources and the experience. He certainly knew where to get supplies. He knew the people who'd already set up supply chains, so setting up another – if that's what he did – was just a question of logistics."

"But those chains originally led to the American mainland through the Caribbean," Weller pointed out reasonably. "Why switch to Europe?"

"The States is already awash with product. Prices have dropped and the inter-gang wars are getting out of control. Everyone wants whatever action is going. We think Henzigger identified a growing market in Europe and saw distractions in the system which he thought could be exploited."

"Distractions?"

"Asylum seekers." Weller looked at Riley. "You know what it's like. From Afghanistan, Iraq, Iran, Pakistan, Bosnia, Albania – you name it. With anti-terrorist measures being prioritised at airports and away from coastal ports, you get holes. Big ones. Henzigger would have seen it without too much difficulty. It's what he was trained for."

Riley waited, but there didn't seem to be anything else forthcoming. She decided to inject some excitement to see what the reaction was.

"What about Walter Asner?" she asked.

The effect on Portius was electric. He almost jumped out of his seat. "Asner? Christ, how –?"

"Who the hell is Walter Asner?" Weller demanded, rounding on Riley.

"He was a deep-cover DEA agent working within the embassy circuit," Riley told him. "His job was to ferret out information at the top of the tree – people who thought they were beyond reach. He committed suicide in his garage after retiring from the agency. Allegedly."

Portius looked shocked. "How do you know this?"

"Henzigger. He told me all about Asner's role with the DEA."

Portius looked stunned.

"Why did he do that?" Weller demanded. The look on his face told Riley he wasn't ignoring the fact that she'd got more information from Henzigger than she'd let on earlier.

"I still haven't worked that out. It was all part of the story he told me about being under suspicion."

Portius shifted in his chair, prompting Riley and Weller to look at him. He took a deep breath and said, "Asner spent several years in Colombia. He moved among the embassy people, socialising, advising, helping smooth paths on trade deals. He was a faceless, harmless civil servant and nobody gave him a second thought, least of all staffers from friendly embassies. As far as they were concerned, he was merely another admin suit in line to have his hand shaken. We think..." He looked up at Riley momentarily. "We think he stumbled on something that really bothered him. Something so big he couldn't carry on. So he resigned. That was all."

"Hardly all," Weller murmured. "It made him take his own life."

Portius gave another jut of his jaw and shot one of his cuffs in indignation. It was clearly an uncomfortable topic, but equally clear that he was under orders. "The belief in the agency is that Asner had done something nobody counted on: he'd uncovered a conspiracy involving our own people. It's the only explanation."

Riley watched his face, trying to work out what was

behind the official mask. "You don't think it was suicide, do you?"

"No. But we can't prove it was murder."

Weller growled, leaping ahead. "Christ, to think we let Henzigger go on your say-so."

"Henzigger killed him?" Riley looked between them for confirmation. "He told me they were friends."

Portius blinked rapidly. "Colleagues in the same pool would be more accurate. Asner was a professional; he must have made records, some notes we haven't yet found. Asking for retirement right out of the blue like he did, it must have struck Henzigger as odd. We think he went to see Asner at his home and Asner either told him what he'd discovered or let it slip. It's possible Asner had discovered what Henzigger was up to."

"Was this part of the trouble Henzigger got into?" said Riley.

"It was part of an ongoing investigation, yes. But we couldn't marry the two." He coughed. "Possibly Asner did."

"How?"

"By joining two ends of the same piece of string. If he found out what contacts Henzigger had with the cartels and FARC, then studied which people on our side Henzigger was seeing regularly, the rest was a matter of deduction. We're still trying to follow the same path."

"How does this affect us?" Weller sounded bullish, but Riley had a feeling he was already there, and was merely nudging the conversation along.

"If Henzigger was arranging shipments, he needed someone to facilitate things down the line: documents, shipping papers, permits, letters of recommendation – it had to be someone with access to papers and people."

"Why couldn't he do it himself?" Riley asked.

"Henzigger didn't have local knowledge of the area where the shipments were going, or the contacts. He'd have had to recruit someone to convince his suppliers he could pull it off, or they wouldn't have touched him."

"So this contact would need knowledge of where he was shipping his drugs to, then?"

"Yes. But this has been going on for a long time. We think he developed contacts in the trade sections of various embassies, spread across Europe to begin with. But the UK was the jackpot. The UK contact, whoever it was, would have been expensive, but the end result would have been worth it. The returns are huge and the markets insatiable. All he had to do was stay clear of the opposition at this end, but I doubt he'd planned on being around too long to care, anyway."

"Do you know the name of this contact?" Weller looked as tense as a gun dog and even Portius picked up on it. But now the tables were turned, and Riley felt the American's relief at being able to point a finger of blame at someone on the other side.

"We're not sure," he replied cautiously. "The evidence points towards Sir Kenneth Myburghe."

Weller looked ready to go ballistic. "Can I suggest, then, Henry," he grated, barely restraining himself, "that you get your team working on it? In the meantime, we'll see if we can't come up with the answer from this end." He threw Portius a look heated enough to weld the American to his seat, then stood up and headed for the door, signalling for Riley to follow.

As she did so, a phone rang on a small table behind Portius. He reached over and snatched it up as if grabbing a lifeline to save him from further humiliation.

"You knew all this, didn't you?" Riley hissed, as they neared the door. "All that claptrap about Palmer and Myburghe and what Henzigger was doing. You've known all the time. How long have you been working on this?"

"Too bloody long," he replied sourly. "I'll be glad to see the back of it."

"Wait." It was Portius, springing up as if jet-propelled.

They stopped and looked at him.

"Something else I was going to tell you," he said quietly, the words coming out reluctantly. "There's another shipment." He replaced the phone gently on its cradle. "A big one. We think Henzigger's behind it."

Riley didn't need to look at Weller; she could almost hear his teeth grinding in fury.

"Another one?" he yelped. "There's a shipment coming in here and you didn't think to bloody tell us?" The words snapped across the room and Portius flinched as if he'd been struck across the face.

Riley felt almost sorry for him. If this didn't create a new period of frosty relations between Washington and London, she wasn't sure what would.

"We had information," Portius muttered defensively. "But it was mostly rumour... nothing substantive." He looked at Riley for support and his voice grew harder in defiance. "You know how it is: it starts as a whisper, with bits here, pieces there. False stories, whispers... even misinformation, until in the end it gets so fragmented you don't know what to believe."

"Is that what brought you over here?" Riley asked. Then it hit her. "You knew what he was up to, didn't you? You asked Immigration to let him go so you could follow him."

"And he bloody side-stepped you." Weller's voice was

loaded with accusation.

Portius looked like a man drowning. "It looks that way, yes." He tried not to catch Weller's eye, and the senior policeman looked as if he wanted to turn the American into a stain on the carpet. "We suspected most of it but nobody would talk. What nobody could come up with was the name at this end."

"Sounds like Asner might have," said Weller sourly. "Doesn't it?"

"That was a mistake."

Weller's anger dissipated as quickly as it had arisen. He let out a deep sigh. "OK. Now what?"

Portius cracked a knuckle and stared at the darkened window. "Henzigger's a planner. He works out everything in advance, discounting risks, putting people in place, setting up escape routes and fallbacks. He uses people for information without them knowing it." He looked at Riley. "We think that's why he approached you. He heard somehow that you and your friend Palmer were close to Myburghe and figured you'd be a source of information." He paused. "There's something else." He nodded at the phone. "I was just advised that they've brought the shipment date forward."

"When?"

"We heard a whisper three days ago. By then it was too late to mount –"

Weller snarled like a terrier with a rat. "I don't mean when did you hear, although God knows, I'm sure it wasn't recent enough to be of any use. I meant when is the shipment due in, and where?"

Portius swallowed hard. "We think it was due today. My people are just checking the ETA." He looked like a small boy in front of a headmaster, and quickly leaned over to scribble on a piece of paper. He ripped off the sheet and handed it to Weller. "That's the ship's name."

"It's tomorrow." Riley said, then looked at her watch. "No – it's today."

Weller's head snapped round. "You what?"

She told him about her earlier meeting with Henzigger by the river. If Weller wanted her head on a plate, it was too bad. "I first suggested we meet up tomorrow, but he claimed he was tied up all day. Doing what? What could keep him more tied up than overseeing a shipment? It must have been somewhere close to London."

Weller nodded. "Right. This has gone far enough." He turned to Portius. "How about you get Marching Boy back here to show us out. I'd hate to get shot by one of your goons for looking down the wrong corridor."

Portius bridled. "What are you going to do?"

"Me?" Weller smiled and waved the piece of paper Portius had given him. "Now you've decided to cough up, I've got some shipping movements to look at."

Portius looked like he'd rather have a full company of US marines come in and jump all over them in their boots. But he picked up the phone to summon an escort out of the building. Seconds later they were chasing the same marine guard back downstairs in double time.

"You were rough on him," Riley said quietly, as they picked up their mobiles from the security desk.

Weller scowled. "Serves him right. If they'd shared their information years ago instead of playing silly buggers, we could have saved ourselves all this trouble." He gave a sly grin. "Did you see his face? Portius thought tonight was going to be all about me pleading mea bloody culpa over Myburghe. Now he's had to admit one of their boys is a real stinker, he's wriggling like a tart on a trapeze."

Riley smiled at the imagery. "How about Myburghe – any sign of him yet?"

"No. His car was found forty minutes ago under the Western Avenue flyover. It was empty."

Riley mourned the fact that none of her time over the past few days was chargeable to the Home Office. They'd certainly had their money's worth out of her. She almost felt admiration for Weller's tactics. He'd played her all along just to stir the waters, and now he'd done the same with Portius. She was ready to bet that the mauling Portius had undergone at Weller's hands was unprecedented. And now he was standing back to see what unfolded.

He handed her a card with his number on it. "Call me if you trip over him."

As he disappeared into the night, Riley's mobile rang.

It was Henzigger.

"I'm real mad at you, Riley!" he wailed, his voice a wild singsong and pitched high as if balanced on the edge of hysteria. The hum of a car engine filled the background, and she realised he was on the move. "I've got the feeling you weren't being straight with me. Am I right? Are they closing in?"

"I don't know what you mean," Riley said. "Where are you?"

"C'mon, don't kid a kidder. I know when something smells bad. I just got a call from a friend. Someone at the embassy wants my passport. Now why is that, I wonder? Still, never mind. I've got someone here who'll make sure they play ball."

Riley felt her throat tighten. She knew instantly what he was saying: he'd got Myburghe.

"Now what do I do, Riley? Do I stick with the plan and hope I can get out in one piece? Or do I let it go and cut my losses? Whaddya say, huh?"

She couldn't reply, unable to form the words.

When he spoke again, she felt a cold tremor running down her spine.

"Or maybe I should let my guys hang Myburghe up in the same place they did his caveman butler!"

33

Riley rang Palmer and told him what had transpired, and that Henzigger was on his way to Colebrooke House.

"I'll take a look," he told her without hesitation. "He might not be there yet. Can you get hold of Mitcheson? We'll need backup."

Riley said she would and dialled Mitcheson's number, knowing full well what Palmer meant by 'backup'.

To her surprise, Mitcheson was on the Bayswater Road approaching Marble Arch. "I had a feeling you might need help," he said. "I'll be five minutes."

He was there within three, behind the wheel of a dark blue Land Cruiser. He was dressed in combat boots, slacks and a cotton windcheater.

"My God," Riley said admiringly, as he turned the car towards west London. "What have you been doing – posing for a gay porn mag?"

He laughed. "I was actually getting ready for a night-time surveillance job. Fortunately, it'll keep. What's going on – and why were you in the Magic Kingdom?" He was referring to the US Embassy.

She told him about the meeting with Weller and Portius, and how Henzigger had been running drugs with Myburghe's help. Now Portius had mounted a watch on his activities, Henzigger was out of options and ready to kill Myburghe unless he got a route out of the country.

Colebrooke House was the only place Henzigger would go. She could feel it. Myburghe's car being found along the Western Avenue was a definite pointer. Other than the M4, it was the main route out of London towards

Gloucestershire. Henzigger must have followed Myburghe and hijacked him once he realised his plans were falling apart, and now he was planning the final curtain.

Once they were out of the London traffic, the motorway was reasonably clear. The few hesitant motorists they encountered took one look at the charging Land Cruiser in their rear-view mirrors and moved out of the way.

Mitcheson jerked a thumb over his shoulder to indicate a steel box in the back. "I stopped off and brought some gear," he said. "I thought we might need it."

Riley felt a sudden tug of concern. The 'gear' he was referring to most likely had triggers and made loud noises, and if they were stopped by police, would be enough to put them both away for a very long time. But she knew Mitcheson wasn't overly bothered by such niceties. Like Frank Palmer, he took the pragmatist's view that you used the right tools for the job. Unlike Palmer, though, she wasn't sure how much control he would exercise in an all-round fight. She felt guilty for even thinking it, but hoped he would keep casualties down to single figures.

"Is it traceable?"

He gave a half smile in the glow from the dashboard display. "Not to me."

While the road unwound beneath them, Riley filled in the gaps about Henzigger and Myburghe, and how the ambassador had been sucked into the world of drugs and ready money.

"Only he can tell us," said Riley. "But I think he ran up huge gambling debts and realised there was only one way to settle them. Who would suspect a British Ambassador of helping clear the way for the occasional drugs shipment? It must have taken a while to reel him in, but it was worth it."

"Unless he was coerced," Mitcheson suggested. "It wouldn't

have taken much for his family to be threatened."

Riley looked at him in the glow of passing lights. "You sound as if you're making excuses for him."

"I know how they work." He let a few seconds go by, then asked, "What brought this to a head, anyway?"

"I think Christian's death tipped the balance. Myburghe had nothing left for them to hold over him. The girls were out of the way and his wife was no longer a factor." She remembered Henzigger's word. "The leverage was gone."

Mitcheson nodded. If the former diplomat had been operating under extreme pressure to do what he'd done, it made his actions at least understandable. Now, with that pressure gone, he was no longer the help the drug traffickers needed.

"The DEA think Henzigger and his backers have been planning this for years," Riley continued. "He needed someone to make it happen at this end. Someone to help get the shipment through. He met Sir Kenneth and probably learned of his gambling debts. It was a weakness he could trade on."

"So the business with Christian was a bluff?"

"To begin with. When he baulked, they picked Christian up and killed him. Whether intentionally or not, we'll never know."

Riley rested her head against the cool of the window. Somehow, two strands of Myburghe's life and career had come together in an elaborate hoax; the letters and the fake bomb from Jacob Worth, a punishment for what the former Intelligence officer had seen as the ambassador's betrayal in a time of crisis; and the finger and ring from Henzigger and the people behind him, probably preceded by threats of exposure about his gambling debts to keep Sir Kenneth in line.

"I'm not sure," she said finally, aware that she, too, was sounding as if she might be excusing Myburghe's actions, "that the business with his wife and son was as clearcut as everyone thinks."

Mitcheson turned to look at her. He was negotiating a sharp, plunging bend at the time. They made it with a whisper of leaves and a slight squeal of tyres.

"What do you mean?"

She explained how rehearsed Lady Myburghe's explanations had sounded about her husband's gambling, and how readily she had disclosed such intimate details. "I suspect he deliberately cut himself off from his wife because he knew the kind of people he was dealing with. There wasn't much he could do about his son without revealing what he was up to. His daughters were protected by being in London, but Christian wanted to be out in the big, wide world. In the end, Myburghe persuaded him to go abroad, probably convinced he'd be safer out there where nobody could find him. But his wife was a vulnerability he couldn't control, so he did the only thing he could, which was to distance himself from her. It put her out of the picture."

"So she was party to it?"

"She had to be, after all those years. She'd been through worse."

"He still did it," Mitcheson growled, his meaning clear. Whatever his reasons, Sir Kenneth had helped facilitate the importing of drugs to the UK, abandoning his principles, his honour and his loyalty, maybe even his soul. For money.

Riley couldn't disagree. There was no escaping that what must have started out as an occasional harmless flutter all those years ago had eventually turned into something far worse than he could ever have imagined. The only way out was total disgrace – or coming to an arrangement. "Save some of the blame for Henzigger. He helped engineer this."

"How do you know?"

She told him about the failed drugs bust and Henzigger's suspected part in it. "He and his suppliers lost everything. God knows what it cost them, but it was enough for them to put in extra insurance this time to make sure the next one didn't go wrong."

"The Colombian grooms." Mitcheson nodded in agreement. "They killed Hilary."

"He must have known all about the schemes. He was the bodyguard your friend saw with Myburghe in Colombia. Sir Kenneth's attempt at watching his own back."

She shivered, recalling the terrible thing she had seen in the stable block. No man deserved to die like that. Thoughts of Colebrooke House made her wonder where Palmer was right now.

"Can you make this thing go any faster?"

34

Frank Palmer drove his Saab through the village and past the entrance to Colebrooke House. A line of police tape stretched across the gateway, with a metal sign warning visitors to stay out.

He turned the car round and drove back. Across the road from the entrance, he spotted a narrow, disused track overhung with the branches of a horse chestnut tree. He stopped and reversed until the car was hidden beneath the foliage, then turned off the engine and climbed out, allowing his eyes to become accustomed to the dark.

He slipped across the road and over a section of dry-stone wall, and padded through the trees parallel with the long driveway. There was no sound save for the wind in the branches, the flapping of a pigeon somewhere overhead and the bark of a fox in the distance.

He reached the edge of the tree line and stared at the house. The building itself was in darkness, but the security lights in the ground along the front threw up an unearthly glow across the walls and windows. In contrast to the glamour and glitz of the wedding party, the effect was cold and unwelcoming, as if all life had been sucked out, leaving a mere skeleton in its place.

He waited five minutes, totally immobile. Satisfied he was unobserved, he slid along the tree line to his left and crossed the drive, making his way to the rear of the house. If it turned out he was wrong, and Henzigger and his men were already here, their vehicles would be in evidence somewhere.

No cars.

He jogged back to the Saab, hugging the trees all the way. He might need a fast exit from here, and his car was too far for a quick getaway. He climbed in and drove out of the track and straight for the main gate.

He slowed before the tape, steering past the police sign and allowing the plastic strip to slide up the bonnet and over the roof. It was a tight stretch, but he made it without snapping the tape. He doubted if the local police had the resources to send an officer to check the place around the clock, but leaving signs of a forced entry would certainly raise the alarm that someone was on the premises. And Henzigger could read those signs just like anyone else.

He followed the drive to the rear of the house, pulling in alongside an old coachhouse which he knew was now used as a maintenance workshop. He edged the car back out of sight and went to check the house and surrounding gardens.

Ten minutes later, he'd covered the gardens and stables, and was about to try the house when he heard the hum of vehicles approaching. Headlights flared across the front of the house as two cars barrelled up the drive, spitting gravel. Both cars skidded to a stop near the front door and a tall figure carrying a shiny briefcase jumped out of the first one and began shouting orders.

Palmer guessed it was Henzigger.

The American was joined by three armed men. One was carrying a large canvas bag, grunting with effort. The other two men reached into the second car and dragged a figure from the rear seat, bundling him roughly towards the side of the house under Henzigger's directions. The man was having trouble walking and had to be supported by the others.

In the glow of the security lights, Palmer recognised Sir Kenneth Myburghe.

He followed their progress to the rear of the house, where they pushed Sir Kenneth down against the wall. He sat uncomplaining, his head lolling back against the brickwork, and Palmer guessed they had sedated him.

Henzigger issued orders in Spanish, and two of the men ran across the gardens carrying the canvas bag between them. None of the motion-detector lights came on, and Palmer realised they must have been disabled. The men disappeared from sight, to reappear moments later in the distance, now several yards apart. As they ran, they each set something down on the ground, following parallel lines running from the house to the woods in the distance. Each object they left glowed brightly.

They were laying out a landing strip.

Palmer was surprised. It looked far too short a space for a plane to land and take off. If the pilot misjudged his approach and speed even by a fraction, he'd hit the house or the trees. Unless, he reflected, it wasn't the first time they'd done it. It explained why the security lights at the back had been disabled: the glare would have interfered too much with the pilot's night vision.

The two men returned, the canvas bag discarded, their breathing laboured. Behind them, the twin line of lights curved away down the slope across the open ground.

Palmer pondered what he could do to stop the plane taking off once it landed. His options were limited. Four armed men were suicidal odds, and he wasn't keen on ending his life just yet. He might be able to stop the plane physically, but that would mean using his car to ram it. And unless he timed it just right, when all the men were on board, that still placed him in danger of being riddled with gunfire in the process.

He stayed where he was. He'd deal with that problem

when it happened

Henzigger, meanwhile, was pacing up and down, glancing repeatedly at his watch. He seemed in a state of high anxiety, his movements erratic. At one point he took out a mobile phone and made a call. Whatever the response, he clearly wasn't happy, because he took the phone away from his ear and swore at the top of his voice: "God damn you to hell!"

His men were looking at him nervously. One of them asked a question. The reply was furious and curt, and the three Colombians exchanged looks and began shuffling their feet. Palmer didn't need a translator to know they'd been given bad news.

The plane wasn't coming.

Henzigger waited another fifteen minutes, staring up at the sky. Then he walked over to Myburghe, still lying slumped against the wall. He said something to the former diplomat, but Palmer couldn't hear. Then he bent down and cuffed the older man savagely about the head. When there was no response, he followed it with a vicious kick to the ribs and a torrent of abuse in Spanish and English. The assault ceased only when Myburghe toppled over sideways and lay still.

Palmer watched, gritting his teeth, sickened by such casual brutality. He had little sympathy for Myburghe; having got into bed with these people for his own ends, the diplomat was now having to experience the down side of the arrangement. Even so, it took all Palmer's self-control not to go out there and give Henzigger some of his own medicine.

The American turned and issued orders to his men. They stepped forward and reluctantly dragged Myburghe off the ground and hustled him indoors. It was clear they would sooner have left him there, but Henzigger clearly had further use for him. He followed, his phone clamped to his ear.

Palmer waited until they were out of sight, then slipped round to the front of the house. The lights here were now dead too; one of the men must have come round to knock them out as a precaution.

The two cars had been left with their doors open. Making sure he wasn't being observed, Palmer leaned in and took out the keys, then hurled them away into the darkness.

He made his way back to the maintenance workshop and rooted around in the dark until he found what he needed. It was time to prepare a diversion and reduce the numbers.

35

Riley estimated they were only minutes from the village of Colebrooke when her phone rang.

It was Henzigger.

"I guess you know where we are, right?" he said without preamble. He sounded angry but in control – just. "Don't bother saying anything pointless about how I'll never get away with this, Riley, or I'll go ahead and finish him off."

Myburghe was still alive. She switched on the loud-speaker so Mitcheson could hear.

"How was Henry Portius?" Henzigger continued. "I know you've seen him – not that he'll help you any." There was a hint of false bravado in his voice, which made Riley wonder what had happened. He still had an edge of hysteria in his tone, but it sounded even more strained than his earlier call.

"You're right," she replied. "Portius was a waste of time." Instinct told her that if she gave the impression she'd hit a stone wall at the embassy, Henzigger might feel less pressured. The fact that he knew she'd been to see the DEA man confirmed that he still had a contact on the inside. She made a mental note to let Weller know.

Mitcheson reached out and turned down the air conditioning, slowing down so she could hear more easily. Henzigger's breathing instantly filled the car, a rasping indication of stress that sounded almost painful.

"What do you want?" she asked calmly, to keep him talking. Give him too much time to think and he might simply cut his losses and kill Myburghe anyway.

"I know you're somewhere near, Riley. How far away?"

"A few minutes."

"Good girl. You alone?"

"Yes. I left Weller at the embassy." She was counting on his informants having told him about the presence of the senior policeman. A little show of information from her might persuade him to lower his guard.

She was right.

"That's good," he said. "We don't need any more cooks at this table. Make sure it stays that way. What about Palmer?"

"I don't know where he is," she replied truthfully. "I think Myburghe told him he could go."

"OK. When you get here, drive up to the house." The way he almost purred the instructions down the phone made Riley think he was smiling at how clever he was. She felt a shiver at the change in tone. Whatever control Henzigger had once possessed, he was losing it. In such a state of tension, he would doubtless be unusually aware of his surroundings, like a cornered animal. Maybe, she thought, he'd been sampling his own product.

"What about Myburghe?" she pressed him, hoping he or his friendly informant in the embassy hadn't become aware of John Mitcheson in the background. With Toby and up to three armed killers scattered around the place, they needed every advantage they could get.

"He's good. But he won't be if you get stupid."

"What do you want, Toby?"

"Salvation," he said with a ragged laugh that ended on a high note. "How about that? I want out of here and I figure you're the gal to help me. You do that and you'll get Myburghe back in one piece."

"How can I believe you?"

"Aw, shit, Riley. You're kidding me, right? Like you could care less about that high-class maggot. I need your help…

just for a few hours. We've got ourselves a serious problem, y'see, and we need a way out."

"Problem?"

"Yeah. Portius coming over has lit a fire under their asses. It seems the guys in Grosvenor Square have decided I have the plague." A voice spoke in the background and Henzigger broke off and muttered something in rapid Spanish. "Thing is, I got these three vaqueros with me and they're breathing down my neck, too. They say they came over to put the bite on Myburghe, but they don't fool me none – they're watching me, too. Fucking paisanos... they ain't got the first idea. Like it matters a whole hell of a lot now." He snorted and muttered something unintelligible under his breath.

Riley exchanged a look with Mitcheson. Henzigger was rambling. Two minutes ago he'd been cocksure and arrogant. Now all that had changed.

She looked up and saw the main entrance to Colebrooke House coming up fast, the headlights catching a flash of fluorescent sign and broken tape. She signalled for Mitcheson to pull in to the side of the road. "OK, so I arrive. Then what?"

Her question seemed to bring the American back to earth. "Then we talk business. You help get me out of here and we're like best buddies. I might even cut you in on a deal. What d'you say?"

"Depends what the deal is, doesn't it?" She watched Mitcheson climb out and walk to the back door. He leaned in, opened the lock-box and pulled out a shotgun and two automatic pistols. "It's got to be worthwhile."

"Uh-uh," Henzigger grunted. "You'll find out once you're here. But you'd better make it quick or His Excellency gets retired!" With a high-pitched laugh at his own sense of the dramatic, he hung up.

Riley slid across into the driving seat and looked out at Mitcheson. He held the shotgun in one hand and one of the pistols in the other. The weight of the second pistol dragged his windcheater down on one side, and he looked different. It was as if he'd suddenly become an integral part of the leaf-and-branch fabric behind him. She felt sorry for anyone he met in the woods.

Something in her expression must have alerted him. "You won't talk him round, Riley," he said softly. "Or the people with him. It's gone too far." He handed her the automatic. "This is just in case. Keep it out of sight. If you have to use it, click off the safety, point and shoot." He was aware of her reservations about using guns, but he also knew that there were times when even she would acknowledge there was no way round it.

"Maybe," she said breezily, tucking the pistol into the back of her jeans, "I'll bore them into submission."

He grinned briefly, then stepped away from the car and disappeared into the bushes at the side of the road. It was as simple as that; one second he was there, the next he'd gone. She waited, hands on the wheel, giving him a couple of minutes to get inside the grounds and observe her arrival at the front of the house.

When her inner clock said time was up, she drove the Land Cruiser past the broken police tape and up the drive. She skirted the fountain where Henry had taken his early bath and cruised the last two hundred yards to the front door. She turned and stopped with the nose of the car facing back down the drive.

As she turned off the lights and ignition, she looked up through the Plexiglas sun-roof and caught a flicker of movement against the sky. A silhouette of a man showed up on the roof of the house, peering over the parapet.

As she stepped clear of the car, she detected a smell of petrol in the air, and something burning, like old leaves.

Toby Henzigger opened the front door and beckoned her forward. He held a gun in one hand and was keeping most of his body behind cover. Riley walked across the gravel, taking care to keep her hands well away from her sides. She felt her scalp crawl at the idea of the man on the roof above her, and realised that if she'd stepped out of the car with a weapon in her hand, she'd have got no more than a few feet before being killed.

"Jacket off." Toby signalled with his gun for her to stand against the wall just inside the door. "Let's see what you've got under there." He sniggered at the double entendre.

Riley slid her jacket off and turned round. He took her mobile and dropped it into a tall Chinese vase on a side table. When he found the automatic, he looked surprised. He gave her a sharp look, then ejected the magazine and threw the gun to one side. It bounced off the marble floor and skidded under a chair.

"You're full of surprises, you know that? Guess you had to try, though, huh? I don't blame you – I'd do the same." He gestured towards the stairs with his gun. "OK, now we're going upstairs, nice and slow. You try anything, like mule kicks or any of that chop-socky shit, I'll shoot you in the back of the knee and let my three vaqueros finish you off. Then Myburghe gets it. You don't need telling how they like to use knives, right?" He chuckled nastily and stepped back a pace.

Riley stared at him, defying her nerves. "Toby," she told him as calmly as she could, "this isn't going to end how you think. Why don't you cut your losses and vanish? It's what you're good at, isn't it?"

There was a two-beat pause. Henzigger blinked as if he might be seriously considering the idea, then shook his head once. There was a rancid smell about him, of stale sweat and cooked food. Riley decided personal hygiene probably took a back seat when someone was facing the ruination of all their plans. Especially when operating at the deep, murky end of the pool.

She slipped her jacket back on and walked up the broad stairway past the row of Myburghe ancestors, their eyes following in grim disapproval. Once on the landing, Henzigger grunted and motioned her to the right. The air smelled musty up here, as if the house needed a good airing, and she guessed Myburghe hadn't bothered getting a cleaner in for a while. Henzigger kept his distance all the way, allowing her no opportunity to get too close.

He grunted again and indicated a room on the left, which Riley thought overlooked the rear of the house. It was plush and warm and the size of a small football pitch, and contained, among other things, a huge double bed. Somebody was lying on it.

Sir Kenneth Myburghe.

He was positioned with his body tilted sideways, and Riley thought he was dead until he opened his eyes and glared at Henzigger. Then she saw his hands were tied tightly behind him by a length of curtain rope. The former ambassador was dressed in shoes, pale trousers and a crumpled blue shirt. There was a vivid red mark on the side of his face, rapidly turning into a bruise. At least, she thought, he's still alive.

"What's this," she said. "Did thieves fall out?"

"Something like that," said Henzigger genially, settling himself against a large, ornate dresser, from where he could command the room. He lifted one foot and rested it on a steel briefcase, of the sort favoured by trendy city types. It looked heavy. "His Excellency here has just decided he doesn't want to play with us blue-collar types any more. That's a shame, because he's been instrumental in clearing a route for us to ship in our product." He looked at Riley with a faint grin. "But I guess you know all about that, right? Portius is a real piece of work, isn't he? I still have friends in the agency... they keep me up to speed about who's doing what. Maybe I should get someone to visit with old Henry and do a number on his arms and legs. That'd stop him interfering. I do hate people who mess with my plans." He turned his head and looked at Myburghe, then raised the gun and sighted down the barrel. His finger tightened on the trigger.

Riley tensed, knowing there was nothing she could do to stop him. The distance between them was far too great, and with all his experience, Henzigger would kill Myburghe and calmly take her out as well before she got halfway across the room.

On the bed, Sir Kenneth stared dumbly at the gun, anticipating the bullet. The fact that he kept his eyes open was the nearest thing to courage Riley had seen him display, and she felt a grudging respect for him.

Henzigger grinned and made a loud 'pow' noise, then lowered the gun.

Myburghe flinched. His body seemed to deflate like a collapsing air mattress, and his face burned red with shame. It was soon obvious why, as a dark patch began to spread across the front of his pants.

"For Christ's sake, Henzigger!" Riley protested, and felt contempt for Myburghe's tormentor. Right then, all she wanted was for Palmer or Mitcheson to come through the door and shoot him.

"Oh, dear," said Henzigger, and looked at Myburghe with an expression of disgust. "Wonder what your Queen Elizabeth would say about that? Anyway, what was I was saying? Oh, yes... Lord Pisspants here wants to renege on our deal, which, by the way, Riley, is paying for this pile of shit to be kept standing a few more years. Did you know that? So much for the honour and integrity of the diplomatic corps, hunh? Thing is, the deal also included a plane out of here, nice and private. Just me and my friends. Only it's all gone wrong and there ain't no plane. Still... I got some of the money." He tapped the briefcase with his foot. "Unfortunately, I have no way of getting out of here. Which means I still need his help. Or yours."

He turned and pointed the gun at her and smiled.

"You must be joking," Riley muttered.

Henzigger shed the smile in an instant, his eyes going dark. "Joking? Actually, no. Let me show you."

With that, he turned and shot Myburghe.

36

The blast was deafening, and the shock waves made Riley's ears ring. On the bed, Myburghe took the full force of the bullet and was flung over on to his front, a fine spray of blood fanning out across the bedspread, bright and vivid against the pale fabric. He groaned once and lay still.

Riley was stunned but took care not to move. Henzigger was watching her like a hawk, the gun now aimed at her. His hand was as steady as a rock.

"That was a demonstration. I only winged him. You refuse me again, he gets another one. And believe me, I can keep this up for hours without killing him. I've done it before. Want to see?"

"No!" She felt nauseous with anger. She couldn't see where Myburghe had been hit, but even a slight wound could kill him with the shock.

"Perfect." Henzigger relaxed and blew down the gun barrel in a sick parody of an old-style gunfighter. Suddenly he was all geniality again. "Now we have a working understanding. Ironic, really, because those Colombians have been itching to do that for weeks. They may be peasants and have shit for brains, but they know how to read a man, you know? Low animal cunning, I guess. They figured he was going to be a liability long before I did. In fact, I was the only thing stood between them and him getting a taste of the blade."

"I'll make sure he recommends you for a medal," she said with unrestrained sarcasm.

It rolled off his back like water. "First things first: I need to get out of the country. Seems my former employers –

the DEA – never quite bought the story about my innocence, and they've slammed most of the doors on me. I bet they've got photos up at every port, too. But I figure a kick-ass reporter and a former British Ambassador might know where all the gaps are – am I right?"

Riley stared at him. He was actually expecting her to get him out on a boat or plane? He must be mad. She had no more idea of a back door out of the country than he did. At best she could take a guess, like stealing a boat and hoping to get across the channel without being run down by a super-tanker. But that wasn't what he meant.

He wanted a plane, preferably something with a lot of range to put himself quickly beyond the reach of Weller and Portius. That meant a corrupt pilot or a busy commercial flight, neither of which could be rustled up in the middle of the night on a whim.

But if she suggested that, Myburghe would get another bullet.

She had to stall for time. Time for Mitcheson or Palmer – and where the hell was Palmer? – to come and narrow the odds. And time for Weller's men in black to come abseiling through the windows.

"I need to think about it," she said, hoping it sounded convincing. "There are a couple of places, but I'd have to check."

"OK. That's cool." He surprised her by agreeing readily, then added the killer line: "Say, twenty minutes. That do you?" His smile was a cold, empty facial gesture, like a death mask in a museum, and she realised that sometime in the past few hours, maybe even days, Toby Henzigger had strayed over the borderline from paranoia into the cloudy realms of madness. "Ten seconds longer and he dies."

He picked up the steel briefcase and walked out, leaving

Riley staring after him. At least he hadn't tied her up. Then she realised why as the key turned in the lock.

She hurried over to the bed. Myburghe was groaning softly, his body quivering with shock. Gently, she eased him over so she could locate the wound. He cried out, his voice shrill as a child, and she felt for where the stickiness was worst. It was a stomach wound, and deeper than Henzigger had probably intended.

Riley fought to quell a rising sense of panic. Unless she got him out of here, he was going to die.

She crossed to the window. What she could see of the garden showed nothing likely to help her out of the room. She didn't fancy her chances of climbing down, as there was no handy drainpipe, merely a glass conservatory roof below, waiting to break her fall.

And if she survived that, there was the man on the roof; he'd have her in his sights the moment she appeared. It would be like potting lame ducks.

She went over to the door and listened. No sounds from out there, but it didn't mean Henzigger wasn't within reach, waiting for her to make a break. It would be what he'd expect her to do. She tried the handle, anyway. Locked.

She heard a sound behind her. Myburghe was watching her from the bed, his face creased in pain. "I have a spare key," he said with surprising clarity. "In the dresser." He moved his eyes to indicate the piece of furniture beside which Henzigger had been standing.

"Don't move," Riley urged him, and checked his stomach. It was seeping blood in a faint but steady flow. His skin was horribly pale and covered in a film of perspiration, and she could feel a faint tremor running through him, as if an internal motor was chugging away but gradually running down, starved of its vital fuel. Grabbing a pillow off the bed, she ripped off the covering and wadded it under his shirt, pressing it tight against the wound. It wasn't ideal battle-trauma treatment, but it was all she could think of for the moment.

"Top... top drawer left," Myburghe whispered. "Socks."

Riley stepped across to the dresser and pulled open the drawer. Under a pile of socks she found a large, ornate bronze key with a cloverleaf top. She hurried over to the door and tried it. It turned with a slight grating sound.

She inched the door open, praying the hinges stayed silent. The landing was clear. She pulled the door shut behind her and ghosted across the thick carpet to peer over the banister. No sound from the foyer downstairs, no sense of anyone waiting to blow her head off. On the other hand, that didn't mean they weren't there. It was a stark choice: either go down and face whatever was there, or stay up here and wait for Henzigger's twenty minutes to tick away.

She checked her watch. Two minutes gone. Eighteen more and Henzigger would be in here with his tame vaqueros. She didn't want to be here when that happened.

She crept down the stairs as quietly as she could. If Henzigger or his men put in an appearance now, she wouldn't stand a chance, unless she pelted them with the portraits of Myburghe's ancestors, still glaring down at her as if she was responsible for everything that was happening right under their starchy noses.

The Chinese vase. Her mobile was still inside where Henzigger had dumped it. The top was too narrow to get her arm in, and when she turned it upside down, the mobile wedged across the neck. With a sigh, she looked round for inspiration, and spotted a narrow run of Persian carpet. She eased the vase on to its side and rolled the carpet around it, then stamped on it as hard as she could. She was rewarded with the muffled sound of breaking porcelain. She unravelled the carpet to find the vase in a million pieces, with the mobile among the fragments. Hopefully, Myburghe would think the sacrifice of the vase worthwhile.

As she scooped up the mobile, she spotted the automatic lying on the floor. There were no bullets because Henzigger had slipped the magazine in his pocket. She grabbed it anyway. If things got truly desperate, she could always throw it at someone. She was contemplating going to see what else Mitcheson might have in the rear of the Land Cruiser when there was a double-tap in the distance. She froze.

A handgun?

There was silence, then the heavier boom of a shotgun. Palmer or Mitcheson?

Alarmed voices echoed close to the house in urgent Spanish. One of them had to be the lookout on the roof, directing operations for his colleagues below.

Riley ran back upstairs, abandoning all attempts to keep quiet. Now Henzigger's men knew Riley had company, they would be coming back in double-quick time to begin a classic hostage situation. She hit the bedroom door on the run and made straight for the bed. She had to get Sir Kenneth out of here, whether he was ready to move or not. Without him, Henzigger and his men couldn't do much but stand and fight or turn and run. Either way, they wouldn't be able to use hostages if they couldn't find them.

"Come on," she said, and shook Myburghe gently by the shoulder. He didn't respond, so she slapped his face. He gave a start and looked up at her, eyes dulled with pain and shock. He looked even worse than before, yet she'd only been gone a couple of minutes. Riley realised he must be losing blood at a terrifying rate, his energy and life-force seeping away with it. "We have to move," she told him fiercely. "If we stay here, Henzigger will kill us."

He gave a faint nod and tried to lift himself off the bed, gasping in pain. Riley put her arm beneath him and eased him upright, then helped him to stagger towards the door.

The only problem was, where to go?

The roof? It's where everyone goes in films, she thought, when they're being pursued by bad guys. God knows why, because they always get caught. Downstairs, then. It would also be easier for Sir Kenneth than climbing up.

But he didn't see it that way.

"Up," he gasped, and pointed with a mottled hand to a stretch of blank wall, where no furniture stood. She thought he'd lost it completely, because she couldn't see anything. Then she realised there was the faint outline of a door in the heavy embroidery-style pattern. It must lead to a stair-case to the roof.

"You can't climb," Riley told him. There was also the gunman up there, waiting for them to show their faces.

"Yes... can," he insisted. "Fresh air... please." He looked sideways at her, his eyes flickering in a beseeching manner, and she nodded. Hell, why not – it was his house.

They crabbed through the narrow door and out on to a small landing, with the stairs leading upwards. The stairwell was cold and dark, and every small sound seemed to echo with terrifying loudness. Riley slipped the automatic out of her pocket and helped Sir Kenneth sit on the stairs. He nodded and urged her on, apparently understanding that the next bit was best done without carrying a dying man.

She flexed her arm, already aching from the strain of supporting the injured man, then crept up the stairs and tried the door. It gave with a faint click of the lock, reminding her of the last time she'd come this way. She waited a few seconds, but there was no sound of movement. There was nothing for it but to step outside and investigate.

She pushed the door open and felt around on the floor with her free hand. Nothing. The wind must have swept it clear of any remaining nutshells. She stood up and stepped through, closing the door behind her, then flattened herself against the wall of the stairwell structure. Up here the night sky had never seemed so attractive, or so far away. A breeze drifted through the treetops beyond the parapet, and a plane droned somewhere high above her. There was no sound to indicate the presence of the enemy, although she knew he was up here somewhere. And his gun carried live rounds.

She peered round the corner of the structure and immediately spotted a darker shadow against the parapet a few feet away. She waited, her eyes adjusting to the poor light. The shadow shifted and became a heavily built man. He was peering over the edge in the direction of the stables.

She couldn't see a weapon, but she knew it must be in his hand.

She thought about Myburghe, his life leaking away on the stairs behind her. And Palmer and Mitcheson, moving around below in the darkness, possibly even now being watched by the gunman. There was no other choice.

37

The man was so busy watching the gardens below, he had no time to react. Riley swapped the gun to her left hand, took three long paces and jammed the barrel into the side of his throat, grinding it hard into the flesh.

He froze with a shrill cry of pain, and she grabbed his right arm just above the elbow and jerked it sharply backwards. But his hand came up empty. She realised with a sickening feeling that he was left-handed.

Sensing her mistake, he began to turn, shoulders bunching with effort. Riley made a split-second decision: it was all or nothing. Since she couldn't very well shoot him with an empty gun, she did the next best thing and slammed it hard across the side of his head. Twice. The shock of impact travelling up her arm sickened her, but it was preferable to letting him gain control.

With a groan, the man slumped to the floor, his weapon clattering to one side. Dropping the empty gun, Riley felt for his shoes and quickly stripped out the laces. Seconds later, she had his fingers lashed tightly together behind his back with no room for movement.

She scrabbled around until her fingers encountered his gun. It had a chunky, compact feel, but was surprisingly light, and she thought it might be a machine pistol called a MAC10. A horrible weapon at close quarters, it was favoured by gunmen who weren't fond of selecting their targets with care.

The gun had a slim flashlight clipped to the barrel. She snapped it on and looked over the gun-sight into the man's face. He was square-jawed and unshaven, with lank, greasy hair and a bruise down one side of his face. It was too mature for the one she'd just given him, and she guessed he must be one of the men Mitcheson had encountered by the river in London.

Her hands began to tremble with reaction, and she killed the light, taking several deep breaths. Then she hurried back down the stairs to where Sir Kenneth was lying curled in on himself. His breathing was hoarse and growing fainter, and she debated leaving him where he was rather than risk killing him by hauling him up on to the roof.

In the end she decided that leaving him to suffer more of Henzigger's venom was no contest, and helped him up the stairs as gently as she could.

Once through the door, she lowered him behind the cover of a skylight and made him as comfortable as possible. She switched on the flashlight again for a quick check. He was breathing in short, laboured gasps, his face creased and turning grey. A red bubble appeared at the corner of his mouth and his throat made a gurgling sound. When she shifted his legs into a more comfortable position, her hand came away sticky with blood.

"Keep still," she said, although she doubted he could hear her. She dug out her mobile and dialled Weller's number. Dialling 999 would probably only have summoned an unarmed community support officer in a Vauxhall Astra, more accustomed to dealing with sheep stealing and travellers on cannabis. She didn't want to be responsible for sending an innocent into certain death at the hands of Henzigger and his Colombian cronies. Weller would be able to whistle up the armed heavy mob at the drop of a hat.

The signal was poor. She stood up and moved about until she got a good dialling tone.

As Weller answered, a shot rang out and chipped away a

hand-sized piece of parapet near Riley's head. She swore and ducked, the ricochet zipping past her ear like an angry hornet.

"Jesus," Weller muttered. "Was that what I think it was?"

"It's the gunfight at the OK Corral," Riley shouted back. "Colebrooke House, on the double… four handguns and Myburghe seriously wounded." She scuttled back to the door and took out the key, closing and locking it from the outside. Then she returned to Myburghe's side.

"What do you expect me to do about it?" Weller sounded peeved but she knew he was just sounding off. In the background she heard him banging on something to attract attention, and guessed he'd got the phone on broadcast and was urging his troops into action.

Another shot whined overhead. She leaned over Myburghe and flicked on the flashlight. He looked even worse, his breathing now almost undetectable and a line of blood worming its way from his mouth down his chin. If she didn't get him to hospital soon, he wasn't going to live.

"Come on, Weller!" she shouted back. "This is the Royal Triangle. There are armed response units less than fifteen minutes away. And you'd better get a medevac chopper in – Sir Kenneth's on the roof and about to quit the diplomatic corps for good."

"How bad?" His voice sounded shaky, as if he was jogging.

"Lung damage, I think. He's breathing blood."

Weller uttered several obscenities then asked, "Is Palmer with you?"

"Yes. He's holding the Alamo downstairs." She decided not to mention the shotgun or the automatic pistol. Or John Mitcheson.

"And Henzigger?"

"Alive and spitting. He's got three Colombian helpers with him, all armed." Just then, the man she'd hit with the pistol groaned, reminding her of his presence. "Correction – make that two; I've got one tied up."

"Have you, by God?" He laughed outright. "Well, make sure you stay out of the way. When the armed response units come in, they won't be checking IDs. Any person carrying anything more threatening than a teapot gets one warning. After that, they're a statistic."

Riley took that to mean that Weller knew Palmer was more prepared than she had let on. A door slammed in the background and a motor warmed up with a high-pitched whine and settled into the whop-whop-whop of a helicopter's rotor blades. She smiled. Weller had been ready and was travelling in style.

The connection died.

She turned to find Myburghe watching her. He gave a weak shake of his head and reached out to grasp her arm.

"Too late, Miss Gavin," he whispered, and dragged himself up a little until his shoulders rested against the skylight frame. It must have taken enormous will, but she guessed the pain was no longer registering.

She moved to brush his hand away, not in the mood to listen to any pleas for forgiveness. Too much misery and death had flowed from his actions already, and it wasn't over yet. But his fingers dug into her arm with renewed strength.

"Just hear me... out," he murmured desperately. "I'm not going to... make excuses... It's too late for that. I want to put things right... for the girls."

"Better make it quick, then," she suggested coldly. She switched on the flashlight to check his face. "Or they'll be taking two bodies off this roof."

Myburghe managed a half smile, the blood on his chin giving him the appearance of a carnival ghoul. "Dear me. And I thought Hilary and Palmer were hard-nosed." He tried not to cough and inhaled deeply, his eyes rolling with a fresh burst of pain. When it receded, he tried again. "I was foolish, Miss Gavin. May I call you Riley?"

She nodded although she doubted he could see her. "Why not?"

"I thought I could play cards and couldn't. Thought I knew horses but didn't. Lost everything. Have you ever lost everything, Riley? I suppose not... you've... probably more sense. I nearly lost my wife, God bless her... but I did lose all her money." He sucked in more air. "I got into debt at a casino in Bogotá, you see. Many years ago and... big money. Too much to wipe off. Someone... someone suggested I speak to a local 'facilitator'. Turned out to be a money man for one of the cartels. Sure you know all about them... more than me, probably."

"Just a bit," she lied. "How was Henzigger involved?"

"Hen...zigger?" His head dropped and she thought he'd gone, but he looked up again and nodded, sucking in breath. "Met him at a local embassy thing... he appeared to know about my... problems. Told me what he could do to help. I refused... at first... then I couldn't any longer. In too deep. He set up the meeting, and from there... was downhill all the way." He gave a sickly grin as if acknowledging his own weakness. "Won't bore you with details. They paid me a lot of money to put my name to... to making the logistics work. Needed a shipping company for the boat and freight... freight forwarding for the papers. Easiest money I ever made." He coughed and a gob of blood landed on his chest and his eyes bulged. "Damn... bloody... bloody mess... Hilary was... was my man. Didn't want to get involved...

drugs... but he was running from a rape charge in Belize when I... took him on. I was advised to get a good man... twenty-four hours. Then, when it was all happening... I got... cold feet. Should have turned myself in... but they tracked down Christian. Didn't count on that... bloody stupid of me. Thought he'd be safe away from here."

"Why didn't you tell us?" she asked him. Down below there was shouting as Henzigger and his two remaining men searched the grounds, their echoing voices making it impossible to place their whereabouts. She hoped none of them thought about the scaffolding as a way on to the roof, or she and Myburghe were finished.

Myburghe stared blankly at her.

"If you suspected Christian was dead, why didn't you say something?"

"Couldn't do... anything else. Needed you two to help protect the girls. They said they would go the same way... if I didn't co-operate. Other papers to fix, you see... more shipments to come. Henzigger knew his career was done... and... was going private. He needed my help." His voice dropped to a murmur, and Riley guessed he was on auto-pilot, his head doing the talking while his body ran down like an old clock mechanism. "Didn't want to do it... must believe that. Far too late for heroics." Something like a sob came from him, but it could have been air escaping from his damaged lungs.

"How many shipments, in all?" she asked, leaning close to him.

He grunted and moved slightly. "Three sizeable... don't know the details... Several smaller. Rest of the time... they used my name for papers..." His voice faded.

A shotgun boomed out below, and she began to be fearful for Palmer and Mitcheson. With Henzigger and two

Colombians left, they could easily get caught in the cross-fire. And Henzigger had the aggression, experience and motivation to make it happen. He also had absolutely nothing to lose.

There was more shouting, and she recognised Henzigger's voice, pitched high and challenging, echoing through the trees and rising above her rooftop position.

"C'mon – Palmer, is it? I know you're out there. This isn't your kinda game, you know? Give it up now while you can!"

She left Sir Kenneth and risked a peep over the parapet, but couldn't see anything. Wherever Henzigger was, he was being cautious enough to stay out of sight. But someone must have been watching for her. There was a flash and another chunk of masonry exploded painfully near her hand, sending a jolt of pain the length of her arm.

The MAC10 went spinning off into the darkness.

"Was that you, Palmer?" Henzigger's voice floated up again, taunting his unseen opponent. "You ain't got what it takes for this!" Two more shots whistled close by the edge of the roof to emphasise his contempt, accompanied by wild whoops from two other voices out in the darkness. Then Henzigger called again: "Francisco? Where the hell are you, compadre? Get that bastard off the roof NOW!"

Riley rolled behind the parapet, clutching her hand to her chest. Without the flashlight, she couldn't see what damage had been done, but there wasn't time to dwell on it. She wasn't sure who Francisco was, but she was prepared to bet it was the man she'd hit with the gun. Henzigger might send one of his other men up here to investigate any minute, and she couldn't afford to get trapped up here.

She scrambled to her feet and sprinted for the far end of the roof, skidding on fragments of grit. She clambered out on to the scaffolding. It was open and risky in the dark, but better than the enclosed environment of the stairs. The structure rattled beneath her, vibrations carrying through the planking and sending down a shower of fine stone dust around her. Ten seconds later she was on the ground, peering round the edge of the building.

Nobody in sight. She scuttled along the front of the house, hugging the shadows and hoping that if Palmer was out here he didn't mistake her for one of the bad guys.

She reached for the car keys. With luck, Mitcheson might have left something else on the back seat.

No keys.

Damn. She was sure she'd put them in her pocket. They must have fallen out somewhere. It was too dangerous to go back and look.

Standing out in the open trying to jemmy the car open was a passport to the afterlife, so she did the next best thing and made her way towards the kitchen. If nothing else she could throw meat knives until the police arrived.

Then she remembered the shotgun they'd taken off the unfortunate Charles Clarke on the night of the wedding party. Rockface had locked it in a metal cabinet in a storeroom behind the kitchen. It was risky entering the house to get it, but it was better than waiting out here to get shot.

As she rounded the corner near the entrance to the kitchen, she came face to face with a bulky figure waving an automatic pistol.

38

It was too late to duck back. Riley kept going, straightening her forearm and swinging it into the man's throat with all the power she could muster.

He made a harsh, choking noise and hit the ground on his back, leaving behind an aroma of fried onions. His gun flew away and hit the wall of the house, where it went off with a bang and a flash, lighting up the surrounding area like a flare. With no time to scoop it up, Riley kept running, bouncing off the doorframe and falling inside.

Behind her, the man clambered to his feet and scrabbled away, shouting in a hoarse voice for someone called Baga. Or maybe he knew some English.

It was deathly quiet inside the house after the sound of the shot, with just the heavy tick of a clock somewhere nearby. She was in the kitchen. There were no lights on, but the room was saved from total darkness by a couple of red pilot lights on the wall above the cookers.

Riley waited until she got her breath back, then inched through the gloom, feeling her way across the stone-flagged floor until she reached the door of the storeroom. She pushed it open and stepped inside.

"You took your time." The voice came in the same instant that the light came on, and Riley thought her heart was going to stop. She spun round, flattening herself against a wall.

It was Palmer, leaning against the metal cabinet as if he was waiting for tea to be served. He looked unruffled but serious.

"I've been up on the roof waiting for you to do something!"

Riley muttered scathingly, determined not to show how scared she was. She brushed him aside and opened the gun cabinet. It gave her something to do while she hid her enormous relief at seeing him, and to steady her breathing. If she even thought about what she was doing right now, she'd probably fall to pieces.

To her relief, the cabinet still contained the shotgun and the box of cartridges. "Why?" she asked. "What have you been doing?"

"Waiting for you, mostly. I figured you'd be along soon –" He broke off, staring at her chest. "Christ, what did you do up there – slaughter a heifer?"

"What?" She peered down and was horrified to see her jacket and shirt were drenched with darkening blood, with more on her hands and arms. It must have come from helping Sir Kenneth up the stairs to the roof. She also had a cut on one hand, probably caused by the piece of flying masonry. Fortunately, it wasn't serious. "I didn't realise… damn – my favourite jacket!" She tugged at a large tear in one sleeve, and felt a chill in her stomach as she realised how close the bullet had come.

Palmer cast around and grabbed a sweatshirt hanging on a hook behind the door. He gestured to a small sink on the other side of the room. "You might want to wash your hands and put this on. I'll watch your back while you change." He gave a tight smile. "Glad to see it's not your blood." Then he turned away to watch the door, suddenly awkward.

Riley nodded, feeling nauseous at the sight of the blood, but oddly touched by Palmer's concern. "Thanks." She stripped off her jacket and shirt, unselfconscious about him turning round and seeing her in her frillies. Now, she figured, wasn't the time for girlish modesty. She washed

273

her hands and arms thoroughly, turning the water pink, then dried them on a handful of paper towels. "What were the shots I heard?"

"You mean apart from the ones they were firing at you?" He handed her the sweatshirt. "No idea. I think they were getting nervous and making noises for the sake of it."

"There was something burning when I got here. Was that you?"

"Guilty, m'lady," he admitted. "By the fiendish application of paper, old leaves and rubbing two sticks together, I created a diversion and Henzigger sent one of his gunmen to investigate. We bumped into each other, but he didn't want to dance."

"Bumped?" She wanted to ask if the man had got up and walked away again, but decided against it. If Palmer was still on his feet and unharmed, it seemed doubtful.

He hefted an automatic pistol she hadn't noticed before and smiled regretfully. "Only bumped, I'm afraid. He was too quick on his feet. Have you seen Myburghe?"

"I had to leave him on the roof. Henzigger shot him."

"Christ. How bad?"

"He needs a hospital, but I don't think he'll last long enough." She described where she'd left Myburghe and the Colombian, and told him of her brief exchange with the man outside.

"Damn," Palmer said calmly. "I must be getting deaf – I didn't hear that one coming." He checked the magazine of the automatic and said, "So we've got one man – possibly two – and Henzigger."

"And Mitcheson. He's armed, by the way."

Palmer nodded, unsurprised. "I had a feeling he was out there. Thanks for the warning."

"I also called Weller. He's on his way in with an armed

response team."

"How much time have we got?"

"Fifteen minutes, at a guess. Why?"

"Too long. Henzigger's not going to sit around waiting. They had a plane arranged to take them out, but it failed to turn up. That's why he's so pissed. He'll want to finish this, and the longer we leave him, the more likely he is to find us. The odds aren't great."

"Why won't he run?"

"He will, eventually. But we're not dealing with rational men; he'll want to silence us, and his Colombians won't dare go back without knowing Myburghe is dead."

"What do you suggest?"

He took the shotgun out of the cabinet and loaded it, then handed it to her with some spare cartridges. He jerked his head towards the roof. "You'll be better off back on the roof watching Myburghe. Try to keep him awake. I'll see if I can hook up with Mitcheson without him blowing me away. Anyone comes over the roof or through the door without singing out who they are, point and pull."

Riley resisted the idea. "But –"

"But nothing." John Mitcheson's voice came from right outside the door. "This isn't your thing, Riley. It's ours. We need to know you're safely out of the way. Go now. We'll watch your back."

Riley did as instructed, waving at Mitcheson's dense shadow against the wall as she passed.

Palmer watched Riley go, ready for the first sign of movement by the trees. He waited for her to disappear among the scaffolding, before turning towards Mitcheson.

"You heard?" he said. "We've got company coming."

"Yeah. Not soon enough, though. Let's finish it."

Palmer nodded. "It might be best if you aren't seen here."

Mitcheson grunted. "I'll deal with it when it comes, don't worry."

Palmer scanned the gardens for signs of activity. But if Henzigger was out there, he was keeping his head down. And probably becoming more desperate by the minute. Men like Toby Henzigger were resourceful, and with a briefcase full of money, there would be plenty of takers with boats and small aircraft willing to provide an escape route, no questions asked.

For the moment, though, he knew Henzigger wanted to finish it on his terms. Without Riley, Palmer or Myburghe to testify to his involvement in the drugs shipments, the American probably reasoned on having a good chance of getting away free. He also had to satisfy his Colombian watchers that he had control of the mopping-up, or they might have orders to demonstrate their displeasure in an extreme way.

Which made Riley and Myburghe the main targets for his anger.

The only spoiler was him and Mitcheson, stuck here clutching weapons when any minute now Weller's men might come swarming down out of the night sky. Awkward wouldn't even come close.

"Lead the way, Hawkeye," he called. He hoped Mitcheson would have the sense to keep his head down when the shit hit the fan. With his past record and his previous involvement in Colombia, the last thing Mitcheson needed was to be found in the middle of a drugs scam originating from the same corner of the world. "I'll take the stable," he added. "You watch the trees." He waited for an acknowledgment, but there was silence. "Hello?"

Palmer swore softly and slid outside. Everything was quiet, save for a soft breeze ruffling the foliage in the trees. An owl hooted somewhere and a night creature gave a high-pitched squeak. Without all the shooting it could almost have been a normal evening.

He made his way across the lawns to the stable block. Being out in the open set all his alarm bells screaming, but there was no alternative. Going round via the trees would be noisier and take too long. And Henzigger wasn't going to wait forever. He also had help, which gave the American a considerable edge when it came to hunting in the dark.

He reached the corner of the stalls and paused. If he'd been in Henzigger's shoes, he would have been waiting outside, knowing there were others out here who had to make the first approach. But as he'd said to Riley, Henzigger wasn't rational.

A sound came from a stall halfway along the opposite block. Nobody showed themselves, so he slipped back and round to the rear of the accommodation block and found an open window into one of the rooms. It was a tight squeeze, but he took a deep breath and hoisted himself on to the ledge. He slid through and waited to see if someone came to investigate. Nobody did.

Short as the corridor was between the room and the anteroom where David Hilary had died, it was the longest walk of Palmer's life. He stepped carefully along the cold floor, checking each room was clear. Each tiny sound he made seemed magnified a hundred times. Every step of the way he expected Henzigger or one of his men to appear. His shoes crunched on minute dirt particles as he emerged into the anteroom, and his stomach locked tight at the thought that he might be walking into a trap.

It was too dark to see if the anteroom had been cleaned.

He could smell the sickly aroma of blood overlaying the sharp tang of chemicals, and guessed the forensic teams hadn't yet finished. This was confirmed when he saw the fluttering outline of plastic crime scene tape stretched across the open doorway.

He peered through the gap between the door and the jamb. It gave him a narrow view out across the yard. If Henzigger's men weren't in here, they must be out there somewhere. And being very patient.

He checked his watch. There wasn't much time left. Any minute now, a helicopter would be dropping armed men behind the trees. Anyone moving would be spotted through image intensifiers. No doubt they would have been alerted about the shooting, and in spite of their rules of engagement, Palmer didn't place too much reliance on first warnings. In a hot fire-zone, anyone with a weapon would be classified as the enemy and taken out.

In the distance a shot slammed out, followed by a stuttering rattle. A high-rate automatic, he guessed, and felt his shoulders bunch at the thought of the hail of bullets slicing through the night. It was followed by a double-tap, then silence.

Mitcheson?

Palmer edged round the doorjamb and ducked out into the yard. With this end clear, he could now check the stalls. He was barely halfway there, when he saw movement across the yard in a doorway. A tall shape came charging out of the gloom, the gleam of a pistol in his hand.

Henzigger. The American had caught him blind-sided.

Palmer threw himself flat, instinctively making himself as small a target as possible. As he did so, the gun in Henzigger's hand flared, lighting up the yard momentarily, the sound of the shot reaching Palmer a nano-second later.

As he hit the ground, a burning sensation seared his back. He yelped involuntarily and rolled away in desperation. Thrusting out the pistol, he pulled the trigger three times, the shots merging like a drum roll. The yard lit up again and he heard a scream and the thump of a body falling.

The American swore. It was a harsh, featureless word ending in a sob.

Lying here, Palmer knew he was just as exposed as Henzigger, especially if the American had anyone backing him up. He flexed his shoulders and a sharp pain lanced across his back. But at least he could still move. So far, he thought wryly, so good. He checked his surroundings. The dark bulk of a stall was just inches away. Rolling over, he reached up and felt for the bolt on the door, easing it across. If he could get inside, he'd be safe.

But Henzigger had other ideas.

As Palmer pulled himself towards the door, there was a click in the dark. A light came on and the muscles in his neck went rigid. He looked round.

Toby Henzigger was hanging off one of the opposing stable doors, his hand on a light switch. In his other hand was a gun.

The man looked almost demented. His clothing was dirty and ripped, and one arm was hanging down, the sleeve shredded. His shirt was soaked in blood, which was dripping from his stomach and forming a small, glossy puddle at his feet. He had a wild look in his eyes. For a man who'd just been shot, he looked livelier than he had any right to.

Palmer stayed very still. His gun was by his side but pointing the wrong way. It would take a visible effort to bring it round. If he tried, Henzigger, even in his state, would kill him without blinking.

"Looks like you've lost this one, Toby," Palmer said, with more confidence than he felt. His voice was shaky and he felt an insane urge to giggle. His back was burning badly now, and he was beginning to feel light-headed. He tried to rationalise his situation; either he'd taken another shot without realising it and was sinking into shock, or he was just over-excited.

He wondered how Riley was getting on. He hoped she'd got out all right.

Henzigger nodded slowly. His body shuddered. He took a couple of great gulps of air and swayed a bit, but the gun in his fist didn't waver by a millimetre. Palmer gave him full marks for cool; no denials, no threats, no claims about how he was going to get out of here and live the high life somewhere in the Caribbean. He simply stared in what could have been bewilderment or anger, but which Palmer guessed was just good old, plain disbelief.

"Damn," Henzigger said at last in a breathless whisper, as if reading his mind. "I should have listened to Hilary. He said you were bad news. You and your girlfriend." He coughed and spat something on to the floor, where it lay glistening wetly in the dirt. "Say, as a matter of interest, she's not butch, is she?"

Palmer shook his head, eyes on Henzigger's gun muzzle. He knew what the American was doing: the question was meant to provoke him into an unwise move. But he wasn't going to play. They were thirty feet apart, which was quite a distance for a pistol shot in dubious light. But it was still like staring into a black bucket, and he didn't doubt that Henzigger knew how to shoot. One wrong flinch and that would be the end of it.

"Yeah, well... who cares, right?" Henzigger coughed again and shook his head. "Are the cops coming?"

Palmer nodded once. "Not just ordinary cops, either."

"Yeah?" Henzigger sounded genuinely interested, in spite of the rattle in his throat. Palmer thought he might be balancing on the edge of hysteria. "Black-hats, huh? Say, is it right they still carry truncheons over here? Hell of a way to arm cops, you ask me. If they tried that in LA, they'd get the crap beat out of them." He tried to laugh but it brought on a fit of coughing instead. He nearly doubled over with the effort, but the gun never wavered, and Palmer had to marvel at the other man's control.

He heard a noise from out in the darkness. A footfall. Deliberate. If Henzigger heard it, too, he didn't react. If it was one of the Colombians, Palmer knew he was in trouble. If not, he didn't want to get in the way. But he might as well play for time.

"Why did you have to do that to Hilary?" he asked.

Henzigger shrugged. He didn't seem to be in a hurry. "Shit, that was the Colombians, not me. He got in the way and let Myburghe slip away. That wasn't supposed to happen. I woulda just given him a slap, but they had their orders. That's how they do things back there. It's called — what's it in French?"

Palmer supplied the answer. "Pour encourager les autres." He'd been right. Hilary's death had been punishment, not torture.

But Toby didn't appear to have heard him. "Well, can't stand talking here all day," he said suddenly. He staggered away from the stable door and stood directly beneath the light illuminating the yard, suddenly larger than life. He even had a semblance of a smile on his face. "Things to do, places to go… " He was talking louder than before, and making no attempt to hide, as if bidding goodnight to a fellow drinker in a bar.

281

Palmer stared at him. What was he playing at?

Then he had his answer. John Mitcheson stepped into the pool of light. He looked calm and steady and dangerous and was carrying his automatic by his side. He eyed Toby carefully, assessing the possible threat.

"Whoa," grunted Toby. "Who've we got here?" He turned his head unsteadily to stare at Palmer with almost comical accusation. "A new boy? You been playing sneaky, Palmer. That's not cricket." He turned back to Mitcheson and said, "What've you done to my vaqueros, huh?" He waved a vague hand, like a drunk talking to a lamppost. "No need to answer that. Believe it or not, they were supposed to be good. Top notch. Just shows, you can't trust anybody these days." His voice trailed off into a faint gargle and he spat again, then shuddered as if in revulsion.

"Put it down," Mitcheson urged him quietly. "It's over."

"Uh-uh." Henzigger winced, then spoke in a rush, his chest heaving. "Can't do that. If the black-hats get their hands on me, they'll lock me up for a zillion years. And that ain't me. I'm too keen on the open air… and the wind in my face." He smiled softly. "Sorry."

As he finished speaking, he swung the gun with an almost casual air towards Palmer. And pulled the trigger.

The shot was shockingly loud. But the bullet hit the ground a long way beyond Palmer and whined off into the darkness like an angry hornet, embedding itself in a stable door and tearing off a large slice of wood.

Henzigger swore and went to pull the trigger again. Mitcheson didn't flinch. He fired twice. Both shots took Henzigger high in the chest and slammed him backwards against the stable wall. The gun fell from his hand, and with a long sigh, the American toppled lazily forward.

He was dead before he hit the ground.

39

By the time the first of Weller's blacked-out Range Rovers arrived and the troops scattered throughout the grounds with guns and torches, Palmer was standing with Riley at the front of the house under the porch light, hands empty and in clear view. Mitcheson had disappeared, pausing only to press the guns he and Palmer had used into the hands of Henzigger and the Colombians. When the forensics team came to match gunshot wounds with weapons on the scene, there had to be none that could not be accounted for.

Weller's helicopter dropped in as Palmer and Riley were being searched and documented, and the body count being logged.

The man Riley had encountered up on the roof was still alive, although he'd taken a tumble off the scaffolding while trying to get away and was now nursing a broken shoulder and jaw. A member of the armed support unit had tried talking to him in broken Spanish, but he had remained sullen and defensive, claiming he was the victim of a misunderstanding.

His two fellow-countrymen were found dead among the trees. Both had died from gunshot wounds.

Riley glanced at Palmer when she heard this bit of news. He shrugged innocently. "I blame it on the films me dad took me to when I was a kid," he said disarmingly.

"Jesus, you two were lucky," commented Weller, after he'd been briefed by his senior man, a tall, grizzled figure in a dark jump-suit who gave Riley and Palmer a sceptical look before walking away to find someone to intimidate. "Especially with the rest of them managing to shoot each other so conveniently." His expression didn't change as he stood over them, but it was plain he knew the scene wasn't as clear-cut as it seemed. He stared at Riley in her borrowed sweatshirt. She still had a smear of Myburghe's blood on her cheek. "You look like you fought a battle on your face." He turned to Palmer and added knowingly, "But you don't. How's that, then?"

"I always carry a rabbit's foot," explained Palmer, when the silence had lengthened to an awkward degree. "My mum swore by them."

Weller almost smiled. "A resident in the village said he saw a vehicle leaving the scene shortly before my men arrived. Reckons it was a Toyota Land Cruiser going like the clappers." He took out a bag of mints and popped two together. For him, it was probably a sign of the stress he was undergoing. He didn't offer the bag round. "You wouldn't know who the driver was, I suppose?"

They shook their heads. With luck, Mitcheson would have got clear of the area before the police managed to throw up a cordon.

"Didn't think you would." Weller stuffed his sweets back in his pocket and lifted Palmer's hands then Riley's, sniffing at them in turn. If he had any thoughts about the unusual aroma of Swarfega cleanser, a large tub of which they'd discovered in the main kitchen, he kept them to himself. "When we look – and we will look, believe me – are we likely to find any fingerprints where we shouldn't?"

"Yes," said Riley. "Mine. There's a small machine-pistol thing somewhere by the side of the house. I threw it over the parapet because I couldn't work out how to use it." She kept her face blank. "And I handled a shotgun the other day, but I'm not sure where it is now."

Weller nodded sourly. "Regular little Annie Oakley, aren't

you?" he murmured.

Up on the roof, a party of medics was preparing to bring down the body of Sir Kenneth Myburghe. He had died of blood-loss, which Riley thought was probably the best outcome. A trial would have served no useful purpose other than to hurt the wrong people. She felt sorry for Lady Myburghe. She really had now lost her husband for good, and her daughters their father.

The steel briefcase, which turned out to be packed with money, caused a stir when it was discovered in the stable where Henzigger had been lying in wait for Palmer. Not as much of a stir, however, as a confessional piece of paper in Sir Kenneth's pocket listing details of where the money had come from and who else was involved in the drugs operation.

"Looks like His Excellency decided to take a few people down with him," Weller commented, studying the list. He gave a carnivore's smile. "There's a Yank I know who's going to owe me a lot of favours by the time I get through with this little lot."

Portius, Riley thought, feeling almost sorry for the State Department man. The list must have been Myburghe's last-ditch attempt to account for his actions, and to gain some revenge for what had been done to his son. If only, she reflected sadly, he'd thought of it sooner.

"How much of this is going public?" she asked Weller.

He threw a pointed look at the helicopter clattering about overhead. Its searchlight beam was lighting up half the county as it checked the woods and fields for further bodies or runaways, and the noise of the rotors must have echoed for miles. No doubt the press corps of half the world would soon be on its way in, opening up the sleepy area of Colebrooke to the glare of international scrutiny.

"Bloody difficult to hide any of it at this rate," Weller said bluntly, and gave her a hard look. "But I decide what doesn't get reported. Got it?"

"OK," said Riley. She was happy to let the tabloids and news crews fight over the stark headline details, just as long as she got to write up the full background story. She didn't much like the idea of Weller having any kind of say in what got published, but that was a fight she'd leave to Donald Brask. A good argument with the establishment might be just the tonic he needed. "Can we go?"

Weller nodded. "Yeah, get lost. But stay available. And don't plan any sudden long-haul flights. Or we might wonder whether you're ever coming back."

When they arrived at Palmer's Saab by the maintenance workshop, he gave an exclamation of dismay and poked his finger through a neat hole in the rear window. There was a corresponding hole in one of the side windows.

"That should entertain my insurance broker for a while," he grumbled, climbing behind the wheel. He winced as he did so, a hiss escaping from between compressed lips.

"Do you want me to drive?" Riley asked him. She had noticed he was holding himself oddly just before the police arrived, and discovered a long burn mark across his back, with a thin line of blood dots where the skin had broken. It had been a close call. After some resistance, she'd persuaded Palmer to let a police medic give him a quick check and put on some plasters to prevent his shirt sticking to his back, with a promise to go to a doctor later that day. Neither of them had mentioned how the burn had occurred.

"I'm fine," he insisted, adjusting the seat until he was comfortable. "It's only a flesh wound." He laughed, wincing as the movement brought a stab of pain. "Damn. I always wanted to say that without wimping out."

They didn't speak much on the way back to London. There didn't seem to be much to say. In between adjusting his position to ease his back, Palmer kept an eye on Riley until she caught him doing it and told him to stop or she'd slap him. He smiled and did as he was told. Her spirited response was a good sign.

"What happened at the stables?" Riley asked, as they approached the end of the motorway near Chiswick. She'd been dying to ask ever since Palmer had walked back from the stable block.. His mood had been clearly sombre. Mitcheson, encouraged by Palmer to leave before the police arrived, had already disappeared into the night. "All that shooting. You could have been killed."

"I was lucky," he said shortly, then added, "If Mitcheson hadn't been there…" He rolled his head in place of a shrug, and she wondered what he wasn't telling her.

"He shot Henzigger, didn't he?"

Palmer nodded.

"Wasn't there any other way?"

"He did what he thought was right. He thought Henzigger was going to shoot me."

Riley stared at him, trying to read his expression in the poor light. There was something in Palmer's voice that didn't sound right. "But you don't think he was?"

"I was lucky. He missed."

Riley knew instinctively that it was all she was going to get out of him. He wasn't defending Mitcheson, but neither was he condemning him. She guessed it was all she could expect and was grateful for it.

After dropping her outside her flat, he drove away into the dawn with a promise to keep in touch.

40

They kept their heads down, urged by Weller to maintain a low profile. The press furore grew like an insatiable monster, feeding on every scrap of information that emerged, real or imagined. Initial reports of an armed siege at a country house gave way to lurid accounts of firefights in the Royal Triangle and terrorists carried off in body bags, then drug smugglers tracked across three continents before being cornered in rural Gloucestershire in what was described as a co-ordinated undercover police operation.

Riley lay low for more specific reasons. She was busy working on the wider story, drafting and re-drafting words which she knew would be subjected to the closest scrutiny by Weller and his people, and even then might never make the light of day. Donald Brask, healthy once more and fired with enthusiasm, left his electronic hideaway to sit with her in her flat, helping her put together the story for maximum effect. He made a series of phone calls, narrowing down the list of editors to be approached when – and if – they were given the green light.

"What if they kill it?" she said sombrely, meaning the Home Office. A momentary lull in activity had deadened her optimism. She had deliberately not gone to press with the account of the shoot-out in Colebrooke House in favour of producing the wider story later – but if the authorities didn't let her publish soon, she would be too late.

But Donald seemed impervious to doubt. "Trust me, sweetie," he told her, "they won't kill it. They can't. They might quibble over bits and pieces... a name here, a detail there. But they can't stop this ball rolling, I promise.

It's already gone too far."

When she saw the twinkle in his eye, Riley felt a knot of excitement in her gut. Donald was planning something. "What are you up to?" she asked him.

He replied by placing a finger alongside his nose. "Building expectation, sweetie. Enough of this is in the public domain to have gained its own momentum. Even Weller must know that. The shootings, Myburghe's alleged involvement, the Colombians. But the dots need joining, or it's a series of random events. And that's what you're doing: joining up the dots." He smiled like a cat with a large bowl of cream. "I'm merely letting it be known in certain quarters that I have access to the full story, and that it will come out. And Donald Brask, sweetie, as everyone knows, never makes claims he cannot deliver."

It wasn't until the second week after the shootings that Weller put in an appearance. He was cheerfully open about the progress of the case.

"The Yanks are smarting a bit," he told her, "on account of having to admit that one of their people went bad. So are we, of course, only we don't make such a song and dance about it. Myburghe was a blue-blood, and everyone knows they're as mad as snakes, anyway."

Mention of Myburghe reminded her of the funeral. Sir Kenneth's ex-wife and two daughters had been captured on camera, attending a private service at Colebrooke village church. Pale and nervous, they had flitted briefly across the public consciousness, before disappearing behind a solid screen of friends and wider family. Starved of willing subjects, the press had soon discovered other targets for their attention in the shape of official releases in the UK and the US about new measures to tighten up accountability in government and state agencies, to ensure nothing like it happened again. Quite what it was that had happened, however, hadn't yet been fully disclosed.

Weller watched the cat, which was circling Riley's living room with its tail erect, eyeing the policeman with a cold, flat stare. "What's his problem?"

"I think he fancies you," said Riley. "Why haven't Palmer and I been interviewed?"

"You will be, don't worry. We've been collating background facts, making sure we don't trip over our feet. There's a lot of muck to sort out." He noticed Riley's laptop on the table. "I'd like to read your notes when you're done. I can't demand them of course, but it would help me fill in a few gaps. Confidentially. You happy with that?"

Riley wondered if this was Weller's way of giving official clearance on the story. For some reason she trusted him. "As long as I get approval to publish."

He shrugged. "Don't see why not. Somebody has to. As long as I get my photo in there for the grandkids, of course." He grinned wickedly and waited for her answer.

"I'll email it to you."

He nodded and walked to the door. "We found the guns you mentioned, by the way. The automatic is a MAC10 – a nasty little bleeder of a weapon. It doesn't shoot, it sprays. We'll need your fingerprints, just to eliminate you. Good job you mentioned them when you did, or my superiors might have their suspicions about your involvement. Take care, now."

One day, Palmer called and left a parcel for her. She took it off the doorstep and opened it. And smiled.

It contained a new jacket and a blue cotton shirt, identical to the ones spoiled at Colebrooke. There was also a note.

I know all about favourite jackets. FP.

John Mitcheson came and went at intervals. He had

invested in a new car to replace the Land Cruiser, which he claimed had been mysteriously stolen the day after the fire-fight at Colebrooke, and was unlikely ever to be recovered. She didn't believe a word of it, but decided it was probably a good thing.

They ate out occasionally and stayed in sometimes, which didn't please the cat. It would sit and stare at Mitcheson, and he stared right back. The two of them stayed like that for a long time.

The cat usually won.

Gradually, Mitcheson's visits became fewer as work intruded. She missed him at first, then she realised his absences were growing longer… and the missing became less. She began to recognise that something intangible had changed between them. She wasn't sure if it was Mitcheson or herself.

Neither was she sure what to do about it.

But it gave her a chance to think about the events of the past weeks, and what lay ahead. It helped to write it down. The shadows and stark images began to recede, like fog slowly dispersing.

When she sent the file to Weller and received a brief 'OK', it was with a sense of relief.

The last thing she did was to send an email to Tristram/ Jacob, telling him it was all over.

She received a one-word reply:

JUSTICE.

More gripping Gavin/Palmer adventures from Adrian Magson

AVAILABLE FROM A BOOKSHOP NEAR YOU

No Peace for the Wicked

Old gangsters never die – they simply get rubbed out. But who is ordering the hits? And why?

Hard-nosed female investigative reporter Riley Gavin is tasked to find out. Her assignment follows a bloody trail from the south coast to the Costa Del Crime as she and ex-military cop Frank Palmer uncover a web of vendettas and double-crosses in an underworld at war with itself.

Suddenly facing a deadline takes on a whole new meaning…

ISBN: 978-0-9547634-2-8   £7.99

No Help for the Dying

Runaway kids are dying on the streets of London. Investigative reporter Riley Gavin and ex military cop Frank Palmer want to know why. They uncover a sub-culture involving a shadowy church, a grieving father and a brutal framework for blackmail, reaching not only into the highest echelons of society, but also into Riley's own past.

ISBN: 978-0-9547634-7-3   £7.99

No Sleep for the Dead

Riley has problems. Her occasional partner-in-crimebusting Frank Palmer has disappeared after a disturbing chance encounter, and she's being followed by a mysterious dreadlocked man.

Frank's determination to pursue justice for an old friend puts him and Riley in deadly danger from art thieves, black gangstas, British Intelligence – and a bitter old woman out for revenge.

ISBN: 978-0-9551589-1-9   £7.99

Gritty and fast-paced detecting of the traditional kind, with a welcome injection of realism.

- Maxim Jakubowski, The Guardian

GRIPPING DEBUT CRIME FICTION
FROM DAYS GONE BY

A new strand from the UK's
most innovative crime publisher.

BROKEN HARMONY   **ROZ SOUTHEY**

Charles Patterson, impoverished musician in 1730s Newcastle-upon-Tyne, is accused of stealing – then his apprentice is found murdered.

As the death toll mounts Charles fears for his life, and it becomes clear things are not as they seem...

a truly magnificent historical crime story... I cannot recommend it enough...
- Amazon reader review

ISBN: 978-0-9551589-3-3   £7.99

TRUTH DARE KILL   **GORDON FERRIS**

The war's over – but no medals for Danny McRae. Just amnesia and blackouts: twin handicaps for a private investigator. Newspaper headlines about a Soho psychopath stir grisly memories in his fractured mind, and he is soon running for his life across bomb-ravaged London.

ISBN: 978-0-9551589-4-0   £7.99

THE CRIMSON CAVALIER   **MARY ANDREA CLARKE**

Pre-Regency London is a dangerous place for an independent young woman. When an unpopular magistrate is murdered, apparently by highwayman the Crimson Cavalier, Miss Georgiana Grey sets out to track down the real culprit.

ISBN: 978-0-9551589-5-7   £7.99

NEW TITLES FOR 2007 FROM OUR BESTSELLING AUTHORS

From MAUREEN CARTER: Birmingham's feistiest detective is finding things tough again in HARD TIME

Detective Sergeant Bev Morriss doesn't do fragile and vulnerable, and struggling to cope with the aftermath of a vicious attack, she is desperate not to reveal the lurking self-doubt.

But her lover has decided it's time to move on and the guv is losing patience. And her new partner has the empathy of a house brick. But she can scarcely trust her own judgement, so what's left to rely on?

A toddler is missing, police officers are dying – and when the ransom note arrives, hard doesn't begin to cover it.

ISBN: 978-0-9551589-6-4   £7.99

From LINDA REGAN, popular actress turned crime writer: DI Banham and DS Grainger take a walk on the seedy side of Soho in PASSION KILLERS

A convicted murderer has recently come out of prison, to the horror of six women who were involved in his crime. Twenty years ago they were all strippers in a seedy nightclub. Now some of them have a lot to lose.

Two of the women are found murdered, each with a red g-string stuffed in her mouth. D I Paul Banham, ace detective but not so hot when it comes to women, focuses his enquiries on the surviving women, and finds that no one has a cast-iron alibi. Everyone is a suspect and everyone is a potential victim...

ISBN: 978-0-9551589-8-8   £7.99

M. JT

A KIND OF PURITAN   **PENNY DEACON**
Claustrophobic futurecrime chiller, first in a series which nods towards
J D Robb.

A subtle and clever thriller - Daily Mail

ISBN: 978-0-9547634-1-1   £7.99

IF IT BLEEDS   **BERNIE CROSTHWAITE**
Chilling murder mystery with authentic newspaper background.

Pacy, eventful… an excellent debut. - Mystery Women

ISBN: 978-0-9547634-3-5   £7.99

A CERTAIN MALICE   **FELICITY YOUNG**
Taut and creepy crime novel with authentic Australian setting.

*a beautifully written book… draws you into the life in Australia… you
may not want to leave.*
- Natasha Boyce, bookseller

IS   £7.99

LLITO
ancing

£7.99

ISON
south

ations

7.99

DEMCO